MURDER
AT THE
JOUST

A HARLOWE & FITCH HISTORICAL MYSTERY

ELIZABETH ROSE

OLIVERHEBERBOOKS

Cover art by Dar Albert at Wicked Smart Designs

Published by Oliver-Heber Books

0 9 8 7 6 5 4 3 2 1

A Note to My Readers:

Dear Readers,

The **Harlowe & Fitch Historical Mystery Series** is ongoing with a main thread that continues to develop throughout the entire series. Mixed in with each story is a new murder mystery, that is solved before the book is finished. While every installment can be read as a stand-alone, it is advised, and also ideal, to start from the beginning with **Murder at Mablethorpe Castle**, Book 1, and to read them in order. If not, there will be surprises ruined along the way.

There might be cliffhangers, but never for the current murder. And while these are murder mysteries and not romances, there is still a romantic thread woven in as well.

See more notes at the end of this book, but for now, welcome to the world of Harlowe & Fitch, where investigations into murders in Mablethorpe and the surrounding areas are underway. A headstrong noblewoman searching for justice with her bloodhound at her side, and a stealthy sheriff trying to secure the safety of his town, team up to uncover that which is hidden but needs to be brought to the surface.

Elizabeth Rose

Chapter One

Mablethorpe Castle, Late 1300s, England

The cloaked figure silently slipped inside the tournament tent that held the competitors' lances. These men would be participating in the tournament's jousting competition, being held right here at Mablethorpe Castle. And to make things even better, the tournament would include King Edward III.

A certain lance was needed for this next job. A special one that had to be identified before the start of the joust. Now, which one was it and where to find it? Making sure no one was around, this was the time to attend to every detail. With a hurried glance through the lances that were stacked on the rack, it was crucial to find the proper one. There would only be one chance to bring this plan to fruition. Revenge was at hand. The patience to get it had been strong and long in the making. But now it would finally happen. This would be the sweetest revenge of all.

The lances were decorated and painted with the crests of each knight. They were made of wood that was designed to break away on impact. Metal tips, usually in the shape of a fist, or three prongs like a crown, were designed to lock onto the opponent's shield to redirect the force of the hit.

However, a heavy, concealed blade, mounted beneath the end

of the lance and covered by the breakaway end, was what was required to make this kill. All lances were supposed to have blunted tips for the competition, but there would be one that did not heed the rules when a certain joust began. This lance would be so much more than just a tool in a knightly sport of skill and courage. It would be a weapon of destruction. A means to an end. Yes, it would be part of a plan to commit the perfect murder, and never be caught.

Running one gloved hand along each of the groups of lances with the knightly crests painted on them to prove ownership, the searching suddenly came to a halt. Ah, yes, this was the exact one needed, and it would do the job nicely. No one would suspect what was about to happen. Nay, no one would ever see it coming! And when the deed was finished, no fingers would ever point back to the true killer, because that secret would stay hidden. Forever.

Accidents happened during jousts on occasion, but this time, there would be no doubt that what was about to happen was not an accident at all, but something planned with purpose and intent. That is, a well-conceived idea by a devious murderer with a heart filled with revenge. A smile curved up the corners of the mouth of the cloaked intruder. This was going to be so easy that it was almost humorous. And by the time the truth of the matter was discovered ... there would be a death on hand. It would be a death that could not be ignored and neither would it be accepted easily by anyone. Yes, very soon now, everything would be in place and things would progress ... just as planned. Someone was about to die. Finally, revenge would be served!

~

LADY VIVIENNE HARLOWE stared out her open window, feeling strong, pent-up emotions of frustration and high confusion. Her life was about to change drastically, and there seemed to be nothing she could do to stop it from happening. If there was ever a time she needed a miracle, it was right now.

"My lady, are you looking forward to the tournament that will be starting tomorrow?" asked Maleine from across the room. The tall, dark-haired handmaid of six-and-ten summers had recently had a harrowing experience at Maltby le Marsh Abbey where she had been a postulant and had planned on taking her vows. After the discovery of a corpse in the abbey's wall was made known, it had intrigued Maleine enough that she decided to make a change in her life. Instead of becoming a nun as initially planned, she now wanted to be an investigator like Vivienne. Maleine was Vivienne's new handmaid, and already proving to be a very good friend. She was also very observant and had been a true asset regarding the abbey murder.

"Looking forward to it?" repeated Vivienne with a forced laugh. "Nay, not at all." She let out a deep sigh. "Dreading it, is more like it, Maleine." Vivienne tired of watching the knights' tents go up outside Mablethorpe Castle's walls in preparation for the grand tournament. With one quick motion she slammed closed the shutters and spun around to face her handmaid. "For the past two weeks now, I've watched more and more competitors and their squires arriving each day, securing a good spot for the tournament by pitching their tents early. Even their weapons for the tournament have been brought ahead of time. The tiltyard has been filled with knights practicing their skills, night and day. With the competitors arriving and registering for the events of the tournament, it is all becoming so real." Her hands waved in the air of their own accord, her body's actions mirroring what she felt inside.

"Yes, I know," said Maleine with a nod. "I have been watching it all unfold as well. The competitors, their squires, and even their servants all seem very eager to be here. Mayhap the King's scheduled presence has something to do with that?"

"I'm sure it does. Part of the King's household has already showed up, and there will be more people accompanying him when he arrives." Vivienne brushed at her skirts, irritation tightening her chest. "Lots more, my dear, and prepare yourself, as some could be quite insufferable. That is often so—with the entourages of kings. Even the lowliest of such folk think themselves above the rest of us."

"Yes, I heard. Cook has been complaining that some of the King's kitchen help is already trying to tell him how to do his job, and he doesn't like it in the least."

"Nay, I suppose he wouldn't. Cook takes his job seriously and prides himself on what goes on in his kitchen—and what arrives on our table. Similarly, the castle blacksmith now has to share his smithy with the King's blacksmith during this time, and he hates it too."

"I was told by Leif the jongleur, that the King's juggler is already here too. The man doesn't even play an instrument, but takes all the attention away from the castle's musicians. They aren't happy about it at all, since the knights have been tossing coins to the juggler instead of the musicians."

"Well, how about the squires and knights the King sent ahead of him?" asked Vivienne. "I couldn't even get into the tilt-yard to practice, because they have overrun the place and act like they own it. My uncle is furious about their rude behavior!" Vivienne let out a deep sigh. "Maleine, I have to admit to you that I am frightened out of my mind."

"Frightened, my lady?" Maleine reached to pet Vivienne's bloodhound, Grunt, who was lying on the bed. "I don't understand why. You are always so confident and sure of yourself, and are the bravest person I know. I've never seen you scared."

"Well, I am this time," Vivienne answered.

"I don't see anything frightening about the tournament, since we are naught but onlookers. Actually, I think the whole idea of the competition happening right here at Mablethorpe Castle is rather invigorating and exciting! I've never been a spectator at a tournament before. I am truly looking forward to it. I especially can't wait for the joust."

"You wouldn't feel that way if you were the one being offered up as the grand prize," scoffed Vivienne.

"Oh, that. Yes, I almost forgot about that part," answered Maleine with a pout. "I see your point." Maleine still petted the dog, who had now rolled over on his back, wanting his stomach rubbed too. Vivienne's bloodhound was usually always at her side. Plus, he had a good nose for sniffing out trouble and helping her find clues where murders were concerned. "Do you think you can change your uncle's mind and get out of having to marry the winner, after all?"

"I wish that were so," said Vivienne. "But unfortunately, I don't see how that will ever happen." Vivienne plopped down on a chair.

"Why not?"

"I've tried to convince Uncle Gilbert not to do this. Every day for the past two weeks now, I've begged him not to offer me up as anyone's bride. However, he's made his decision and there is nothing anyone can do to change his mind. Still, I just can't stop trying. My future is at stake here!"

"My lady, you've changed Lord Mablethorpe's mind in the past. Are you really sure you cannot do it again?"

"You must remember that I wasn't the one to control his choice to marry me off in the past. I mean, with the murder at the castle, it was more like fate took hold of that decision last time. My uncle was forced to let the idea go, against his will. But even so, this time is different. I highly doubt that fate will step in yet a second time to save me."

5

"I believe in fate, my lady." Since Vivienne was already dressed, Maleine picked up her shoes and brought them to her.

Vivienne got up and settled herself atop the bed, reaching out to scratch Grunt behind his ears. "Fate or not, this time, Lord Mablethorpe has made certain that I can't get out of the betrothal," she explained, speaking about her uncle. Upon the death of Vivienne's parents, her Aunt Ellen and Uncle Gilbert took over as her guardians, and she'd lived right here at Mablethorpe Castle ever since. "This time, Lord Mablethorpe has given his word to the King that I will marry the winner of this tournament! Because of the King's planned arrival, as well as me being the grand prize, it has caused quite a stir. It is already attracting a big crowd. My uncle likes a lot of attention, you see. Especially from nobles and the King. Nowadays, it seems like nothing else matters to him."

"So, you're saying your uncle can't change what's about to happen even if he wanted to? That it's too late?"

"Yes, that is right. My fate is sadly already sealed. Since King Edward has offered to fund this tournament, and because he's agreed to be here at all, there is no turning back now. The only thing that could possibly save me is a miracle. However, I don't seem to be any good at attracting miracles into my life, I'm afraid."

"Nay, don't say that. It isn't so, my lady," Maleine protested. "After all, don't forget about the miracle that brought your baby boy back to you after seven years of him being lost."

"Yes. You are right, Maleine. And I didn't forget. I will be ever grateful that I've been reunited with my son. I never expected that Martin was still alive. Ever since the day my parents were murdered on the road by bandits, and my brother and son disappeared when the spooked horses ran off with them in the wagon, I didn't expect to ever see my family again. That awful night haunts me still."

"My heart breaks for you, my lady." Maleine sat at Vivienne's feet. After helping Vivienne don her shoes, she reached up to hold her hand. "No one should have to lose their entire family the way you did."

Suddenly, Vivienne felt selfish. After all, Maleine had just lost her entire family as well.

"I'm sorry, Maleine. My head is filled with thoughts about myself when you are suffering just as much as me." She tightly gripped the girl's hand in hers.

Maleine bit her lip, then pulled her hand away, quickly brushing at a stray tear. "So King Edward will actually be here and you will have a chance to meet him then?" She quickly got to her feet. "I must say, that *is* a little nerve-wracking. Not only for you, but for everyone at Mablethorpe Castle. I mean, after all, he is the King!"

"Yes, everyone is nervous and anticipating our sovereign's arrival," agreed Vivienne, glad to have the conversation steered away from either of their families. "Even Cook and Maria have been at each other's throats lately in the kitchen. Cook is terrified of all the new dishes he's expected to create. And Maria is afraid her pregnancy will slow her down and that mayhap it will get both of them dismissed from their positions."

"I am sure no servant will be dismissed at such a crucial time. Will they, my lady?" Maleine seemed suddenly concerned for her own new position as Vivienne's handmaid.

"Nay, all the help will be needed at this busy time," Vivienne replied. "And you don't need to worry about your position, Maleine. As I've told you, it is secure."

"Thank you, my lady." Maleine straightened up the room, seeming relieved.

Vivienne's hand went to her chest where she wore the King's ring on a chain concealed under her clothing. It had been given to her by her mother just before she died. Her mother had revealed to her that Vivienne was the King's bastard. There was every reason in the world to feel nervous about that! Especially since Vivienne planned on confronting King Edward about this subject during his visit. She wanted to tell him exactly who she was, in case he didn't know. Her mother hadn't actually said if the King even knew he'd sired a bastard daughter. It surely didn't seem so. Would King Edward be happy or angry about finding out that he had a daughter by one of his past mistresses? Just thinking about it scared her even more.

She supposed this newfound fear came from the story that was lodged in her brain. That is, the story of King Edward III's bastard triplets and how he ordered the babies killed at birth because of superstition. Those baby boys, Rowen, Rook, and Reed, were her half-brothers even though she had yet to meet any of them. Word was that at one time they and their armies had raided from the King. Under the guise of the Demon Thief, this had gone on for years, in an act of revenge. Now, even though they had never been legitimized by King Edward, two of the three bastards had made alliances with him. They now served the King instead of fighting against him.

The Legendary Bastard Triplets of the Crown were said to be coming to the tournament as well. They were married with children now, but would be competing in a special joust for married knights. That is, a competition that didn't offer her up as the grand prize at the end. It was rumored that even the King himself might participate in an event, but no one really knew for sure.

Vivienne had questions for King Edward. Questions regarding his feelings toward his illegitimate children, and also about having had a mistress who happened to have been her late mother. Why did he couple with her mother in the first place? How did they even know each other? And was there any love between the two of them, or was it lust only? She wished more than anything that she could ask her mother these questions, but it was too late now. Vivienne had no idea why her mother had kept from her the fact that her true father was King Edward. She'd only learned about the secret with her mother's dying breath.

Even with all these questions filling Vivienne's head, her main one was, did King Edward know that she existed? He had to know! Didn't he? If not, why had he given her mother his expensive, ornate golden ring with the huge ruby embedded in it? Her mother's last words were that this ring would help Vivienne and her baby. She'd also told her that her *father* would help and protect her and her child. Of course, she'd meant the King. Her mother also warned her to tell no one this guarded secret. It was almost as if she felt that Vivienne's life would be in danger if anyone knew. Vivienne's questions were overwhelming and also ones that only the King himself could answer.

"My lady, excuse me for saying so, but you seem to have your mind on other things today. I mean, besides having to marry a man you neither know nor love." Maleine picked up a boar's-bristle brush and gently ran it through Vivienne's loose hair.

Vivienne really wanted to tell her handmaid about the ring. And about the King being her father. But her dying mother's warning was to keep this information to herself. Only Vivienne's aunt and uncle knew the truth. Of course, Nairnie, the old woman who served as nursemaid to the sheriff's daughter, knew as well. But it was only because the old woman was too observant and had figured it out on her own.

A knock sounded, and the door opened a crack before Maleine had the chance to walk over to see who was there.

"Mother?" Little seven-year-old Martin poked his head into the room. "May I come in?"

"Yes, of course. Come in, Martin," said Vivienne with a

smile. "This is your room now too, remember." Since discovering that the page boy was truly Vivienne's son, whom she'd lost when he was a newborn baby, she'd let her son sleep in the big bed with her and Grunt every night. Maleine had a pallet she used at the foot of the bed, directly on the floor. "You don't have to ask permission to enter."

"I keep forgetting," said the boy, walking into the room and dropping to his knees. He held out his arms for a hug. Not from Vivienne, but from her bloodhound, Grunt. The dog jumped off the bed with tail wagging, bounding over to lick Martin's face. The dog and Martin were best friends now. It did Vivienne's heart good to see her son smiling and laughing. This was something that she never thought she'd ever get to witness in this lifetime.

"Martin, did you have a message for me?" asked Vivienne, getting up and walking over to hunker down in front of her son. She gave him a hug and a big kiss on his cheek.

"My face is all wet from Grunt and now from you, too." Martin used the back of his hand to wipe away the kisses, wrinkling his nose as he did so.

"What's the matter? You don't like my kisses?" she teased, standing back up.

"I don't think knights are supposed to be kissed," the boy answered. "And I'm going to be a knight someday, you know."

"It will be a long time before that happens," Vivienne informed him.

Maleine laughed. "I don't agree with you, Martin. I think knights do like kisses. However, I suppose it all depends who they are from."

"Oh, really," said Vivienne, looking over her shoulder at her handmaid. "You both mean no kisses from mothers, but just from the pretty girls?"

"Nay, no girls either!" Martin blurted out, quickly jumping to his feet.

"Not even if they're pretty ones?" she asked. "Like ... Starah, mayhap?" Vivienne giggled, liking the teasing, and the look of horror on Martin's little face.

"Nay! Starah doesn't like kisses either," said Martin, speaking of the sheriff's seven-year-old daughter. He wrinkled his nose again, and shook his head so hard that his long blond bangs fell over his eyes.

"How do you know what Starah likes?" asked Vivienne. "Did you ask her about it?"

"Nay," he answered, looking up through his bangs with shy, but curious bright blue eyes. His eyes, just like Vivienne's, were so blue that it almost seemed unnatural. "Mother," said Martin. "If you want to know if Starah likes kisses, you can ask her yourself. She, the sheriff, and Nairnie, are all down in the great hall waiting for you."

"The sheriff is here?" Vivienne's heart skipped a beat. While Zachariah Fitch had been her best friend since childhood, Vivienne had recently started feeling an attraction to him. They'd both lost their spouses and had young children to raise on their own. Yes, they had a lot in common. Plus, Vivienne had been working with the sheriff lately on murder investigations. Spending so much time at his side made her sometimes wonder what it would be like if they were always together.

She quickly pushed that thought right from her mind. She and Zachariah were friends and partners in business, and that was all either of them wanted right now, she reminded herself. Even if she'd started feeling romantically attracted to him on occasion, she was still not sure she forgave him for not being able to solve the murders of her parents from seven years ago. Not to mention, even though her son miraculously came back into her life, her younger brother, Adrian, was still missing. Adrian had been nine years old when he'd disappeared. He'd be six-and-ten years old now, and Vivienne couldn't help wondering how Adrian would look or act as a young man. Her heart ached for her brother every day. She never gave up hope and still longed to find him, even if by now it seemed improbable that it would ever happen. Vivienne also dearly missed her departed parents. The worst part was that even seven years in passing, she was still having nightmares about what happened that awful night that took away everyone from her that she'd ever loved.

The herald's straight trumpet from the courtyard resounded, the shrill cry penetrating right through the closed shutters. It was an announcement of the arrival of someone important who was about to enter the castle walls.

"I hear the herald's trumpet!" Martin ran over to the window and threw open the shutters before Vivienne could tell him not to do so. "I wonder who has arrived now?"

"I announce the arrival of Lord Rowen of Whitehaven and Lord Rook of Naward," shouted the herald, blowing the horn once again.

"Martin, Lady Vivienne wants the shutters closed," Maleine told the boy, as she walked across the room to do so herself.

"Nay, wait!" Vivienne heard the announcement that two of her half-brothers had arrived. She was curious, wanting to know what they looked like, and exactly who they were. Yes, she wanted to know everything about them.

Hurrying over to the window, Vivienne curiously peered out, not being any different from her young son with his insatiable curiosity. There, riding high and mighty atop their horses were two of the King's triplet bastard sons. One had blond hair like her. It was pulled back into a queue. The other had hair as dark as a midnight sky, and that he wore long so that it fell around his shoulders. They both seemed so regal and were dressed in fine clothing. Long cloaks were thrown over their shoulders, the sumptuous material billowing back behind them and falling over the rear end of their horses. Around their waists they wore thick leather belts that carried an assortment of weapons. Their longswords, sometimes referred to as bastard swords, were strapped to the sides of their mounts. The thought of this made her smile.

"Lady Vivienne, I think those men might be the Legendary Bastards of the Crown," said Maleine in awe, her eyes lighting up as she leaned out the open window to get a better look at them as well.

"Yes, that is who they are," affirmed Vivienne.

"Bastards?" asked Martin. "What does that mean, Mother?"

Suddenly, Vivienne felt embarrassed. After all, she was a bastard too. And from the same man who sired these men. She didn't want to explain bastards to Martin right now, since she wasn't sure what he'd think of it all. Or of her, once he discovered the truth that her birth parents had never been married.

"Martin, you need to get back to Sir Guy's side," she told him. "After all, he is your mentor and I am sure he needs your help to get things ready for him regarding the tournament. He will be competing as well."

"Naw, he won't need me. He has his squire, Milo, for that," said the boy, stretching his neck to see out the window. "I wonder if I'll be able to meet the bastards. Don't they look important, Mother? Mayhap being a bastard means you're someone important."

"Martin, that's enough." Vivienne pulled her son away from the window and hurriedly closed the shutters. "You are a page-in-training and should be doing something other than gawking out the window all day long. Now go find Sir Guy and tell him you will do whatever needs to be done."

"Aw, do I have to?" Martin looked down and kicked at the

floor. "I'd rather go meet the rest of the competitors. They're knights and that is exciting."

"Sir Guy is a knight as well," she reminded him.

"Aye, but Sir Guy is stuffy and boring," complained the boy. He looked up and suddenly his eyes took on a new shine. "I just had a thought, Mother! If those men who just arrived are called the Legendary Bastards of the Crown, they must be related to the King, right? I mean, I've heard the King called the Crown."

"We'll talk about this later, Martin. Right now, you have work to do, and I have people waiting for me in the great hall."

They all left the room with the dog following on their heels. Vivienne couldn't help feeling just as excited as her son about meeting the Legendary Bastards. Then again, at the same time, the idea of meeting her true father, the King, still had her scared to death.

Chapter Two

Sheriff Zachariah Fitch impatiently paced the great hall, waiting for Lady Vivienne to arrive. His seven-year-old daughter, Starah, was with the nursemaid, Nairnie. The two of them sat at a trestle table talking with some of the kitchen servants, as the space was cleared from the morning meal.

Zachariah was here today not just for the tournament, but also at the request of Vivienne's uncle. Lord Mablethorpe spotted him from across the great hall and came rushing over. His wife followed right behind, being the perfect, ever-obedient, quiet noblewoman that most noblemen coveted.

"Sheriff, so glad you're here." Lord Mablethorpe's voice boomed through the crowded and noisy great hall. His big hand clutched a tankard of ale as he approached.

"My lord," said Zachariah, with a bow as was required of any commoners who greeted nobles. "You sent for me?"

"Yes. Yes, I did," Lord Mablethorpe answered in a low voice. "With the tournament starting tomorrow and King Edward arriving, as well as many other important noblemen, I think it is crucial to have as much protection around the castle as possible."

"I agree," Zachariah answered. "I am sure you've already seen to the measures of posting extra guards?" He couldn't imagine why the lord of the castle was involving him in any of this. Zachariah's job had to do with the town, not the castle.

"I did see to posting more guards," answered Lord Mablethorpe. "However, I thought it would be wise for you to be here too, Sheriff. I mean, if anything goes awry, I'd like to have the town sheriff on hand."

"Really?" he asked. "Are you by any chance expecting trouble, my lord?"

"God's eyes, I hope not!" spat Lord Mablethorpe. "However, one can never be too careful. It is always good to be prepared, with this many people and our ruler arriving inside the castle walls."

"I see."

"Can I count on you to stay here through the tournament then, Sheriff Fitch? I will give you a chamber inside the keep where you can stay."

Zachariah noticed that Lord Mablethorpe hadn't said he was hiring him or promising to pay him anything at all. Lady Vivienne did say her uncle was tight with the purse strings. Zachariah didn't know how to answer. His duties were in town, not at the castle. Besides, he didn't work for free.

"I'm not sure," he mumbled, shifting from foot to foot. Where the hell was Vivienne? She would make sure he got paid, if she were here. It wasn't his position to question a noble about such matters. "I do have a responsibility in town, my lord, and cannot leave the people and businesses there unguarded," he said, stalling for time.

"Don't you have constables for unimportant tasks like that?" asked Lord Mablethorpe, belittling Zachariah's job whether he did so purposely or not. "After all, this is a great opportunity for you, Sheriff Fitch. The King is going to be here, and you'll most likely get the chance to meet him. Don't you understand?" He frowned. It was as if he thought Zachariah was being ungrateful to him, and that wasn't a comfortable position to be in at all.

"I understand, my lord," Zachariah answered. "And while I do have two constables working with me, one of them is more like a filing clerk than anything else. Handling the town isn't an easy chore, you understand. Especially not with everything that goes on regarding Rotten Row. I am sure you've heard about the recent murders there."

"Yes, I've heard. However, there's been a murder here at the castle recently too, unless you've already forgotten."

"Nay. Of course not, my lord. How could I forget something as awful as that?"

"Well then, it proves my point of how important it is that you are here during the tournament, Sheriff. If you have two constables, then bring one of them along with you and leave the other behind to watch over the town. I need all the protection possible with the King's arrival." Lord Mablethorpe lifted his tankard and downed the rest of his ale. It was evident that he wasn't going to take *no* for an answer. Zachariah had known Lord Mablethorpe for his entire life and he'd usually been more than accommodating. However, since the man took in Vivienne as his ward, his demeanor changed somewhat, and he was more inconsiderate than usual. Perhaps it was because his children had all died that he seemed so protective over Vivienne. Or mayhap it was because Vivienne, as everyone knew, never acted quite the way that was expected of a noblewoman. He supposed it could be Vivienne's outlandish ways that brought on this side of Lord Mablethorpe, and Zachariah supposed he couldn't really blame him.

"Sheriff Fitch, my husband will of course pay you and your constable for your services regarding the tournament," Lady

Mablethorpe spoke up, causing her husband to spit ale across the room, almost choking.

"Ellen, please! Stay silent," scolded her husband. "I will handle this. You have no right to talk over me."

"I'm sorry, Gilbert," apologized his wife, becoming suddenly sullen and obedient again. Women had no rights, and it wasn't heard of to speak over their husband or go against his word. Zachariah supposed Vivienne's aunt had learned to do this from Vivienne.

"Sheriff, my funds are limited since this tournament is already costing so much. Otherwise, of course, I'd pay you," said Lord Mablethorpe, as if that made it all right for Zachariah to work for free.

"Uncle, the King is paying for most of the tournament expenses, and you cannot ask the sheriff to not only give up his time but to work for free on top of it." Thankfully, Vivienne walked up just then, not afraid to speak her mind, coming to his aid. Her hound, Grunt, was at her side as always.

"Lady Vivienne," said Zachariah. "And Grunt." He leaned over and patted the dog on the head. Grunt wagged his tail and seemed to smile.

"Why can't I?" argued her uncle. "After all, the town will be nearly empty since everyone will be here at the castle. With me feeding them," he added under his breath. "The sheriff can watch over the townsfolk this way as well. After all, that is his job, isn't it?"

"The King is paying for food and drink as well," Vivienne boldly pointed out, not letting her uncle's snide remark go unaddressed.

"Excuse me, Gilbert," Vivienne's aunt spoke up again, even though she seemed reluctant to go against her husband's wishes. "Vivienne, is right, dear. Sheriff Fitch has a lot of responsibilities and we need to pay him well for his time."

"Yes," said Vivienne. "I actually think that in this case, the sheriff should be paid double the normal amount. After all, this will be a huge event."

"Double?" gasped her uncle. "How can you even suggest such a thing, Vivienne? That is ridiculous!"

"I'm afraid I have to agree with Vivienne, dear," said his wife once more. "After all, it will be a big job with so many people present."

"Who asked you?" snapped Lord Mablethorpe. "I don't need either of you telling me what to do!" His face became red and he banged down his empty tankard on a nearby trestle table.

"Sheriff Fitch, you, as well as your constable, will be paid double whatever price you are normally paid," Vivienne assured him, ignoring her uncle altogether.

"Thank you. I accept," said Zachariah with a nod and a smile.

"Vivienne, stop it," growled Lord Mablethorpe. "After all, I just offered to let the sheriff stay here at the castle during the tournament. He'll already be taking up a room that a noble could be occupying."

"Gilbert, you know the competitors are all staying in tents since we are holding the rooms for King Edward and his people," Vivienne's Aunt Ellen said, then lowered her head and stepped back a pace, wringing her hands in front of her.

"I think it is wonderful that the sheriff will be staying here at the castle," remarked Vivienne, with a soft smile toward Zachariah. "As a matter of fact, I think his daughter and nurse-maid should stay here throughout the tournament as well."

"Lady Vivienne, I make the decisions around here," warned her uncle, wagging a finger in her face.

"You make the decisions?" asked Vivienne. "You mean, just like you did by betrothing me to the winner of the tournament

19

without asking me about it first?" was her reply. Her eyes narrowed and her jaw clenched as she glared at her uncle in unspoken challenge. Zachariah admired her bravery, but felt a little uncomfortable that she was challenging her uncle so openly. Her actions really were unusual.

"Don't start with that again, young lady." Her uncle glared back at her. "I don't have time for this nonsense. I have important things to do. Sheriff, you and your family are welcome to stay, but not your constable. And I cannot give up any more rooms so you'll only have the one."

"And his pay will be double?" asked Vivienne, obviously just wanting to hear her uncle agree, since he'd already accepted the job at those terms. Her hands slowly went to her hips.

Lord Mablethorpe's jaw clenched as he perused his niece. Then he finally let out a big sigh. "Yes, I'll pay you double your normal fee, Sheriff. But only you. Your constable will be paid a single amount only." He turned on his heel and stormed away without another word.

"Sheriff, I apologize for my husband's gruff behavior," said Lady Mablethorpe in a soft, kind voice. She was always so friendly and caring about everyone. "Gilbert is just anxious and on edge about the tournament because the King is coming."

"Aren't we all," said Vivienne under her breath.

"It's all right, Lady Mablethorpe. I understand completely," said Zachariah. "The terms Lord Mablethorpe has named are acceptable. I will return to town to gather some of my belongings, and then be back. Will I be able to access my chamber today?"

"Yes, of course," said Lady Mablethorpe. "And your daughter can stay with you. However, I'm afraid it wouldn't be proper for your nursemaid to stay in the same room as you. After all, what would people say?"

"Aunt Ellen, it's just Nairnie! She's an old woman," Vivienne reminded her. "Besides, Nairnie already lives in the same house as the sheriff, so what does it matter?"

"Nay, Vivienne. I'm afraid it wouldn't be proper, and would not reflect well on us." Lady Mablethorpe seemed worried. Probably more worried about how her husband would react when gossip started regarding this situation.

"It's not a problem. Nairnie can stay with me in my chamber," Vivienne spoke up, finding a solution to the dilemma.

"Vivienne, you already have Martin and Maleine staying in your chamber," her aunt reminded her. "And we don't have any extra pallets to give one to Nairnie."

"Nairnie can share the bed with Maleine then, and I will sleep on the pallet with Martin," Vivienne answered, not backing down in her decision. "After all, it is only going to be for a few days, so I think I can handle it."

"Nay, Lady Vivienne," said Zachariah, feeling bad for her now. "You are a noble and shouldn't be sleeping on a pallet on the floor. I can't agree to that."

"Sheriff, if I have to, I will sleep in the great hall or outside the castle gates in a tent—it doesn't really matter. But I am not going to have an old woman who can probably barely get up off the floor, sleeping anywhere but in a bed."

"Just don't tell your uncle about it," warned Lady Mablethorpe, looking across the great hall. "Oh, he's summoning me, Vivienne. I must go." She hurried off, making straight for her husband. Once she left, Zachariah spoke up.

"Now that all is settled, I wish you a good morning, Lady Vivienne, and thank you for coming to my aid," said Zachariah. "I was starting to think you weren't going to join us."

"Good morning to you, as well, Sheriff. You are welcome, and yes, I overslept again, if that is what you are hinting at."

"Was it the nightmares again?" he asked softly, knowing that for the past seven years she'd been haunted by the unsolved murders of her parents and the disappearances of her baby and brother. Even though Martin had now been found.

"Nay. I was just ... concerned," she said, making him think that it most likely had to be about her being a prize bride. He'd had bad dreams about that, as well. "Have you had anything to eat yet? It seems the meal is over already but I am sure I can find something for you in the kitchens."

"Nay, I'm good," he told her with a raise of his palm. "Nairnie fixed me a big bowl of porridge and some fresh bread before leaving to come here. However, since it seems you missed the meal, perhaps you'd like to go and find yourself some food?"

"Nay," she said, her hand going to her stomach. "I'm afraid that I am too upset to eat."

"Lady Vivienne, I can see that being a prize bride is destroying you. I think you should confront your uncle again and convince him that you don't want to be married."

"It doesn't work that way," she told him. "Besides, I have tried just about everything, and can't seem to budge his decision, even a little."

"Is there anything I can do to help?" Zachariah gazed into her bright blue eyes, thinking how jealous he was going to be once she was pawned off to be the bride of a noble. Even if he couldn't have her, it still bothered him to think of his good friend as being the wife of a man she didn't know or love. Vivienne had a hard life and deserved better than that. Especially after what she went through, first losing her husband and then her parents to death. That awful night her family was attacked on the road was something neither of them would ever forget.

"Sheriff Fitch, you can be here as my rock. My support, as always," she said, taking his arm. "I don't want you to leave my side from now until the end of the competition. Let's walk, shall we?" She directed him to the door of the great hall and out into the corridor. Grunt followed on their heels, panting since the day was already becoming quite warm.

"I suppose once you're married off that you'll be leaving Mablethorpe then, my lady?" he asked, not wanting to even think about this happening, but feeling as if it needed to be discussed between them.

"Leave Mablethorpe?" Her gaze flashed over to him and a shadow darkened her face. "Nay, I never plan on leaving here. Why would I?"

"Oh, I see," he answered. "Then you're planning to live here at the castle with your new husband." This was starting to feel more than uncomfortable to him. Zachariah wanted to tell her how much he'd miss her, but he couldn't. True, he was her best friend as well as a partner more-or-less in solving murders, but he was a commoner and she, a noble. That is something that would never change between them. Even if they wanted to, they could never end up together.

"I prefer not to speak of this anymore." She quickly released his arm.

"Of course not. I'm sorry." He cleared his throat and looked to the ground. "I suppose I'd better collect my daughter then, and head back home so we can pack a few things for our stay here at the castle."

"Yes. I guess that would be in order."

"Until later then, my lady." He bowed, quickly turned away from her, and headed back to the great hall.

"My lady? Is everything good between you and the sheriff?" asked Maleine, rushing to Vivienne's side as soon as Zachariah had walked away.

Vivienne's focus was on his back as she replied. "Of course, Maleine. Why shouldn't it be?"

"I just wondered, because he seemed so upset about something. What were you two just talking about, if I may ask?"

"Of course, you can ask," said Vivienne, liking to have someone she could confide in. "I want you to always feel as if you can speak freely around me, Maleine."

"Thank you, my lady. That means a lot to me." The honor as well as gratefulness showed on the girl's face.

"The sheriff was inquiring about my new living arrangements once I am married off to the winner of the tournament," Vivienne explained.

"Oh, I see." Maleine's smile faded. "Will I be losing my position as your handmaid once you are married? Or will I perhaps be leaving Mablethorpe to go along with you and your new husband?" Vivienne could tell by the girl's words and tone of voice that both of these predicaments bothered her.

"Why does everyone keep saying I am leaving Mablethorpe? I am not going anywhere," Vivienne assured her.

"Excuse me for saying so, my lady, but won't you have to answer to your new husband and go wherever he orders? Noblewomen are expected to heed their husband's wishes, are they not?"

Vivienne's anger rose to the surface. She was not going to let that happen, even though it was the normal, expected way. A noblewoman was supposed to do whatever her husband wanted and not question his choices, that was true. However, Vivienne decided she could never live that way, noble or not. It just wasn't right that a woman was given no authority to have thoughts or feelings of her own.

"Between you and me, Maleine, I am not yet done trying to get out of this horrible situation I have found myself in."

"Then you're going to confront your uncle about it again?" asked Maleine, seeming happy and hopeful by the thought.

"Well, nay, not exactly," she answered, throwing her chin in the air.

"What does that mean?" Confusion washed over Maleine's face. Grunt dropped down at Vivienne's feet and put his nose between his paws.

"It means that I plan on going over everyone's head and straight to the top about this."

"Straight to the top?" Maleine's eyes popped open wide. "You don't mean you are going to talk to the King about it, do you?" The girl might not know how to read or write yet, but she was a bright one when it came to figuring things out on her own. Maleine was always observant about what was happening around her.

"Why shouldn't I go to the King with my concerns?" Vivienne asked her handmaid.

"Because, my lady. He is the King! That's why."

Vivienne wanted more than anything to tell Maleine that King Edward was not just the King, but also her father. However, this wasn't the time or place to do so. She needed to stay silent about that and keep it a secret for now. Or at least until after she confronted the King about things first, she decided. That is, if she didn't faint from fright at thinking of making such a bold move.

"Mother, did you see the bastards?" shouted Martin, running up to her and tugging on her tippet, the long sleeve of her gown that almost reached the ground.

"Shush, Martin. Don't say that word so loud." Vivienne scanned the courtyard that was filled with people preparing for the tournament that would start first thing tomorrow. Nobles strutted around, throwing a coin or two every so often to the commoners and those who arrived from the town or village to see them. Children squealed and raced after the coins, pushing each other aside to try to get to them first. Servants scurried to and fro doing their expected chores. Washwomen passed by holding large woven baskets containing clean linens that would be used by the chambermaids to make up beds for their special guests. The stablemaster walked by with a bridle over his shoulder and a pitchfork in his hand. Several scullery maids hurried back to the well to fetch clean water to wash the morning dishes.

A shepherd boy herding half a dozen sheep and two goats directed the animals toward the kitchens, most likely to be used by Cook and his helpers in preparing the King's feast. Then the castle blacksmith moved through the throng, checking with one knight after another to see who needed their swords sharpened or repaired before the tournament started. A scribe trailed behind him, recording all the events. Even merchants and craftsmen from town were starting to arrive, curious about the tournament and trying to sell their wares ahead of time to the participating nobles. Vivienne saw Cook and Maria starting out the door to the keep, while Leif, the jongleur, walked around plucking tunes on his lute. There were tables set up by the main gate where the competitors were to register for the tournament, deciding which events they'd participate in once it started. The winner of the tournament, the man who would get Vivienne as his bride, would need to compete in each of the events in order to qualify to be the grand prize winner.

"Mother, I found out that the bastards' names are Lord Rook and Lord Rowen," said Martin with excitement in his voice, sounding proud to even know this. "I was with Sir Guy when he actually talked to them. Sir Guy is helping behind the tables with the registration. He said he already knew the bastards before today. Isn't that exciting?"

"Please don't call them that, Martin. Where are Lords Rook and Rowen now?" asked Vivienne, scanning the area, but it was too crowded to even find them. She kept looking down to make sure Grunt was still with her and that the poor dog wouldn't get trampled in the crowd.

"Right there. There they are. See them?" Martin pointed to the registration tables at the gate. "They are still signing up and talking about a special joust against the King."

"Really?" This interested Vivienne immensely. She didn't know that the King was going to joust at the tournament. Normally, no one wanted to go up against King Edward, since it wouldn't be good to actually beat a king at anything! It would only make the King look weak in others' eyes. Also, no knight wanted to lose on purpose, so avoided situations like this if they could. Then again, Lord Rowen and Lord Rook were the King's own sons. They would probably relish jousting against the father who once ordered their lives taken when they were naught but defenseless newborn babies. Perhaps besting their father was what they had in mind. "I'd like to meet them," she said, picking up her skirts and heading over to the table.

Martin happily led the way while Maleine held back, walking in Vivienne's shadow. Grunt saw another dog and ran off, distracted.

"Sir Guy, Sir Guy, my mother wants to meet the Legendary Bastards!" shouted Martin as they approached the competitor's sign-up table. Vivienne tried to keep up with her son, but had a hard time getting through the hoard of people.

"Martin, don't call them that!" scolded Vivienne, finally approaching the table.

"Why not call us bastards?" asked the tall, handsome man with long black hair. "After all, that's what we are. Lord Rook at your service, my lady." He bowed to her and reached out and took her hand, kissing the back of it, all the while keeping his eyes interlocked with hers.

"Rook, quit showing off," grumbled the other man with long blond hair as he pushed Lord Rook out of his way. "I am Lord

Rowen, my lady. And who might you be?" He bowed, but didn't take her hand and kiss it the way his brother had.

Vivienne looked up at him and gasped. Both men had the same exact faces, the same build, and those same bright blue eyes. The same color eyes as her and Martin. The only thing different between the men was the contrasting color of their hair. They seemed to be about five or six years older than her age of three-and-twenty summers.

"This is Lady Vivienne. She's my mother," said Martin proudly, before she even had a chance to say a word.

"Did you say, Lady Vivienne?" Rowen stood up straighter, seeming surprised. "The daughter of Lord and Lady Mablethorpe?"

"Yes, and nay," she answered. "I am Lady Vivienne Harlowe. Lord and Lady Mablethorpe are my aunt and uncle, not my parents. They are my guardians as well."

"Then you're the ... I mean you are ..." started Rook, not sure how to say it.

"Yes, Lord Rook, you can say it aloud. I am the prize bride, being used as bait to lure competitors to my uncle's door like a worm on a hook to catch a fish."

"My, I've never heard it put that way before," commented Rowen, a grin spreading across his face by what she'd said aloud.

"Prize brides who are noblewomen usually are quite a draw. Especially if they are as pretty as you," said Rook.

"Pretty or ugly, it doesn't matter, because I don't intend to really see it through," she announced to them.

"You don't?" Rowen raised a brow. "But isn't that using false pretense to get knights to sign up, then?"

She shrugged. "Like I said ... a worm on a hook as bait to lure a big fish."

"Lady Vivienne, you have to go through with it," Rook told her. "After all, the competitors are expecting a bride to be the

28

grand prize, as promised. You wouldn't want to disappoint them."

"Lord Rook, I don't care who is disappointed by it, but I am no one's grand prize and never will be!" She crossed her arms over her chest, feeling like wringing both their necks for not being on her side regarding this. Then again, if they knew she was their half-sister, mayhap they would stand behind her.

Rook and Rowen looked at each other and grinned. "Brother, I like this lady," said Rook with a chuckle. "She has a fire burning deep within her."

"Yes, me too. She rather reminds me a little of us, in our younger days," agreed Rowen.

"Mother, Mother, introduce me now." Martin tugged on her sleeve and jumped up and down, not able to contain his excitement.

Vivienne took Martin by the shoulders and pulled him up with his back against her.

"Lords Rowen and Rook, this is Martin. He's my son," Vivienne introduced him.

"I'm a page!" exclaimed Martin, smiling so widely that everyone could see the gap in his mouth where he'd recently lost a front tooth. "Someday I'll be a knight just like the two of you," said Martin, bubbling over with such strong emotions that he couldn't seem to stand still, so Vivienne was glad she was holding him down. With Martin's enthusiasm at meeting these men, she wasn't sure he wouldn't pull out his wooden sword and try to challenge them to a duel next.

"A knight, huh?" said Rook with a chuckle. "Keep on working at it, little one. Mayhap someday you'll be jousting in a tournament too." He reached out and ruffled the boy's hair. Martin blushed and lowered his face.

"Oh, and I'd also like you to meet my handmaid, Maleine," said Vivienne, moving to the side to introduce the girl standing quietly behind her, not making her presence known the way Martin was doing.

"Nay, my lady!" Maleine looked up with frightened eyes, still trying to stay hidden behind her. This was a shy nature that Vivienne hadn't seen from Maleine before.

"Greetings, Maleine," said Rowen.

"Maleine," said Rook with a nod of his head.

When the men seemed to be about to leave, Vivienne decided she needed to do something quickly since she wanted to talk to them in private.

"Maleine, will you and Martin please go look for Grunt? I wouldn't want him to get lost in this crowd. Perhaps it'd be best to keep him in the kennel for the time being."

"Yes, my lady. Come on, Martin. Grunt will come to you if you call him." Maleine reached out for the boy's hand, but Martin pulled away.

"Nay, I want to stay and talk to the bastards," Martin protested.

"Martin, go find Grunt. Right now," ordered Vivienne, embarrassed that her son was calling these men bastards to their faces when the little boy didn't even know the meaning of the word.

"Yes, my lady," said Martin with a frustrated look, heading through the crowd with Maleine. Since he'd called her *my lady* instead of *Mother*, it was obvious Martin wasn't happy with her decision.

"What's a ... a Grunt?" asked Rook, with a silly look on his face.

"Oh, Grunt is my bloodhound," explained Vivienne, flashing him a quick smile, realizing how silly it must have sounded to him. "And I apologize for my son's disrespect, my lords."

"You mean because he called us bastards?" asked Rowen, chuckling.

"Yes. That was uncalled for and I will talk to him about it later."

"No need to scold the boy," said Rook with a quick swipe of his hand through the air. "We are known as the Legendary Bastards of the Crown, and by right, that's what we are. So, he wasn't wrong at all in calling us that."

"Rook, we're knights now and nobles," Rowen softly reminded his brother. "The page boy should show respect. Lady Vivienne is right. Come on, let's head over to the tiltyard to practice before it gets too crowded."

"If you'll excuse us, my lady," said Rook with a nod as they started away.

"Oh, so you're all knights now?" asked Vivienne, hurrying to keep up with them as they walked, trying her hardest to keep them in conversation.

"Well, not all of us. Our brother, Reed, is not," explained Rowen. "He refused to ever pay homage to dear old dad."

"Is Lord Reed here too?" Vivienne looked around.

"Nay, he's still in Scotland where he lives with his wife and children," said Rook. "He doesn't like anything to do with King Edward, and it takes a lot of convincing from us to bring him to England at all."

"That's a shame, because I was hoping to meet him too."

"You were?" asked Rook, looking at her from the corner of his eye. "Why?"

"Because ... because ..." She didn't know how to approach this subject except to just come right out and say it. Before she had the chance to change her mind, she blurted out the words. "Because I wanted to meet all three of my half-brothers."

Rook and Rowen stopped walking and turned and stared at

her. Their jaws dropped open. It was obvious that they were the ones now who did not know what to say.

Chapter Three

"Did you say ... half-brothers?" asked Rowen.

"As in ... you're the King's bastard, too?" Rook spoke up.

She nodded, feeling tongue-tied and uncomfortable and very hot.

"Nay, you must be mistaken," said Rowen with a quick shake of his head. "After all, I heard your parents were murdered seven years ago."

"They were," she told them. "I mean, my mother and stepfather were murdered. You see, I never knew about my real father being the King. My mother first told me about it with her dying breath."

"If she was dying, she might have been confused and talking nonsense," said Rook, seeming to want to dismiss this idea.

"Nay, she wasn't delirious. My mother knew exactly what she was saying," protested Vivienne. Just to prove her point to the men, she quickly looked around and then removed the hidden ring hanging from a chain around her neck, holding it up for them to see.

"What's that? It looks like the King's ring," said Rook, reaching out to touch it.

"Yes, it is," she told him.

"It has his royal crest on it and everything, including the big, precious stone worth a lot of money," added Rowen, leaning forward to get a better look at it. "Where did you get this? Did you steal it?" He narrowed his eyes, perusing her as if he thought she were a thief.

"Nay! Of course not," she gasped, pulling the ring away. "I am not a pirate!" That comment made Rowen stand up and clench his jaw, since he'd been raised by pirates and even had his own ship at one time before he was a knight. "My mother gave it to me just before she died."

"Did I hear someone mention pirates?" Nairnie walked up holding on to Starah's hand. "Och, it's good to see ye, boys. How are ye?"

Vivienne quickly hid the ring back under her clothes.

"Nairnie! So good to see you, too," said Rook with a big smile. "Where's that unruly beast of a husband of yours?"

"He's no' a beast, Rook, he's a kind man. And Bear is at sea, on a mission for the King," Nairnie told them. "I'm hopin' he'll be back soon, since I miss the old buzzard."

"Nairnie, I see Martin and Grunt," said Starah, pulling at the old woman's arm. "Can I go play with them? Please?"

"I dinna ken. I'm sure Martin has work to do, since he's a page in trainin'," said Nairnie in a firm voice.

"It'll be all right," Vivienne told her. "Starah, just be sure to stay in the courtyard, and don't leave Martin or Grunt's side. Meet us in the great hall in half an hour."

"Thank you!" Starah happily skipped away, meeting up with Martin and Grunt.

"Now, what's all this talk of pirates, I heard?" said Nairnie, looking at Vivienne with one eye squinted.

"Lady Vivienne was just telling us that we share the same father," said Rook, using no discretion at all.

"Shhh, please, not so loud," gasped Vivienne, seeing the sheriff making his way toward them. "I don't want anyone else to know."

"Now you did it, Rook," said Rowen. "You shouldn't have said that in front of Nairnie."

"Och, I'd already guessed who she really was, so it was no secret to me," said Nairnie, looking over at Vivienne. "Lassie, ye need to tell the King."

"Aye, it might do you well to let Father know he's sired another child," agreed Rowen.

"I'm not so sure about that," said Rook. "After all, his mistress is coming with him to the tournament, and I don't think Alice would like to hear about Father's infidelity, or see proof of it, for that matter." He held out a hand to motion to Vivienne as the proof.

"Dinna worry, I'm sure Vivienne willna show Alice Perrers the King's ring," said Nairnie. "Besides, if Alice saw it, she'd want it for herself, since she is so greedy."

"Nairnie, that is no way to speak of the King's mistress," said Vivienne.

"Well, it's true," said Rook with a shrug. "But when I said proof of Father's infidelity, I was speaking about Lady Vivienne, not the ring," Rook corrected the old woman.

"The King's mistress is coming here? To Mablethorpe Castle?" Vivienne wasn't thinking about the ring anymore. She was thinking about the mistress of the King now. Suddenly, she felt as if things had just gotten a lot worse. Surely one mistress wasn't about to accept another, if Alice heard about Vivienne's mother. Her stomach clenched the way it always did when something bad was about to happen.

"We can mention all this to the King for you if you'd like," offered Rowen.

"Nay!" Vivienne's gaze flashed over to Zachariah, who was picking his way through the crowd, slowly making his way toward them. He stopped to speak to a few people every few steps he took. The sheriff was a well-known figure and loved by everyone in town. Now that the townsfolk were showing up to watch the tournament, she was sure they felt delighted that their sheriff would be there as well to protect them. "I don't want anyone to mention it to the King. I don't want anyone to know about this. My dying mother told me to keep it a secret."

"Then why did you tell us?" asked Rook, looking as if he thought she were addled.

"I'm not sure." Vivienne's heart drummed in her chest. "I suppose I just wanted to know what it was like to be someone in ... in our position. But we can talk about it later. Please. The sheriff is on his way over here and I would prefer that he didn't know about this. For now."

"Boys, keep yer big mouths shut," warned Nairnie, her hands going to her hips. "Lady Vivienne doesna want trouble. I'm sure she will tell Edward when she feels the time is right."

"All right, then," said Rook. "Rowen, shall we head to the practice yard? After all, I really want to beat Father in the joust."

"I'm jousting with him, not you," Rowen corrected his brother.

"Nay, you're not. I am. I'm better at the joust and you know it," was Rook's reply.

"Ye can both joust with him ... now go. Shoo," said Nairnie, brushing her fingers through the air, trying to send them away. As soon as they left, Nairnie turned and looked directly into Vivienne's eyes. "If ye dinna tell Zachariah about this soon, lassie, I swear I will do it for ye."

"Nay, Nairnie, please don't." Vivienne grabbed the old woman's arm. "I plan on telling him. But just not yet."

"Then when? He needs to ken about this. Ye two are supposed to be good friends."

"We are."

"Well, good friends dinna keep secrets from each other."

"I know," said Vivienne, flashing Nairnie a smile that didn't reach her eyes. "Mayhap after I talk to the King, I'll tell Zachariah everything. But I'd like to speak to King Edward about it first to get his reaction."

One corner of Nairnie's mouth lifted and she continued to peruse Vivienne with one eye still squinted. "Ye'd better no' change yer mind about this, lass. And while ye're talkin' to the King, see if he can get ye out of this silly idea of bein' a prize bride. That is, unless ye want to marry a man who isna the sheriff."

"What?" gasped Vivienne just as Zachariah walked up to join them.

"Are you two talking about me?" asked Zachariah with a sexy grin. His smile faded when neither of them answered. "I was only jesting. I didn't mean anything by it, I swear. Why? Were you really talking about me?"

"Sheriff Fitch," said Vivienne. "It's a nice day we're having, isn't it?"

"Yes," he said, looking at her in a suspicious way. "Nice weather for a tournament, that is. Where is Starah, Nairnie?" He glanced around for his daughter. "I don't want her lost in this crowd."

"Och, she's just fine, Sheriff. The girl is off playin' with Martin and Grunt."

"The children are alone? You shouldn't have left them alone." Sometimes Zachariah could be overprotective, and this was one of those times.

"Starah is safe. You don't need to worry," Vivienne assured him. "She is inside the castle walls and I've instructed her not to leave."

"I still don't like this. She's too young and shouldn't be without adult supervision."

"Blethers, Sheriff, really," scoffed Nairnie. "I'm goin' to find them right now, so dinna ye worry a bit about the young ones." Nairnie looked over to Vivienne and winked. "Good luck, lass," she said before turning and waddling away.

"Good luck?" repeated Zachariah, shifting to watch Nairnie go. "What did she mean by that? Lady Vivienne, is there something going on that I should know about?"

"Nay, nothing at all." Vivienne looked down and fixed her bodice, making certain that the King's ring was once again hidden.

"Did I see you talking with the Legendary Bastards of the Crown?" asked the sheriff next.

"Yes. Yes, you did," she admitted, not giving him any more information about their meeting.

"Really. Well, what did they say?"

"Not much. I wanted to meet them, and Nairnie knows them so she introduced me." It was a partial lie, but she figured it would sound too bold of her if the sheriff thought she'd introduced herself to such men as these. "Sheriff, I thought you were going back to town to pack your belongings and to get ready for your stay here at the castle."

"I was, but my plans changed," he told her. "Starah didn't want to leave right now, and I figured I'd go back later to do it. Besides, I wanted to start checking in with the guards and securing the premises for the King's arrival just in case he shows up early."

"Early?" Vivienne's eyes widened. "The King might arrive here before tomorrow?"

"It's possible, you never know. After all, the tournament starts in the morning, so he might want to get here a day ahead of time to get settled before things start. After all, most of the competitors have been here for a week already. They're all in high anticipation."

"I understand, it's just that I wasn't prepared for this."

"Prepared? Lady Vivienne, why are you acting so odd? And why does the King's arrival seem to upset you so much? I mean, the tournament starts first thing in the morning, and everyone is getting here a day ahead of time, as is proper. Why would the King being here, too, make you so nervous?"

"Me? Nervous? Nay, I'm not. Not at all. Why would you think that?" She giggled nervously. Her hand went to her chest, resting over the ring hidden beneath her clothes in a form of false comfort. "I'm just a little anxious, I guess. That's all. And excited." She looked up at him and tried to look happy about this. "I mean, it's not every day that someone gets to actually meet the King."

"Vivienne," he said softly, leaning forward, not bothering to use her title. "I know you too well."

"What does that mean?"

"It means, I can tell you are extremely worried about something, and I don't think it is just that the King will be here at the castle. You know you can talk to me about whatever it is you have on your mind. So, tell me what is it that has you so nervous? You are not normally like this, no matter what the situation."

"I'm just ... worried. About the betrothal. And of course, the King's arrival. I mean, this is all happening so fast." It was all happening so quickly that she couldn't even think straight right now. She needed a plan. Bid the devil, she needed to know how to talk without tripping over her tongue right now.

"Yes, I agree that your uncle did throw together this tourna-

39

ment quite quickly," stated the sheriff. "But I have a feeling it is so much more than that. There is something that you are not telling me, and I believe you should. Now, speak up. What is it?"

Vivienne felt as if she couldn't breathe. If Zachariah knew she was the King's bastard, would he hate her for it? Especially since she knew this seven years ago and never told him? Mayhap Nairnie was right. By keeping this information from the sheriff she might have hampered the chance of Zachariah finding her parents' murderers. "Oh, look! Here comes Constable Dorson," said Vivienne, glancing across the crowded courtyard and waving her arm in the air to flag him down.

"Vivienne?" Zachariah's voice was deep and foreboding. He sounded sexy, but at the same time it was almost like a warning. "I need to know. Whatever it is, you can tell me. Trust me, for God's sake. You know I will help you however I can."

"Oh, Zachariah, thank you. And I want you to know that I do trust you, honest I do," she said, feeling her cheeks becoming flushed. "I will talk to you about what's troubling me, I promise. But just not right now." She reached out and gently rested her hand on his forearm.

"If not now, then when?"

"Soon. Just have faith in me. Please. I need a little more time."

"Fine," he said, releasing an exasperated breath. "Take all the time you need." His hand covered hers and a caring smile lit up his face. "I just don't know how much time we'll have to spend together before you're wed to the tournament winner and whisked away from Mablethorpe forever."

"Nay, that is *not* going to happen, I promise you that. I told you, I am not marrying anyone, and neither am I ever leaving here. Mablethorpe Castle is my home now, and where I belong."

"I don't think you have a choice in the matter, sweetheart."

"I do have a choice. It is my life, and *I* will determine what happens. No one else. I'm not sure how I'll stop this insane idea of me wedding the winner, but somehow, some way, it will happen if it is the last thing I ever do."

"I CERTAINLY HOPE SO," said Zachariah, with a slight nod, his emotions starting to choke him and make his throat feel dry as he turned away to greet his constable. He couldn't imagine his life without Vivienne in it. Vivienne was truly amazing in every way. She was a confident, independent woman, so unlike most females. If she set her mind to something, there was no stopping her. He'd learned that about her many years ago. Nothing ever seemed to scare Vivienne. And no one, not even a man ... or perhaps even a king, was going to stop her once she made up her mind about something. That was what attracted him to her, as well as frightening him at the same time. If Vivienne were forced to marry a nobleman, there was no telling how her new husband would treat her. All Zachariah wanted was the best for her. She'd already had so many disappointments and hardships in her life that all he hoped for was for her to find the happiness that she truly deserved.

"Constable," he called out, dodging a few running children, a pig, and an alewife carrying a large tray filled with tankards of ale. The courtyard was bustling with activity as everyone anxiously awaited the start of the tournament and the visit of King Edward.

"Sheriff, there you are," said Constable Dorson, accidentally stepping on the paw of a stray dog and jumping backward as the hound snarled at him before running away. "This looks as if it is shaping up to be quite a huge event."

"Yes, it is and it's important that we keep our eyes and ears open. There will be pickpockets, fights, and mayhap even women being accosted. You never know what will happen with a crowd this size."

"And the King. What about the King?" asked the constable in concern. "How in heaven's name will we protect him? After all, that is what is expected of us, is it not?"

"We are here at the request of Lord Mablethorpe to watch over things concerning the castle and the safety of the onlookers. I am sure the King has his own guards who will be at his side during this event." Zachariah stepped back as a juggler came through the crowd tossing balls over his head. The balls were made of leather stuffed with rags and sewn together with thread. The juggler was dressed in party clothes, consisting of trews and even a tunic that was yellow on one side and blue on the other. He wore a small cap with bells on it, and reminded Zachariah of a court jester.

"As long as we don't have any more murders, this should be orderly and peaceful," said the constable.

"Murder?" asked the juggler, looking over at them and dropping a ball. "Did you say murder?" Zachariah realized just then that this man wore the colors of the King and must have been sent ahead of the King's arrival.

"Nay, you misheard us. Now go on." Zachariah tried to get the man to leave. "Go about your business before I have you arrested."

"Aye, Sheriff." The juggler picked up the dropped ball, and hurried away, looking over his shoulder at the men.

"Don't even say the word *murder* aloud," Zachariah warned the constable under his breath. He scanned the crowd, but no one else had seemed to hear them.

"Sorry, Sheriff," apologized Constable Dorson. "I suppose gossip like that could create quite a stir if the juggler starts a rumor. And it'll be naught but hearsay."

"Hopefully, that's all it will be. But something tells me that this tournament will be anything but orderly or peaceful."

"What are you saying, Sheriff? Do you really expect something bad to happen?"

"I always expect something like ... you-know-what to happen when Lady Vivienne is involved," said Zachariah, not wanting to say the word *murder* aloud. "After all, if you haven't noticed, everywhere she goes, trouble seems to follow."

"Are you saying Lady Vivienne is cursed?" asked the constable, with wide eyes. "Does she attract trouble to herself somehow?"

"I'm not saying anything of the sort," Zachariah clarified, even though he had been thinking that exact thing in the back of his mind. "All I'm saying is that she's to be a prize-bride and doesn't want to be one. I am not expecting her to accept that fate without fighting back somehow. That alone will create a stir. And as much as I hate to admit it, I have a feeling the end results will be anything but peaceful."

Chapter Four

The herald's straight trumpet sounded, and Vivienne jerked her head around, eager to see who entered the gates of Mablethorpe Castle now. Every time someone was announced, she was sure it would be the King. But it wasn't. However, the traveling party entering the gate at the moment seemed to have something to do with the King. She picked up her skirts and hurried across the courtyard, wanting to know more.

"The servant household of King Edward III," announced the herald, as a traveling party of people mainly on foot entered through the front gates. A guard atop a horse led the way. The guard's horse was wearing trappings decorated with the royal crest of the King.

"Excuse me. Let me through." Vivienne picked her way through the horde of people who congregated around the entrance of the castle, eager to see their noble ruler. "Move aside, please." She was having a difficult time making her way to the front gate. That is, until Nairnie stepped through the crowd of people with Starah, Martin, and Grunt with her. Maleine straggled behind.

"Didna ye all hear the noblewoman?" shouted Nairnie. "Now move yer blasted arses and let Lady Vivienne through. This is her home, no' yers."

"Nairnie," said Vivienne in surprise.

The crowd started to turn to see what was going on, but still didn't make way for Vivienne.

"I said move yer doups! Didna ye hear me?" Nairnie started pushing her way through the people and to the front gate.

"I'll help, Nairnie." Martin ran up beside her and waved his wooden sword in the air. "Make way for my noble mother," said the boy. People started grabbing their children and moving aside, not wanting to be hit by the boy's swinging sword, even if it wasn't a real weapon.

"Martin, nay," said Vivienne, but her words fell on deaf ears. Mayhap it was because Grunt thought it was some kind of fun game and started barking and jumping at Martin, and running in circles around him, even knocking into onlookers.

"Grunt, stop that!" Vivienne was about to run after them when she noticed Starah standing there with tears in her eyes. She held on to her new, big black cat that used to be the rat-catcher's cat. She called her Midnight.

"Oh, Starah, are you scared?" asked Vivienne, making her way over to the girl.

"I don't like the crowd and neither does Midnight." She started bawling. "I want to go home."

"You'll be safe with me." Vivienne took Starah's hand. "Come on, we might get a glimpse of the King. Wouldn't you like that?"

"Nay! I don't care about the King. I'm scared. I want my father."

"I'm here, my lady. I've got her," said Maleine, rushing up and taking Starah's hand from Vivienne. The cat squirmed in the little girl's arms and Starah almost dropped her.

"Lady Vivienne, hurry up!" shouted Nairnie, with a wave of her arm through the air. "I canna hold back the crowd forever. Ye need to get up on the dais with Lord and Lady Mablethorpe. I think the King is arrivin'."

"Yes. Of course." Vivienne looked down at Starah and then back to Maleine. "Will you two be all right if I go up on the raised platform?"

"Of course, my lady," said Maleine, hardly heard over Starah's crying.

"I can't leave. Not now," said Vivienne, bending over to put her arms around Starah.

"Starah? What's wrong?" It was Zachariah pushing his way toward them. The constable was right behind them.

"Father!" Starah ran to the sheriff and he scooped her up in his arms. But when he did, the cat jumped out of the girl's hold and meowed loudly.

"Midnight! Get her, Father," cried Starah. "She's going to get stepped on."

"Not the damned cat," grumbled Zachariah. "I told you to leave that thing back in town."

"Midnight wanted to come and sneaked into the wagon when I wasn't looking," Starah told him.

"Somehow, I doubt that. Starah, we're going to have to have a little talk about obedience, but not now." He kissed her head and put her on the ground. "Right now, the constable and I have to provide security. With the King's arrival, we need to be on our toes. Where the hell is Nairnie?"

"I'm here, Sheriff," said Nairnie, making her way back through the crowd toward them. She swung a metal ladle in the air, making people jump back and away from her. Martin followed on her heels, still waving around his wooden sword. "Get back! Move away," commanded Nairnie, using the ladle to clear her path.

"What on earth are you doing, Nairnie?" Zachariah ripped the ladle out of the old woman's hand, thinking she'd gone mad. "You're going to hurt someone with that. Be careful."

"Och, that's my good ladle," proclaimed Nairnie, grabbing it back from him. She blew on it and shined it on her skirt. "It always kept the pirates in line. I'm sure it'll work with this unruly bunch too."

"The constable and I will see to the visitors. That is not your concern," he scolded. "Now hold on to Starah and don't let her go. I don't want my daughter lost and crying in fear from this chaos."

"I'll protect Starah," said Martin, holding up his wooden sword bravely. "I'm going to be a knight someday, you know," said the boy, never letting anyone forget it.

"Martin, you stay with Nairnie for now as well. And put down the sword," Vivienne scolded. "Where is Grunt? And Midnight?"

"I don't know," said Martin with a shrug. "Grunt was here a minute ago."

"Nairnie, you and Maleine please take the children back to my chamber," instructed Vivienne, talking to them, but keeping her attention on the procession coming through the front gate.

"Now, my lady?" asked Nairnie. "But I'm sure the children want to see the King. I ken I do."

"Nairnie, please. It is for their own safety," said the sheriff.

"But I'll watch them. They need to see the King."

"You heard Lady Vivienne, now go," demanded Zachariah, not wanting to be distracted with the children when he was supposed to be protecting the castle grounds. Now was the most important time, since the King was at the end of this long procession.

"Hrumph!" said Nairnie with a sniff. "Come along, children. They dinna want us here."

"But I need to find Midnight," complained Starah. "She's lost."

"And I need to find Grunt," added Martin, looking around. "Grunt, where are you?"

"We'll find them for you. Now go back to Lady Vivienne's chamber where you'll be safe, and stay there until I come to get you." Zachariah didn't like being so distracted while he was supposed to be working.

"Me too, my lady?" Maleine looked up at Vivienne.

"Yes, Maleine. Just for now," answered Vivienne. "When things calm down, you'll all have a chance to meet King Edward, but just not now."

"Aye, my lady." Maleine took Martin by the shoulder as Nairnie picked up Starah, who was still crying and whining about her cat. Once they left, Zachariah walked up close to Vivienne.

"You should be out of this madness as well, for your own safety, my lady." He took her by the arm and plowed his way through the onlookers, heading for the dais. "Move aside, by order of the law," he started shouting. It worked. People recognized him as the sheriff and moved and let them pass. In a matter of minutes, Zachariah had escorted Vivienne up to the raised platform where Lord and Lady Mablethorpe stood, watching the entourage of the King enter through the front gate. The bastard sons of the King, Lords Rook and Rowen, were up on the platform as well. People cheered and pushed their way closer to the front gate, hoping to get a glimpse of King Edward.

The herald's trumpet sounded again, followed by the next announcement. "Please welcome King Edward III, our ruler, our protector, the King of England."

The people all clapped and shouted in excitement as the King rode through the gate next, surrounded by guards on horses on either side of him. A man rode on a horse right next to the King and also a woman at his other side.

"I don't see his mistress," said Constable Dorson, coming to Zachariah's side. "Where is Alice Perrers?"

"I don't know," he answered. "Perhaps she doesn't like tournaments and decided to stay back."

The King was helped by the man riding with him, dismounted, and made his way up the platform, waving to the crowd. Zachariah thought Vivienne would be the first to greet the King, but instead, she stepped back behind her aunt. Before he knew it, she'd made her way from the platform and was descending the stairs.

"My lady?" Zachariah rushed over to her side. "Why are you leaving the platform? What are you doing?"

"I thought I saw Midnight in the crowd. I'm going after her," stated Vivienne.

"Now? The King just arrived. Isn't it proper to stay here and greet him?"

"There will be plenty of time for that later, don't worry."

"I don't understand," said Zachariah, thinking she was acting very odd. "It's almost as if you are avoiding your meeting with the King."

"Nay. I told you, I saw Midnight. Oh, there she is. Excuse me." She started to walk away, but Zachariah grabbed her by the arm to stop her.

"Vivienne, I will get the damned cat. You need to get back up on that dais right now and greet the King. It is your duty."

"But I ..."

"Is there a reason you don't want to meet the King?"

"Nay. Why would there be?" Vivienne asked with a shrug.

"I'm not sure, but you are acting very strange. Almost as if you are afraid of meeting him."

"Now, that's silly," she said, brushing off his comment as if it meant nothing. "And I find it amusing that you would even say such a thing, Sheriff."

"Really," he said with a raised brow. "Then you might also find it amusing that your uncle is motioning for you to get back up on the dais, and he looks furious right now."

"He does?" She turned and looked up at her uncle, a lack of enthusiasm evident as her face showed all the signs of defeat.

"Go!" Zachariah told her, turning her by the shoulders and gently pushing her toward the stairs.

He heard her let out a deep sigh as she climbed the stairs with her shoulders slumped and her eyes cast toward her feet.

"Did I miss something, Sheriff?" asked Constable Dorson, a look of confusion washing over him.

"I have a feeling we both did." Zachariah heard the hissing of a cat and turned to see Midnight getting pushed around by the rough crowd as they hurried to try to get closer to the King. Then he heard the barking of Grunt as the dog wove through the legs of the onlookers, chasing after Midnight. "Constable, go get my daughter's cat and take it and also that damned hound to Lady Vivienne's chamber."

"What? Now, Sheriff? But the King just arrived and our assistance is needed."

Zachariah looked up to see Vivienne stretching her neck, peering into the crowd since she heard her bloodhound barking.

"Do it," snapped Zachariah. "Because if you don't, Lady Vivienne will be back down here in a second, and I will warn you, Lord Mablethorpe is going to have our heads over this."

"Aye, Sheriff. I'm going." Constable Dorson hurried away, chasing after Grunt and Midnight.

Vivienne looked directly at him. Zachariah held up a hand, silently telling her to stay where she was. Then he used his finger to make a circle in the air, trying to tell her to turn around and greet the King as was proper. Egads, what was wrong with her? And why, pray tell, was she acting as if she didn't want to be introduced to the most powerful man in the land?

Chapter Five

Vivienne felt as if she were about to swoon when her uncle pulled her forward and introduced her to the King.

"This is our niece, Lady Vivienne," her uncle said, positioning her right in front of her real father, making her want to retch.

"My King. So nice to meet you." Vivienne curtseyed to the tall, regal man. This close up, she could see every wrinkle on the King's face. He had long blond hair with lots of gray mixed in. His beard was down to his chest. The King wore a silk tunic and long cloak lined in ermine. A jeweled crown rested atop his head at a slight angle. The rings he wore graced each of his long, bony fingers. Her eyes immediately fastened on his hand. He wore a ring very similar to the one she was wearing, hidden under her clothes. His, however, had an emerald instead of a ruby. Her hand instantly went to cover the hidden ring beneath her clothing. She had to tell him who she was. Or did he already know?

"Lady Vivienne, is it? Do I know you? Have we met before? You seem familiar," the King said, making her gaze shoot up to his face now. Bright blue eyes, just like hers, stared back at her in a cross between amusement and curiosity. His hair was once blond too, just like both her hair and Martin's. Did he know of her? It made her wonder if he had perhaps met her as a child. Vivienne had so many questions that only he could answer and only she could ask. But now wasn't the right time for any of this, she was sure.

"Funny you should say that, Father." Rook stepped forward, seeming as if he were going to blurt out her secret right there in front of everyone.

"Nay!" Vivienne threw her half-brother a look that warned him to keep quiet. "I don't believe so, Your Majesty. I would have remembered if I'd met you."

The King chuckled. "You are very comely and look to be about the same age as my Royal Mistress, Alice." He lifted his hand to partially cover his mouth. "Don't tell Alice, but you are much prettier, my dear." This was awkward, hearing him say this. She knew King Edward's mistress was half the man's age, so she figured Edward was attracted to younger women. Either way, it was wrong. Very wrong. Was he perusing her as if he expected her to be his next mistress? If so, this man was truly appalling. After all, she was his daughter! But then again, he most likely did not even know it.

"Father," said Rook, clearing his throat, stepping closer to her so the King would have to let go of her. "Rowen and I are looking forward to jousting with you tomorrow."

"Yes," said Rowen, rushing forward and standing close at Vivienne's other side. It gave her a warm feeling inside that her half-brothers were coming to her side to protect her. "We're eager to joust with you. Perhaps we can have a practice session before the actual tournament starts tomorrow."

The talk of the joust and the tournament thankfully took the King's attention off of her. Vivienne released a breath she'd been holding and slowly stepped backward, letting her brothers take the King's interest now.

"Actually, plans have changed," reported the King.

"They have? No one told me," Lord Mablethorpe spoke up. "What's changed, My King?"

"I won't be staying for the tournament after all," said Edward coolly, as if he wasn't really interested in the tournament after all.

"Why not?" asked Rook with a gruff tone. "Have you got something better to do, perhaps?" Only Edward's bastard sons could get away talking this way to a king.

"If you must know, Alice has been feeling ill lately. She wanted me to stay with her instead of even coming here."

"Father, please don't tell me you are letting Alice control your actions and decisions again," grumbled Rook. "Everyone is expecting you to be here."

"Rook, watch your tongue while mentioning my dear Alice," warned the besotted man.

"But Father," said Rowen, seeming for a moment to be lost for words. His eyes interlocked with Vivienne's, but she shook her head slowly, not wanting him or his brother to mention her. "Father, you funded this tournament, unless I am mistaken."

At that comment, Vivienne's uncle became visibly upset. "My good king, you are still going to fund the tournament even if you don't stay, aren't you?" worriedly asked Lord Mablethorpe. "I mean, I cannot afford the expenses of such a large gathering. I am not that wealthy of a man, you understand."

"Don't worry, Lord Mablethorpe. I am a man of my word," Edward assured him with a quick nod of his head. "Yes, I will continue to fund the tournament, like I promised. However, I will be leaving here before the end of the day today."

"Oh, that's a shame," Lady Mablethorpe spoke up, having

been so quiet up until now. "We wish you could stay, Your Majesty."

"Yes. And what about the joust?" asked Rowen. "Shall we notify the master of ceremonies that it'll be canceled then?"

"Nay," said Edward with a slight cough. "But do tell him it'll be moved up to this afternoon instead."

"But, Your Majesty, that is supposed to be the finale of the tournament," protested Lord Mablethorpe. "It was to be the whole reason to make everyone stay until the end."

"Lord Mablethorpe, my joust will take place today, or not at all," said Edward in a stern voice. "I don't care about or need to be anyone's finale."

"Yes, My King. We understand." Lady Mablethorpe spoke up before her husband could say something they'd all regret. With her hand on her husband's arm, she held him close to her side.

"And I'll only do one joust. That is all I am feeling up to today," the King announced.

"Only one?" asked Rook. "But I thought you were going to joust with both Rowen and me."

"Nay. Just one. You heard me."

"Which of us will you be jousting with, Father?" asked Rowen.

"Yes, is it me?" asked Rook. "After all, we all know I am better with the lance, while Rowen rules the sword."

"Mayhap so, but I believe I'll be jousting with Rowen today," said the King.

"Really? Thank you, Father." Rowen looked quite pleased, but Rook seemed angry and put out about the King's decision and not being chosen.

"Father, I'd be a better match for you," said Rook, still trying to convince the King to choose him.

"You also insulted me where my Alice is concerned," the

King reminded him with an angry sneer. "Now, someone show me to my chambers, because this noisy crowd is giving me a headache. The joust will begin in two hours from now. Don't make me wait."

"Two hours from now?" asked Lord Mablethorpe. "That soon?"

"Yes," said Edward. "I want to get back on the road and home before nightfall."

"Oh my, we have so much to do," said Lady Mablethorpe. "We had better hurry."

"Aye, that won't even give our cooks enough time to prepare your feast," Vivienne's uncle continued. "We have some exemplary ornate dishes planned to serve during the feast, in your honor."

"I don't care. I don't want a feast," said the King, seeming as if he didn't want to be bothered. "You can serve those dishes tomorrow instead. Just bring me a tray of whatever food you have ready. Bring it to my chambers anon." Edward didn't seem at all to care that he was ruining all the plans. Vivienne didn't really mind, but she knew this tournament meant a lot to her uncle.

"My King, our steward will take you and your household into the keep and show you where you'll be staying," spoke up Lady Mablethorpe, lifting her hand to motion to John.

"No need to house my entourage since we are not going to be here overnight," said Edward. "And I'd prefer to stay alone in my chamber for now, with just a guard or two at my door."

"Alone? Father, do you think that is safe?" asked Rowen in concern. "I mean, you are the King."

"Should I be worried?" asked Edward, with an edge to his voice. "Lord Mablethorpe, did you set up proper protection for me during my visit or not?"

"Yes! Of course, I did," answered Lord Mablethorpe. "I've

even hired the town sheriff and his constable to help out my guards for added protection."

"The sheriff?" Edward looked around. "Where is he?"

"His name is Sheriff Zachariah Fitch," Vivienne spoke up. "He is very good at his job."

"Really? I'd like to meet him."

"Sheriff Fitch, will you join us?" Vivienne called out, waving Zachariah up to the dais. He seemed hesitant to climb the stairs, but with a coaxing look from her, he finally made his way up to the platform. "King Edward, this is Sheriff Zachariah Fitch," she introduced him.

The King smiled and nodded. "Aye, yes. I've heard so much about you, Sheriff Fitch. That was brilliant work you did catching that menacing rat-catcher, the Pied Piper. Not to mention all the murders you've solved lately. That was you, who did those things, wasn't it?"

"Thank you, it is an honor to meet you, Your Majesty." Zachariah bowed deeply. "And yes, it's true about the murders as well as the Pied Piper ... that was me. However, I must point out that Lady Vivienne assisted me in catching the killers. She is very good with her skills of observation and investigation."

"Lady Vivienne? A girl? She did that?" The King looked shocked, but also a little pleased at the same time if Vivienne weren't mistaken. Hopefully, that would work in her favor. She'd have to thank Zachariah later for mentioning her.

"Well, the sheriff really did most of it," said Vivienne, not wanting to take the credit away from Zachariah, since he deserved the accolades. Plus, she wanted him to look good in the King's eyes.

"Lady Vivienne and her bloodhound were both very helpful," continued Zachariah with a chuckle. "As a matter of fact, the first murder Lady Vivienne helped me solve happened right here at Mablethorpe Castle."

"There was a murder here? At this castle?" The King didn't seem to like that. "Mablethorpe, you didn't tell me about that."

Lord Mablethorpe's eyes opened wide, and then narrowed as he looked over at the sheriff. "My castle is safe, My King, I assure you."

By the look Vivienne's uncle was giving Zachariah, she thought if looks could kill, the sheriff would be dead right now. Her uncle obviously hadn't told the King about the murder here, for fear that Edward wouldn't fund the tournament if he found out.

"Sheriff, are you staying here at the castle for the tournament?" asked the King.

"I am, My King."

"Then I'd like to see you as one of my guards outside my door until I leave."

"Me?" Zachariah looked up in surprise. "I'd be honored, Your Majesty, but I am not sure I am qualified for such an important job as to guard you."

"You are if I say you are—now escort me inside. I need to get out of this blasted hot sun." Edward waved a ringed hand in front of his face and let out a deep breath. He looked tired. Then again, he wasn't a young man. Men his age didn't usually even joust anymore.

Vivienne watched as Zachariah escorted the King off the platform, and then guided Edward and his entourage to the keep, being met by John, the castle steward.

"I cannot believe that I'm not going to have the chance to best him in a joust," said Rook, staring as they disappeared inside the keep.

"Don't worry about it, Rook." Rowen slapped his brother on the back. "I'll be sure to take the praise when I win against Father."

"You'll let him win because he is the King—I know you,

Rowen," said Rook. "You won't want Father to look weak in front of all these people."

"Nay, that's not true. Not this time, Brother. I'll beat him at the joust, and I'll do it just for you."

"You do that!" Rook stormed away and the rest of them followed, leaving Vivienne standing up on the platform by herself. She had hoped to build up her courage enough to tell King Edward her secret, and figured it would take some time. She had thought she'd have until the end of the tournament to do so. Now, she realized that she only had a few hours and then the King would be gone. If he left here without knowing she was his daughter, she might never again have the opportunity to tell him that he had sired her. This made her even more anxious, because she wasn't about to let him leave before she learned the truth about him and her mother.

But would she really have the courage to talk to the man who was not only her king but so much more? And in such a short amount of time? She wasn't even sure how to tell him or what to say. For all she knew, she'd never get a chance to speak to him privately. With Zachariah guarding his door, it would make her challenge even more difficult.

Vivienne's stomach clenched. Now, more than ever, she couldn't wait until this was all over. Descending the platform, she reentered the crowd, deciding to head to the kitchens. Mayhap she could at least bring a tray of food to the King in his chamber. Perhaps then she'd be able to have a word with him in private, since he was staying in his chamber alone.

A short while later, when Vivienne entered the kitchens, she saw Cook arguing with a woman she'd never seen before. The man's hands were over his head, waving above him and his face was red.

"Cook?" she asked, walking over to the fire where they both stood. "Is something wrong?"

"Yes, my lady," said Cook. "This woman is what's the matter. She thinks she can stroll into my kitchens and not only instruct me what to cook, but tell me I am doing it all wrong as well."

"Who are you?" Vivienne asked the woman.

A tall, bony, dark-haired woman who looked to be about ten years her senior turned around with a tray of food in her hands.

"Oh, pardon me, my lady." She curtsied slightly. "I am Gisela. I work for the King," she explained.

"Ah, I see. And what is the problem here, Gisela?"

"I know what the King likes to eat and how he wants it prepared. Sadly, this man is not doing it right," the woman explained.

"My lady, the King wasn't supposed to arrive until tomorrow," said Cook. "And I thought he'd be staying for the whole tournament, not coming and going in the same day. I haven't had time yet to prepare the ornate dishes. After all, do you know how long it takes to cook a peacock and replace all its feathers?"

"I understand," said Vivienne, in a calm voice. "It was a surprise to us all. Cook, do you think you can do whatever it takes to please the King?" she asked in a friendly and calming voice.

"The King, yes. This shrew, nay!" Cook jerked his head toward Gisela. "Not for all the cheese in the world am I going to do something just to please her."

"This will have to do, but the King won't like it," said the woman, holding the tray in one hand and adjusting the lid covering the plate with her other hand. "When the King complains, I will be sure to tell him that you were not at all accommodating."

"Nay, there is no need for that, Gisela." Vivienne needed to intervene fast. "I am sure we can work this out."

"No need?" Gisela's brows raised. "Yes, there is a need. He is king, my lady. King Edward deserves the very best."

"Of course, he does," answered Vivienne. "No one is saying any different."

"Excuse me, my lady. I need to deliver this plate to the King's chamber at once. Can you tell me how to get there?"

"I'll do better than that." Vivienne grabbed the tray from the woman before she could object. "I am going that way so I will gladly bring the food to the King myself."

"But, my lady! That is my job. It is not a job for nobles such as you."

"Mayhap so, but I insist." Vivienne turned and left holding the tray, hearing the woman still protesting from behind her. Then Gisela ran after her, not wanting to let this go.

"You don't understand, my lady. I have to be the one to bring it to him. Only me."

"Not today," Vivienne replied without looking back. She hurried to the stairs, smiling since now she had a reason to be alone with the King. This was the answer to her prayers. Since the King said he didn't want any of his people in the room with him since he had a headache, there would be no one listening when she told him she was his daughter. Vivienne hummed to herself, balancing the food tray carefully, finally approaching the King's chamber. Zachariah and one of the King's guards stood watch at the door.

"Lady Vivienne?" Zachariah looked at her sharply. "What are you doing here? And what is that?" His glance lowered to her hands.

"This is a food tray, Sheriff. I am bringing King Edward his meal."

"I can see that," Zachariah answered with a scowl.

"Nay, my lady," protested the King's guard. "Gisela has to do that. It's her job."

"I know. But I told her to stay down in the kitchens and that I'd attend to it instead." She reached out with one hand and quickly knocked on the door. "After all, I want to be a proper hostess."

"Lady Vivienne, It is anything *but* proper for the lady of the castle to be serving the King his food," said the sheriff.

"Don't be silly. It shows my attempt at hospitality," she stated, determined that no one, not even the King's guard or the sheriff, was going to stop her.

"Who's there?" came the deep growl of the King from behind the closed door.

"It is me, Your Majesty. Lady Vivienne. I have your food tray," she called out.

"My lady, you really cannot do this. You don't understand," protested the guard.

"It's all right," she said, throwing open the door to the King's chamber and entering, and then quickly closing the door behind her. "Your Majesty, I have the food tray you've requested."

"What?" The King was sitting on the edge of the bed in the near dark. He had his face in his hands. "Where is Gisela? That is her job. Why isn't she bringing me my food?"

"She's not here, but I am, My King." Vivienne placed the food tray on the table. "My, it is dark in here. I think a little sunshine and a nice breeze would freshen up this stale old room, don't you?" She walked over and yanked open the shutters. A stream of bright sunshine filled the room, as well as the warm summer breeze. The King groaned, shading his eyes with his hand. "Oh, I'm sorry. Does the sunlight bother you?"

"It doesn't make my splitting head feel any better, if that's what you mean," the King complained.

"Perhaps you are hungry and just need a little food for that headache to go away." When Vivienne lifted the metal lid off the plate, a delicious aroma filled the air. "Mmmm," she said, taking a deep sniff. "Beef pottage with root vegetables in a savory gravy. My favorite." Picking up the spoon, she looked back toward the door. She might only have a minute to talk to the King before someone entered so she needed to hurry. "My King, there is something I wish to speak to you about now that we have some privacy."

"Did you say pottage? Is that pottage on that tray?" snapped the King, wrinkling his nose in disappointment.

"Yes, My King."

"Where the hell is my venison and quail eggs? I like venison and quail eggs. Gisela knows that."

"I am sorry, My King, but those items were not available yet."

"Lady Vivienne, I don't believe this. I am king and yet you are trying to feed me pottage? And after I funded this whole damned tournament? You have got to be jesting! Wait until I have words with Lord Mablethorpe about this."

Vivienne suddenly wondered if she should have listened to Gisela. After all, she'd grabbed the tray from the woman and had never even checked what food was under the lid before bringing it to the King. Now that she thought about it, pottage was not a suitable dish to be served to a king at all. Especially since he paid for everything for this tournament, including all the food!

"Oh, I'm sorry, Your Majesty," she said, looking down to the bowl, feeling totally embarrassed. "It is just that ... you requested to eat your meal earlier than was originally planned. You see, it takes much more time to prepare venison and the food we had intended to serve you. I am sure you'll have some of that later though."

"Nay, I won't. Because I told you that I won't be here later. Oh, hell, just give me the damned pottage. I need food to cure this throbbing head."

"Of course, My King." She held out the spoon for him. "I ... do have a few questions I hope you won't mind answering while you eat."

"What is it?" He inspected the spoon without taking it.

"It's a spoon ... Your Majesty." She wondered why the man was asking such an addled question. Mayhap he'd hit his head and that was why it hurt. Perhaps it was causing him not to be able to think straight.

"Nay, I know what a spoon is, you silly girl." He ripped it out of her hand. "I meant your questions."

"Oh, yes. Of course. My questions." Vivienne released a deep breath, trying to calm her jumping stomach.

"Wait a minute," he said, holding up his free hand. "This isn't right." King Edward put the spoon down on the table."

"My King? What isn't right?"

"I cannot eat the food yet."

"You can't? But I thought you wanted your meal early. To cure your aching head. I said I am sorry about the pottage, but I assure you that Cook makes it taste delicious. The flavors explode right on your tongue."

"That's not what I mean," he all but shouted. "I cannot eat it because I always have a food taster test my food first. In case it is poisoned."

"Poisoned?" She looked at him blankly, blinking several times, not believing what she'd just heard. "You don't really think we'd serve you poisoned food, do you? I assure you, it is not tainted in the least. Now take a bite while I talk to you about something very important." She picked up the spoon and handed it to him once again, but he crossed his arms over his chest and stubbornly shook his head.

"What could be more important than knowing that my food isn't poisoned?" asked the King. "What, I ask you?"

Once again, Vivienne felt foolish. "Nothing is more important," she softly answered. "May I call for your food taster to come to assist you, my good King?"

"I don't know why she didn't just bring the food to me in the first place as is proper."

"She?" Vivienne's stomach churned. "Oh, no. Is your food taster a woman?"

"Yes, that's right."

"Is it Gisela by any chance?"

His head jerked upward and he leaned back a little on the bed. "Yes. Gisela. That's right. Do you know her?"

"Kind of. I mean, I ... met her. In the kitchens, earlier."

"I'll have Gisela dismissed for this, I swear. She knows better."

"Nay, don't dismiss her. You see, it is my fault. She told me she needed to bring your food to you, but I insisted on doing it myself, instead."

"Really."

"Yes, but I didn't know she was your food taster. Honest, I didn't. Please don't punish her, My King."

He mumbled something inaudible.

If I may, I'd like to tell you about something that happened to me seven years ago."

"You do it."

"Pardon me?"

"Since you insisted on bringing the food, you taste it for me. Go on." He held out his open hand, motioning to the food.

"Me?" Vivienne's heart ran rampant. "You want me to taste your food?"

"Yes, that's right."

"Oh, but I couldn't."

"Why not? After all, you assured me you'd never serve me poisoned food at Mablethorpe Castle, so why are you even hesitating? Go on, Lady Vivienne. Taste it. I am hungry and want my meal, as meager as it might be."

"I ... I ... Is that really what you want me to do, Your Majesty?" She prayed that he'd change his mind, but he didn't. Instead, he nodded.

Seeing no way out of this, and knowing he'd never answer a single question for her until this was done, Vivienne dipped the spoon into the pottage, hoping to hell that no one was really trying to poison the King. If so, she was about to die, and it was no one's fault but her own. Slowly, she lifted the spoon, closing her eyes, and saying a silent prayer. Then she opened her mouth to take in the food.

"Nay! Stop."

"What?" Her eyes popped open. "My King?"

"If the food is really poisoned and you die, I'll never hear the end of it from that big-mouth uncle of yours. My head hurts enough as it is, having had to listen to Alice chastise me and tell me not to come to the tournament. She thought it wasn't safe. Can you believe it?"

"Not safe?" She forced a chuckle. "That is silly. Is that why she didn't come along with you?"

"Nay. I actually told her I didn't want her at my side. It was a compromise in a way. She stayed back, and I said I'd return to her later today. I just needed to make an appearance."

"I see." She still stood there balancing the pottage on the spoon, not knowing what to do. "Did you want me to send someone to fetch Gisela for you?"

"Nay. Don't bother. Guard!" he yelled, and immediately the door opened.

"Did you call, My King?" asked the confused guard.

"Yes. Is the sheriff still out there with you?"

"I am," said Zachariah, poking his head around the guard.

"Good. Come in, Sheriff."

"What can I do for you, Your Majesty?" Zachariah had a smile on his face. Until he heard the King's next words.

"I need you to act as food taster for me. Taste that pottage." His long finger pointed at the spoon of food still raised to Vivienne's mouth.

"What?" Zachariah's gaze shot over to meet with Vivienne's. "Whatever for, My King?"

"He says his food taster always tests his food before he eats it," Vivienne explained.

"Then let me fetch your food taster for you." Zachariah turned to go.

"Yes, that would be good. Thank you, Sheriff," said Vivienne putting the spoon of food back into the bowl.

"Nay, wait," commanded the King, stopping him from leaving. "Lady Vivienne assures me that I would never be poisoned by eating food from Mablethorpe Castle."

Zachariah stopped at once and looked back at them. "I ... I'm sure she's right. Now, I'll be right back with your food taster, just to put your mind at ease." He turned once more to leave, but the King stopped him once again.

"Nay. You will taste the food for me, Sheriff. After all, isn't it your job to protect me?"

"Well, yes, but ..." Zachariah looked over to Vivienne with a worried expression. She had to do something to help him.

"The sheriff is a widower with a young daughter to raise," she blurted out. "He really can't take the chance of something happening. I'll do it."

"Vivienne, nay," said the sheriff under his breath, as she scooped up some pottage on the spoon and brought it closer to her mouth. "You just found your son after seven years. Don't risk it. Martin needs you."

"Her son? What's this?" asked the King. "Lady Vivienne,

does this have something to do with what you wanted to speak to me about in private?"

Vivienne felt trapped now. If she agreed that it was, she'd have to tell him everything in front of Zachariah. But she hadn't told the sheriff her secret yet. It wouldn't be good for him to find out this way. There was only one thing to do to get out of this horrible situation that she found herself in. Vivienne didn't answer. Instead, she quickly opened her mouth and swallowed down the spoonful of pottage, feeling scared out of her mind now, of possibly dying.

The room became suddenly silent. Then an odd twisting sensation churned in her stomach. Her hand covered her belly.

"What's going on? Is she getting sick?" asked the King. "God's eyes, was that food poisoned after all?"

"I—I'm not sure," mumbled Zachariah. "I hope not."

Vivienne took a deep breath and then slowly released it. Thank God she was still alive! "The food is fine, just like I said." In total control, she slowly slid the bowl across the table to the King.

"Then why are you holding your stomach?" The King didn't seem to believe her.

"I sometimes have an odd feeling in my belly when something is about to happen."

"Happen? What does she mean, Sheriff? What's going to happen?"

Vivienne suddenly realized she never should have said that. After all, the King was very superstitious. Wasn't that the reason he thought triplets were bad luck, and why he'd ordered his own sons killed when they were just helpless, newborn babies?

"Oh, it's nothing to do with the food, I assure you," Zachariah told him. "I am sure it is fine to eat. Look, I'll have a bite as well." He followed Vivienne's actions and ate a spoonful of pottage, smacking his lips together after he swallowed. "That should prove it's not tainted."

"Yes. I can see it's the truth now." The King grabbed the bowl and spoon and started shoveling the pottage into his mouth.

"Vivienne's stomach tends to churn when she's nervous," Zachariah continued. "I mean, after all, she is about to become the bride of the winner of the tournament, and is going to have to marry against her will."

"Zachariah, please," Vivienne whispered, but the sheriff held up his hand, telling her without words that he would take care of this.

"I see what you mean," said the King, between bites of food. "That's what you wanted to speak to me about, wasn't it, Lady Vivienne?"

"Well, yes, I suppose it is one of the things," she told him. Her gaze roamed over to the sheriff next. Zachariah stared at her and slowly nodded his head, urging her to say more. When she didn't, he spoke for her once again.

"My King, forgive me for speaking so freely, but Lady Vivienne doesn't want to marry the winner of the tournament, and was never told about this ahead of the planning," Zachariah said, only seeming to make her stomach even more squeamish.

She had wanted to first tell King Edward that he was her father. She figured that might have given her leverage in getting out of marrying anyone against her will. Too late now.

"The fact that Lady Vivienne is a prize bride wasn't my idea, it was her uncle's." The King finished off the pottage and licked his lips. "Damn, that tasted better than I thought it would. Your cook isn't bad at all, Lady Vivienne, just like you said. I'm impressed."

"Thank you," said Vivienne. "I'll be sure to give Cook that

compliment. It'll mean the world to him, especially coming from you."

"And so it should." Edward pulled a flask out from under his clothes next. He uncorked the top and raised it up to his mouth and took a big swig. "There is nothing I can do about your situation, Lady Vivienne. I'm sorry, but it's too late to be changed. The competitors are expecting you to be a prize bride, and it'll mean chaos if the promise is not carried out."

Vivienne was about to protest when the guard knocked on the partially open door. "My King, your blacksmith is here."

"What is it you want, Theodoric?" grumbled the King.

"I just heard that your joust will take place today, My King," said the dark-haired man, bowing low, still in the doorway. Theodoric had a small mustache and beard, and little eyes that were far apart from each other. "I will inspect your horse for the joust to make certain he is shod properly and that his tack is in place and that everything is in order. Did you want me to give your armor to your squire? I have it all polished and ready to go."

"Yes. You do that. And while you are at it, sharpen my sword." He picked up his blade from the bed and held it out. "You never know when I might need to use this."

"Aye, Your Majesty." The man walked into the room. He glanced over at Vivienne and suddenly stopped. "My lady."

"Is something wrong?" she asked the blacksmith.

"I am sorry, I didn't know you were here." He quickly bowed to her. "And Sheriff, you too," he added with a nod, lowering his gaze to the floor.

"Come on, come on, take my sword," said the King impatiently. "I need to get to the joust and head back home before the sun sets."

"Thank you, My King," said Theodoric. "Who will you be

competing against, if I might ask? They might require my assistance with their armor or weapons as well."

"Mablethorpe Castle has its own blacksmith, but thank you," said Vivienne. This man seemed to think he was better or more important because he worked for the King.

"Of course, my lady. I meant no disrespect." With the King's sword in two hands, the blacksmith bowed again. "I was just trying to be helpful."

"Theodoric goes far beyond his required duties, and is one of the best blacksmiths I've ever had," said the King with a satisfied nod.

"I'm sure he is," mumbled Zachariah.

"I can't be late for my joust against my son, Lord Rowen," said King Edward. "Now get moving, blacksmith. I will meet you out on the tiltyard in an hour. And when you see that lazy squire of mine, tell him I want everything ready to go. This will be a fast joust, and then we'll be headed back home."

"Aye, of course, My King. Everything will be ready in time, I assure you." Theodoric walked backward to the door, still holding the sword flat in two hands. Then he bowed once more and quickly left the room.

Vivienne's stomach churned. She started wondering if perhaps something was wrong with the food, after all. She prayed not. If it was really poisoned and the King died, she'd never forgive herself. Of course, she'd be dead too, so what would it matter? And since Zachariah decided to reassure the King by eating the pottage as well, they'd all be in their graves if that were the case.

"Excuse me," came the guard's voice from the door once again. "Your valet is here, Your Majesty. And the pages have brought your trunk of clothes as well."

"Ah, good. Send in Frederick and the pages. And send word

to Lord Rowen that I want him ready and waiting when I arrive. I have no time to waste."

"Yes, My King." The guard bowed and left, as a short man with a mustache entered the chamber.

"Frederick, I need to dress for the joust. Where are my clothes?" asked the King.

"They are right here, Your Majesty." Frederick held out his hand and waved someone into the room. "Hurry up, boys. The King has things to do. Don't tarry." Two boys carried a trunk into the chamber, one of them being in his teens and quite tall for his age. The other looked short and young, and Vivienne couldn't see him well as he struggled with the heavy trunk. She wondered why anyone would send such a little boy to do this job. As they came farther into the room, Vivienne realized the small page just happened to be her son!

"Martin? What are you doing here?" asked Vivienne. She noticed Grunt appear at the door now, sniffing around in the corridor. A lanky, but tall young man dressed like one of the King's squires entered right behind the others.

"Sir Guy said it would be all right if I helped," answered Martin, half hidden behind the large trunk. "Plus, I wanted to meet the King." Since he was small and weak, he dropped his end and the trunk hit the floor hard, almost landing on Zachariah's toe. The sheriff thankfully jumped out of the way in time not to be hit.

"Be careful with my things!" The King shot up to a standing position, scowling at Martin. "You have no respect for the Crown, boy."

"Yes, I do," said Martin with a frown. It looked as if he were about to cry. "I met the Legendary Bastards and I wanted to meet you, too. I can't help it if the trunk was heavy and I don't have muscles yet."

"He's sorry, My King." Vivienne rushed over and put her

73

arm around her son. Grunt wandered into the room, still sniffing around. "My son is just a child, and only seven years old. Please forgive him."

"*This* boy is your son?" The King inquisitively looked at Martin.

"Yes," Vivienne answered.

"Your son is a page at Mablethorpe Castle? That's not proper. He should have been fostered out to another lord at a different castle."

"I didn't know he was my son when he was sent here to train as a page," she quickly tried to explain. "You see, I lost him seven years ago when my parents were killed on the road by bandits. Martin was just a baby. The horses were spooked and my son and my younger brother were in the wagon when the horses took off at a run, taking them both with them. I never saw either of them again. It was just recently that by luck Martin appeared into my life again."

"What a tragic story," said the King, almost sounding as if he really did have a heart, after all. "Tell me, Lady Vivienne, who were your parents? Did I perhaps know them?"

Vivienne didn't know how to answer. There were too many people in the room now, including Zachariah, to tell the King she was his bastard child. That is something she wanted to tell him in private. Besides, she didn't want Zachariah or Martin to find out this way. Thankfully, the King's valet interrupted.

"Excuse me, Your Majesty, but it is getting late. If the others will leave now, I'd like to help you dress for the joust." Frederick flipped open the trunk, digging inside.

"Yes, of course. We'll leave," said Vivienne. "We wouldn't want to get in the way."

Grunt started barking and the King jumped back in surprise. "Who let that mutt in here? Take that hound away. Now!"

"Come on, Grunt, we're not wanted here," said Martin, running to the dog and pulling him out into the corridor.

"Page, go to the tiltyard and check that my squire has readied my lance and shield. I cannot joust without them," commanded the King.

"Yes, My King," said the page, bowing and running out the door to carry out the King's orders.

"Vivienne, you never answered the King's question," said Zachariah softly, resting his hand on her shoulder.

"It can wait," she whispered back, her hand going to her chest, gently touching the King's ring hidden beneath her clothes. "Come on, Sheriff, we need to leave so the King can prepare for the joust."

"And close that door on the way out," shouted the King after them.

"Gladly," Vivienne mumbled under her breath, leaving the room with the sheriff and closing the door behind them. The King didn't seem to be a very formidable man. Mercy, he was mean to a child and cruel to a dog. Even if he did seem to take pity on her after hearing her story, it still made her wonder now if she ever wanted to tell the King that she was his daughter, after all.

Chapter Six

An hour later, Zachariah walked with Constable Dorson to the King's tent, just before the joust between King Edward and Lord Rowen was about to begin.

"Lady Vivienne was acting odd earlier," said the sheriff. "I believe she isn't thinking straight, being so upset about being a prize bride."

"Odd, really? How so?" asked the constable.

"I mean, she had every opportunity to tell the King how she felt, but yet she seemed afraid to speak up about it."

"Mayhap she is nervous, this being the first time she's met the King." The constable watched the crowd around them as they walked, the two of them always being on the lookout for approaching trouble.

"Perhaps," said Zachariah in thought. "But something tells me it is more than that. I'm just not quite sure what she seems to be keeping from me."

"Sheriff," came a voice from behind him. Zachariah turned to see Lords Rowen and Rook. Rowen wasn't yet dressed in his armor, but under his arm he held his helm, which had a long orange plume attached to the top.

"Lord Rowen and Lord Rook. This is Constable Dorson who will be helping me during the tournament," Zachariah introduced them.

"Nice to meet you," said the constable with a bow.

Rowen and Rook just nodded.

"Where is good old Dad?" asked Rook, seeming a little snide with his words. "He's not going to be late for his own joust, is he? After all, each moment counts since he is in such a big hurry to leave here."

"His guards are bringing him here in a few minutes," said the constable. "We came ahead of him to make certain everything was secure."

"Lord Rowen, I have everything ready for you," said Sir Guy from Mablethorpe Castle, as he walked up with his squire, Milo, at his side. Martin straggled behind, with Grunt following on his heels. "You'll be jousting from the other end of the field, and the King will start here."

"Thank you for helping me today, Sir Guy. My squire isn't arriving from Whitehaven until tomorrow, so I appreciate the assistance."

"I'm helping too," said Martin, holding Grunt by the collar.

"Well, thank you, too, Martin." Rowen chuckled and ruffled the boy's hair.

"Och, Rowen ye'd better hurry and dress for the joust." Nairnie waddled up, holding little Starah's hand. "Ye dinna want to keep the King waitin'."

"Father!" Starah ran to the sheriff and he scooped her up in his arms. "Are you going to sit in the stands and watch the joust with us? We have a bench right in the front row. Maleine's holding our spots for us."

"Sorry, Starah, but I can't. I am needed here to watch over the King. But I will catch up with you later, I promise." He kissed her on the cheek and put her down.

"Here comes the King," announced Sir Guy's squire, Milo.

"Come on, lassie, we need to go sit down. The joust is about to start." Nairnie took the little girl's hand. "Grunt, ye'd better come with us or ye'll just get in the way."

"I'm staying with Sir Guy to help Sir Rowen," Martin told the dog. "Go on, Grunt. Stay with Starah and Nairnie."

"Starah, you didn't bring that cat to the joust, did you?" asked Zachariah, already picturing the hound chasing the cat onto the field in the middle of the King's joust.

"Nay, Father. Nairnie made me leave Midnight in Lady Vivienne's chamber."

"Good," he answered. "Speaking of Lady Vivienne, has anyone seen her? I thought for sure she'd be here to watch the joust."

"There she is, following behind the King and his guards." Sir Guy pointed her out.

"Oh hell, no," said Zachariah, having a feeling this meant trouble.

VIVIENNE FOLLOWED behind the King and his guards as they made their way to the tiltyard for the joust. There was a small entourage around him, including Frederick, his valet; Gisela, his food-taster; Theodoric, his blacksmith; Peter, his squire; and two of his knights who she'd learned were Sir Amis and Sir Barclay. She knew if she was going to talk to Edward about not only being his daughter but also about not wanting to marry the winner of the tournament, she'd have to do it now before the King jousted. Edward already made his plans widely known that he was leaving as soon as the joust was over. She was sure he'd rush out of here and she might never see him again.

"Your Majesty," she said, trying to get as close to him as

possible, but it wasn't easy with all of his people surrounding him.

"Lady Vivienne, what are you doing here?" asked the King over his shoulder.

"I need to speak to you in private."

"My lady, the King is about to joust," said Sir Amis. "Please, go now."

"I already told you, I cannot do anything about you being a prize bride," the King said as he walked, his long cloak brushing across the dirty ground.

"I know. But I have something else I need to tell you. It's important." Vivienne's nerves started to get the best of her once again. Her stomach churned just as much as it had right before her parents were murdered.

"Now is not a good time, my lady," said Frederick.

"Please, Your Majesty," she begged. "I will be quick about it."

"If you need to talk to me then speak as we walk. I'm about to joust, and I need to focus," said the King, as they made their way across the crowded courtyard.

Every few steps, another commoner rushed forward to gush over the King, and the King's guards surrounding him had to push the people away.

"I request a private audience with you, King Edward," she said, not wanting everyone listening to their conversation.

"I can't give you that," said the King as they neared his tent. She noticed Sir Guy, Milo, Martin, and Lords Rowen and Rook standing there waiting for them. The sheriff and the constable stood on each side of the King's tent door.

Vivienne froze, her heart slamming against her ribs. It was too late. Now she'd never get a private audience with the King, and this is exactly what she needed. She'd failed. There was only one more thing she could think of that might get her that private conversation. She hated to do it, but had no choice.

"My parents were Abiathar and Flanie Harlowe," she spoke loudly. "I believe you knew them. Or at least, knew my mother, Flanie."

The King stopped at once and slowly turned to face her.

"My King, we need to hurry," said Sir Barclay.

"Yes," agreed Theodoric. "Everyone is waiting to watch you joust. Here is your sword, My King. Sharpened and polished as requested." The blacksmith handed the King his sword. King Edward took it and slowly slid it into his weapon belt.

"Everyone, leave us," commanded Edward. "Lady Vivienne, we can talk privately inside my tent, but it needs to be fast."

"Oh, thank you," she said in relief. Mayhap luck was with her today, after all.

"But what about the joust?" asked Sir Amis. "The master of ceremonies is already heading out to the field to announce you."

"Yes, the people want a joust," agreed Frederick.

"Sir Amis, you will joust in my place while I speak privately to Lady Vivienne," said the King. "That should satisfy the crowd."

"Me? But I don't have my armor here," said his knight. "I wasn't prepared for this, Your Majesty."

"Use my armor, I don't care."

"I can't use your armor. You're the King."

"That's right, Sir Amis, I am the King, and what I say, goes. Now do it! And I don't want to hear another complaint."

"Lord Rowen won't like that, My King," said the blacksmith. "He is expecting to joust against you."

"That's right. He's married and shouldn't be jousting against me to begin with," said Sir Amis. "Besides, you know I can't beat him! He is one of the Legendary Bastards of the Crown."

"Rowen," called out the King, walking up to the rest of the group. Vivienne stayed on his heels.

"Aye, My King," said Rowen with a smile. "Are you ready for the joust? It has seemed to cause a lot of interest with those attending the pre-tournament festivities."

"I'm not quite ready," said Edward. "I need a private word with Lady Vivienne. Sir Amis will take my place and joust against you first."

"So, you want me to joust twice?" asked Rowen in confusion.

"Nay. He'll be too tired. Let me joust against you in his place, Father." Rook tried once again to secure a spot jousting against Edward, but the King seemed as if he didn't want to compete against Rook. Vivienne had heard that Rook was unbeatable at the joust, so mayhap that was why. Plus, he was called Rook the Ruthless. It was more than likely that he wouldn't purposely lose against his father to let the King save face. Not with a name like that. It wouldn't look good for the King to lose against his bastard son, and Vivienne was sure King Edward knew that, too.

"Nay, Rook," said Edward. "Rowen, find someone else to joust in your place against Sir Amis, and we'll compete in the second joust instead."

"I'll do it," offered Sir Guy. "But I don't have my armor here."

"You can use mine," offered Rowen. "We're about the same size."

"But what about my lances?"

"Use my lances too," offered Rowen. "If they break, we'll get more, no worries. Now go." He handed his helm to Sir Guy.

"My King, do you really think this is a good idea?" asked Theodoric.

"Don't question my choices," snapped the King. "Sheriff,

open the tent door. I need a word in private with Lady Vivienne."

"Yes, My King," said Zachariah, opening the tent flap, enabling them to enter.

"Vivienne, what's going on?" the sheriff whispered, and she stopped in the entranceway, the King going on ahead of her.

"Zachariah, I need to speak to you later, and I am only sorry that I didn't do it sooner." She reached up and gently stroked the side of his cheek.

"What does that mean?" he asked.

"It means, I've been a fool. I am sorry I didn't trust you more, like I should have all along."

With that, she entered the tent, leaving Zachariah looking more than confused as she reached back and closed the flap behind her.

"Yes, I knew your mother," said the King, looking in the opposite direction as he spoke. "Flanie was my mistress, many years ago. She was my favorite mistress, too."

"She ... was?" Vivienne already knew her mother was his mistress, so she shouldn't be so surprised. But actually hearing the King say it, made everything so real.

"If you don't mind my asking ... were the two of you in love?" Her stomach fluttered as she waited for his reply.

King Edward slowly turned to face her. "Flanie loved me, yes. However, as you know, I was married to Philippa at the time. Even though I had mistresses, I cannot say I ever loved anyone other than my wife. But I will tell you again that Flanie was always my favorite mistress."

Outside the tent, the master of ceremonies could be heard announcing that Sir Guy would joust against Sir Amis while they were waiting for the King and Lord Rowen to compete. The crowd wasn't happy about that, and some naysayers could be heard protesting loudly.

"How did you meet my mother?" she asked.

"Don't you know?" He sounded surprised that she should even ask.

"Nay. I didn't even know she was your mistress until she confessed it to me with her dying breath."

"Oh. I see." He let out a deep sigh. "Lady Vivienne, I will tell you, but you can never repeat what I say to anyone. Not even your aunt or uncle. Do you understand?"

Vivienne swallowed deeply before answering. "All right," she said, wondering now if she really wanted to have to keep another secret. Especially one that she wouldn't be able to tell Zachariah.

"Flanie ... worked for me."

"She did?" This really confused Vivienne. "How so?" She had never heard that her mother worked in the King's castle. "Was she your cook mayhap?"

"Nay. Flanie was ... my spy."

"A spy?" Vivienne gasped, almost choking on her own spit since she was so shocked to hear this. "My mother was a spy? A spy for the King? This is so unbelievable."

"Shhhh," the King warned her to keep quiet with a finger to his lips. "That is also where Flanie met your father. Abiathar was one of my spies as well."

"Him too? Nay." Vivienne shook her head, almost laughing since this sounded so absurd. She couldn't believe this. Nay, she refused to believe this about her parents. "My father was a foot soldier, Your Majesty. And my mother was just ... just a noble-woman, nothing more."

"That's what they were told to make everyone think," said Edward. "After all, I couldn't let their identities be known or their lives would have been at stake."

"Lives at stake?" she repeated softly. Vivienne's thoughts quickly flashed back to the times her father was away for long periods. Sometimes, her mother would go with him, and they'd be watched by her aunt and uncle until Vivienne had been old enough to look after her brother, Adrian, by herself in their own home. She'd often asked where they went, but her parents had never given her an explanation. They'd just said to trust them. And that everything would be fine, and that they'd return soon. She hadn't given it much thought, actually, thinking they just wanted to go away together to have time alone. Now she realized she'd been more than gullible. But why in the world would she ever not have trusted her own parents?

Her family always seemed to have more than enough money and food and things they needed in their lives, even though her father was just a common foot soldier. Now she realized that King Edward must have seen to funding their expenses. Vivienne's heart ached. How could she have never known this? And how could her parents have lied to her by keeping this secret from her for her entire life? Everything changed in a matter of minutes, and suddenly Vivienne felt as if she'd never really known her parents at all.

"So that is why they were attacked and killed on the road," said Vivienne sadly. "They must have had information that someone didn't want getting back to you."

"I don't know who killed them or why," said King Edward with a shake of his head. "But yes, Vivienne, they were investigating some people and things for me. They were actually on their way to join me when they died. They'd sent a missive saying they needed to divulge something of utmost importance. Something that they had to tell me in person about someone deceiving us all."

"Do you know anything more about it?" she asked him.

"Nay. Not really."

"So they took the secret information to the grave with them, then?"

"Yes, that's right. And I'll never know what they were going to tell me that was of such utmost importance."

"My parents died because of something like that?" She still couldn't believe what she was hearing. Tears formed in Vivienne's eyes and she felt anger rising up inside her. Nothing like this should have ever happened.

"I'm sorry, Lady Vivienne. I miss your mother too. Had I known they'd be discovered and killed, I never would have hired them to help me in the first place. But your mother and father were good at observation and finding out things that were hidden. I needed their help, since I always felt as if someone was plotting to kill me. But alas, I guess I was wrong. Because, it's been seven long years now since they died, and there have been no attempts on my life. Whatever it was they knew might not have even had anything to do directly with me."

"This is all too unbearable," she whimpered, doing her best to keep from crying.

"I know," he said. "It seems two good people lost their lives in vain."

"Did you know about me and my brother and my son?"

"I'm ashamed to say that I didn't. I heard about your parents' deaths, but I received no other information. I hadn't talked to them about their personal lives when they were alive. Our meetings were in secret and very quick. They had to be. For all of our safety, as I've said."

"Why did my mother leave you for my ... for Abiathar?" Vivienne needed to know.

"She was my secret mistress, for a short time only. She stopped being my mistress when she became my spy and married Abiathar. She married the man because I made her do it, Lady Vivienne. Even though she didn't know him at the time, I felt this would be better for her."

"You forced my mother to marry someone she didn't know

or love? That's no different than my uncle forcing me to marry the winner of this tournament."

The herald could be heard outside, announcing the first pass of the joust. It was followed by cheering, and the sound of thundering hoofbeats as the jousting knights headed toward each other with their lances held steady and ready.

"Yes, I suppose that is true," said the King with a shrug. "But Flanie was my favorite. And I decided she needed more in her life than just being my mistress."

"What about me?" she asked. "Are you going to help me so I don't have to marry a man I don't know or love?

"I'm sorry, Lady Vivienne, but I can't help you with that, like I told you earlier. You'll need to marry the winner of the tournament as is planned."

"But you are the King! Surely you can do whatever you want. You can change this outcome."

"The competitors are here thinking they have a chance to win a bride," he told her, smoothing down his long beard. "I can't take that away from them."

"So, give them money instead of me. Please, I beg you."

"Even as king, I really can't get involved."

"Then how about if you get involved not as king ... but as my father?" She pulled out the ring from under her clothes and held it up connected to the chain. It dangled in the air, the deep red ruby reflecting in the crack of light coming in from around the tent flap. Edward's eyes fastened upon it and he slowly nodded.

"That's the ring I gave Flanie the day she stopped being my mistress and started being my spy. I told her if she was ever in trouble and needed me, to get the ring to me and I would be there to help her."

"My mother gave me this ring as she took her last breath after being brutally slain by a killer on the road." Vivienne felt choked and barely able to breathe now. Visions of that horrible incident flitted through her mind as if it had happened just yesterday. "She told me to come to you, and said that you are my father. She also said that you would help me as well as my son."

"She–she said I'm your ... father? Really?" Surprise filled his eyes, but she couldn't read if he was pleased or disgusted by hearing this. "I never knew."

"Yes, that's right. I am your bastard daughter, whether you like it or not." She held her head high and proud, meeting his gaze. Her heart drummed in her chest as she waited for his reaction. Would he smile and take her into his arms? Or would he frown and order her killed, the way he did with his bastard triplets? She wanted this over with, one way or another. Especially since her stomach was churning so badly that it caused her to double over in pain.

Before the King could even respond to what she'd just told him, loud shouting was heard from outside the tent, followed by screaming and a lot of commotion.

"Something's wrong." The King spun on his heel and hurried over to the tent flap and ripped it open. "Sheriff, what is happening out here?" he demanded. "What is all the shouting and screaming about?"

Vivienne followed on his heels, able to see Zachariah stretching his neck, looking over to the tiltyard. His hand was on the hilt of his sword.

"I'm not exactly sure, Your Majesty," said Zachariah. "It looks like Sir Guy knocked Sir Amis off his horse."

"That's not unusual, is it?" asked Vivienne, peeking out from around the King's large body. "Doesn't that mean Sir Guy just won the joust?"

"Sir Amis is not moving!" shouted Peter, running over from the direction of the tiltyard. "And there is blood on him. Lots of blood!"

"Blood?" The King squinted, looking over in the direction

where the joust took place. "That shouldn't be. Not with blunted lances." He stormed out of the tent and Vivienne followed.

She could see the master of ceremonies leaning over the man on the ground as he inspected him.

"I'm going to find out what happened." The King started toward the tiltyard.

"Wait, Your Majesty. It might not be safe," protested Zachariah, but the King didn't heed his warning. "Constable, we need to protect the King," shouted the sheriff.

"I'm going with you two," said the King's guard, Geoffrey, waving to a few more of the King's men to join them. They all ran after Edward.

Zachariah looked back to see Vivienne still standing near the entrance to the King's tent, looking confused or mayhap in shock. He'd highly expected her to be the first one to make it to the tiltyard.

"Lady Vivienne, stay there," he called out, hurrying after the King.

When they ducked under the rope and made their way out to the jousting area, Zachariah saw Sir Amis on the ground and he wasn't moving. Sir Guy, Milo, Martin, and even Grunt were standing there staring down at the man.

"What happened?" shouted the King. "God's eyes, is Sir Amis injured?"

Zachariah ran up to see the end of the lance stuck right through Sir Amis's heart. The buckle on his chest plate had broken and part of his chest hadn't been protected at all. There was blood everywhere, just like Peter had told them. Sir Amis stared up at the sky with unblinking eyes, a look of disbelief and pain on his face.

"He's dead, Your Majesty," announced the master of ceremonies, standing back up.

"Nay! How could this happen?" asked the King, sounding furious.

"Let me pass." Zachariah pushed his way through the onlookers, followed by Constable Dorson. He hunkered down to inspect the body. Sure enough, it was too late. Sir Amis was stone cold dead.

"I didn't mean to kill him!" Sir Guy screamed in disbelief. "I don't know what happened."

"I don't believe this was a blunted lance at all." Zachariah pulled the lance from the dead man's chest, holding it up to display the sharp, thin, but sturdy long blade that was fastened to the end of the wooden pole.

"That's a knife!" shouted Martin, holding on to Grunt's collar. "Is that allowed in a tournament, Sir Guy?"

"Of course not, you fool," spat Milo. "That's why the man is dead."

"If it's against the rules, then why did you give Sir Guy that lance to use?" Martin innocently asked the squire, Milo.

"Me?" Milo seemed suddenly scared. "Sheriff, I only handed him Lord Rowen's lance as instructed."

"That's right," said Sir Guy. "We didn't have time to get my lances, and Sir Rowen said to just use his, as well as his armor. So, I did."

"Is that so?" asked the King as Lords Rowen and Rook ran up to join them, stopping suddenly when they saw what had happened.

"God's eyes, is he ..." asked Rowen, staring down at the body.

"Yes, he's dead," said Zachariah, standing up with the lance in his hand. When he stood, he saw Vivienne from the corner of his eye as she, too, had joined them.

"Someone will pay for this," snapped the King. "Sir Amis was my best knight."

"Who would want to kill Sir Amis?" Vivienne sneaked through the crowd, then came to a halt directly next to the King. She stared down at the body now too.

"No one," said Edward. "Amis was liked by all."

"Why was the blade on the end of the lance, and for God's sake, why didn't anyone notice that ahead of time?" asked Rook.

"It looked like a regular lance when I handed it to Sir Guy," said Milo.

"It was concealed under the coronel." Zachariah picked up a piece of the coronel, the metal end piece that was shaped somewhat like a pronged crown. It was made to break away upon impact. "It seems that when the coronel broke away, the blade was what went into Sir Amis."

"Look at his chest plate." Vivienne hunkered down next to the dead man. "The buckle is broken." She reached out with two fingers and carefully touched it. "It seems to have been severed. Probably ahead of time."

"What are you saying?" asked Rowen. "That Sir Amis's death was deliberate?"

Zachariah stood with the bloody lance still in his hand. "I'm sorry to have to say this, but yes, it seems so, Lord Rowen."

Grunt barked several times, breaking away from Martin. The hound hurried over to Vivienne, sniffing Sir Amis's body.

"Sheriff," said Constable Dorson. "Is it safe to assume that this was a murder? And that there is a killer lurking around somewhere?"

"Aye," the sheriff answered. "That is exactly how it looks."

"That's ridiculous," broke in Rook. "Everyone knows the rules of the competition. All lances need to be blunted."

"Aren't the weapons usually checked as a competitor registers for a tournament?" asked Vivienne, running a hand over her dog's head.

"Aye. They were checked. I watched them do it," said Martin anxiously.

"My lance was blunted, I swear," said Rowen, holding up his hands.

"Och, let me through," came Nairnie's voice, as she pushed aside one guard after the other, making her way to the center of the group. She held little Starah's hand. "What is the holdup with the joust? The crowd is gettin' restless."

"Aaaaaah!" screamed Starah when she saw the dead man and all the blood. She gripped onto Nairnie and hid her face in the old woman's skirt as she cried.

"God's teeth, Nairnie, get my daughter out of here," snarled Zachariah.

"Starah, it's all right," said Martin, running over to the girl. "You'll get used to seeing dead people after a while. I did." That only made her cry more. And her crying seemed to upset Grunt. The dog started barking furiously. Little by little, more people joined them, including the King's blacksmith, his steward, and even Lord and Lady Mablethorpe.

"What's the holdup?" asked Lord Mablethorpe in his deep booming voice. He stopped when he saw Sir Amis dead on the ground. "God's eyes, what the hell happened?"

"Someone murdered Sir Amis," Martin blurted out, before the sheriff or anyone could answer.

"Murdered? Oh, nay, not again," cried Lady Mablethorpe, holding a hand cloth to her nose.

"Your Majesty, Sir Amis was your best knight," said Theodoric. "This is tragic."

"Yes, it is," agreed the King.

"What are you going to do, My King?" asked Peter.

"Someone will have to pay for the loss of Sir Amis," bellowed the King. "This cannot and will not go unpunished."

"Someone?" Rowen looked over and cocked his head. "Father, surely you don't think I had anything to do with this? I didn't even know Sir Amis."

"And yet he's dead, and your lance killed him," said Rook, not helping the situation any. "I'm sure glad I wasn't the one jousting, after all."

"I wasn't jousting either," growled Rowen, sneering at his brother.

"Nay. But I was," said Sir Guy softly, shaking his head. "I didn't know him either. I tell you, I never meant to kill him. I didn't know the blade was concealed at the end of the lance. I was only participating in a joust, like every knight has arrived here to do."

"I'm scared," wailed Starah, turning her head a little to look at the body again, and then hiding her eyes once more, crying even louder.

"Nairnie, go!" ordered Zachariah. "For God's sake, get my daughter out of here."

"Yes, and take Martin and Grunt with you," said Vivienne, getting to her feet. "This is no place for children."

"Aye, Sheriff, and my lady. Come along, children. We'll go back to the castle." Nairnie collected up the crying Starah, and Martin grabbed Grunt's collar.

"I don't want to be sent away," complained Martin. "I want to stay here and help my mother and the sheriff find the murderer."

"Martin, that's enough," said Vivienne, running a hand over her son's head. "Now you go with Nairnie and Starah and protect them until we figure out what is going on here."

"Yes, Mother," said the little boy with a sigh. "I really can't

93

wait until I'm a squire. Then mayhap I won't always be sent away when exciting things happen."

"Come on, Martin. This isna excitin', it is tragic," said Nairnie, pulling the children away with her. Martin took Grunt with them as well.

"Sheriff, the crowd is getting restless," said the master of ceremonies, pushing forward. "The word of a murder has fallen upon their ears, and the women and children are frightened and are starting to leave."

"Nay. No one leaves until I say so," answered the sheriff. "Everyone is a suspect until proven otherwise."

"No one is leaving?" asked Lord Mablethorpe. "You don't really think I'm going to house and feed all these people? And what about the rest arriving tomorrow for the start of the tournament?"

"That's true," said Lady Mablethorpe. "Do you want us to turn them away, Your Majesty?"

"Nay," the King answered. "The tournament will continue as planned. Tell the people Sir Amis has been injured, but say nothing about his death."

"The King is right," agreed Zachariah. "It'll only frighten the crowd if they know a man has been murdered. It could cause a frenzy that might result in injuries or perhaps even more deaths. We can't have that. Not with a crowd this size. We need to stay discreet about what happened here."

"Sheriff, I think we need to move his body," said Vivienne softly.

"Yes," answered Zachariah. "Constable, can you and several of the King's guards carry Sir Amis to the smokehouse?"

"Nay, not the smokehouse again," complained Lord Mablethorpe. "It is in use."

"That's right," said Vivienne. "Cook is smoking meat for the tournament. Perhaps the dungeon would be a better choice this time."

"Yes, I agree," said Vivienne's uncle. "Put his body in one of the cells. They are all empty at the moment so it shouldn't be a problem."

The King cleared his throat.

"Father? What is it?" asked Rowen.

"I cannot allow this action to go unpunished," the King said once again.

"Your Majesty, as soon as I figure out who murdered Sir Amis, I assure you, justice will be served," promised Zachariah.

"As soon as *we* figure it out," Vivienne corrected him.

"In my eyes, Sir Guy is responsible for Sir Amis being dead," said the King. "After all, he is the one who stabbed the daggered lance through my knight's heart.

"Me? Nay, Your Majesty. I tell you, I didn't do it." Sir Guy's eyes opened wide.

"Your Majesty, there are a lot of factors at play here that need to be considered before coming to a conclusion," said Vivienne, but the King didn't listen.

"Take Sir Guy to the dungeon, and lock him behind bars." The King was adamant with his decision.

"But My King, we haven't yet determined who concealed the blade under the coronel," Zachariah reminded him. "You could be locking up an innocent man."

"I could be keeping a killer from striking again, as well," said King Edward.

"Sir Guy is not to blame," Rowen spoke up. "I've known this knight for a long time, and he hasn't got a mean bone in his body."

"Then mayhap you're the one to blame for this, Rowen," said the King. "After all, it was your lance he was using."

"Your Majesty," said Vivienne. "You cannot really think

your own son would kill a man he liked and considered a friend, do you?"

"I don't know. But mayhap Rowen wanted to kill me," said the King.

"You?" Rowen looked more than confused.

"You and I were supposed to joust," Edward pointed out. "When I changed things at the last minute to talk with Lady Vivienne, you suddenly didn't seem to want to joust, and pushed it off on Sir Guy. That is a little suspicious."

"Now wait a minute," Rook spoke up. "My brother is not a murderer. Father, you are the one who tried to murder us as babies, unless you are forgetting. Mayhap you planned this all along, wanting to make my brother pay, looking for justice since we once raided you."

"That's enough," said the angry king. "While you are at it, Sheriff, lock away both Rowen and Rook as well."

"You can't do that!" Vivienne spoke brashly to the King. Zachariah cringed, picturing the King ordering her locked away next. "Lords Rowen and Rook had nothing to do with this and you know it!"

"Vivienne, please," said Zachariah, just wanting her to remain quiet.

"I can't be locked away," protested Rook. "I wasn't the one jousting, and neither was it my lance that killed Sir Amis. Anyone can see that I am innocent."

"I'm the King," bellowed Edward. "I can do whatever the hell I want."

"Oh, really?" Vivienne crossed her arms and bravely stared the King down. "That isn't what you told me a few minutes ago when you said you couldn't change the fact I was a prize bride. Suddenly change your mind about what you can and cannot do?"

"For God's sake, Vivienne, please be quiet," Zachariah

warned her. He had no idea why she thought she could speak to the King in this manner. This wasn't going to end well at all.

"I'm going back to my chamber to pack, and then I am leaving at once," the King announced, oddly not even responding to Vivienne's bold and challenging remark. Zachariah found that odd in more ways than one. "Put Sir Guy as well as Lord Rowen in the dungeon. And Lord Rook, if I hear another word out of your mouth, you'll join them. So stay silent if you know what's best for you." The King turned on his heel and his entourage followed. Except for two of his guards who came to help the constable move the dead body.

"Zachariah," said Vivienne, running to his side. "What are we going to do?"

"We're going to investigate a murder, just like we always do," he responded.

"But you can't let Lord Rowen and Sir Guy go to the dungeon. You have to do something. Please."

"I can't change the King's decision, Vivienne," he told her, wishing he could.

"Well, then, mayhap I can."

Zachariah watched as Vivienne picked up her skirts and stormed away, taking matters into her own hands. Now he was the one with the churning stomach, because he knew without a doubt that Vivienne was at it again, and trouble was sure to follow.

Chapter Seven

"My lady, wait for me."

Vivienne looked over her shoulder to see her handmaid Maleine running to catch up with her.

"Not now, Maleine. I have to talk to the King."

"I heard there's been a murder. Is this true?"

Vivienne continued to walk as she talked. She didn't want to lie to Maleine since they were friends now, and Maleine was always honest and open with her. "Yes, that's right. There's been the unfortunate death of Sir Amis while jousting."

"I also heard Sir Guy and Lord Rowen are being put into the dungeon. Please tell me that is not true."

Vivienne stopped and turned toward Maleine. "My, word sure gets around fast. Unfortunately, that part is true too, I am sad to say. However, we don't want everyone finding out the details of this event. Or mayhap I should say, that is by the King's order."

"My lady, if there is a killer at the castle, I want to help you find him."

"Mayhap we'll talk about it later." Vivienne noticed the

King hurrying into the keep. If she wanted to speak to him before he left, she had better hurry.

"I want to know what I can do to help." Maleine was very persistent.

"Nothing," said Vivienne, turning to walk away, but then having an idea. She stopped and turned back toward Maleine. "Actually, there is something you can do to help speed up this investigation."

"What? I'll do anything, my lady. Consider me at your service."

"I'd like you to give word to the servants of Mablethorpe Castle to keep their eyes and ears open. If anyone hears or sees anything suspicious, they are to report back to me or the sheriff immediately."

"Or me," said Maleine, nodding. "I can do that, my lady." She was ready to run off when Vivienne grabbed her arm.

"Maleine, it is important that you don't let any of the King's people or the visiting knights and guests know about this."

"It is? Why?" Maleine blinked her big brown eyes and smoothed back a curl of her nearly black hair.

"Because, at this time we have no clues as to who the killer is, and I don't want to warn them that we are looking for them."

"I'm sure if the killer is still here, they will know that, my lady. Unless he or she has already left the premises."

"Nay, I don't believe so."

"What makes you think that?"

"I think that Sir Amis was not the intended target. I believe the King is whom the murderer planned to kill all along, but plans went astray."

"You do?"

"I will tell you more later. For now, watch everyone. And especially keep an eye on Starah, Martin, and their pets. You don't know whom you can trust, and I fear for their safety."

"I will, my lady. I promise."

"On second thought, I only want you to tell Leif, Wymond, Cook, and Maria about this. They are the only ones I really know we can trust. After the last murder at the castle, it proved that anyone can be guilty, and right under our noses and we might not know it."

"I will, my lady. I am sure they will be happy to help. So will I."

"Thank you, Maleine. I knew I could count on you. Now go. I need to find the King and try to talk to him once more. I cannot allow Sir Guy and Lord Rowen to be imprisoned. It just isn't right."

Vivienne hurried into the keep, knocking into a juggler and falling to the ground. The juggler dropped the bags of sand he'd been using, one of them hitting her on the head.

"I'm so sorry, my lady," said the man, extending her his arm. "May I help you to your feet?"

"Yes, thank you." She took his arm, noticing he had quite a firm arm with lots of muscles. His hands were also rough and dirty. Not what she'd expect from a man who was not more than a jester. "What is your name?" she asked him, perusing his face next. He was much older than she thought most jugglers would be. Usually, they were young men, since the older ones all had skills or paid professions. This man had dark eyes, a mustache, and short beard. He almost seemed familiar, but then again, most men had mustaches and beards and dark hair, so it was deceiving, she supposed.

"I am Alvin," said the juggler. "I am here from the King's court."

"Yes. I've seen you here for a few days now."

"True. I came early with many others who serve the King. He wanted us to get situated before he arrived."

"Well, thank you," she said, brushing off her gown, meaning to leave.

"I heard there was a murder on the tiltyard and that they've thrown the killers in the dungeon."

"Nay, you've heard wrong," she told him.

"So, Sir Amis hasn't died then? And Lord Rowen and Sir Guy haven't been imprisoned for killing him?"

"Alvin, this is really none of your business. And I warn you not to be listening to gossip and starting rumors when you have no facts about the truth. Sir Guy and Lord Rowen are not murderers, I assure you."

"Then the killer still roams the grounds?" The juggler's eyes widened. "Should we be worried for our safety?"

"Nay, don't worry about your safety. The sheriff and his constable have secured the castle. Plus, Mablethorpe has many guards."

"Then if it is so secure, why was a man killed today?"

That left her speechless. The man was right. Perhaps they needed to heighten the security both inside and outside Mablethorpe Castle.

"You are forgetting that I never said anyone was killed. Please forget what you've heard and go entertain the visitors outside of the castle, since that is your job. You shouldn't be in here right now to begin with."

"I was just roaming the castle to try to bring the joy of enter-tainment to all."

"We have our own juggler, jongleur, and minstrels, thank you."

"I will leave you then, my lady." The juggler nodded and scooped up the sand bags and headed outside.

"I don't like that there one," came a low voice from the door to the kitchens. Vivienne looked over to see Cook standing there wiping his hands on his apron. Maria stood next to him with a large bowl of what looked like broad beans, that were mainly used in soups.

"I don't like that cook, Gisela," said Maria.

"Her, I hate," added Cook, gritting his teeth.

"Gisela is not a cook. She is the King's food taster," Vivienne corrected them. "Please, don't give her any trouble. She has a very stressful and dangerous job. And that juggler might be nosey, but he seems harmless, so just stay out of his way."

"Lady Vivienne, what happened out there today?" asked Cook.

"I'll tell them." Maleine ran up behind her.

"Yes, Maleine will fill you in." She turned and headed up the stairs, meaning to go to the King's chamber. That is, until another voice from behind stopped her.

"Vivienne, wait."

She turned to see Zachariah taking the stairs two at a time, trying to catch up with her.

"Sheriff, whatever it is, it can wait. I need to try to talk to the King once more before he leaves."

He made his way to her and stopped her at the top of the stairs. "What were you talking to the King about when the murder happened?"

"Why does it matter?"

"It matters, because your talk is what foiled the killer's plans. If it weren't for you, King Edward would be lying there lifeless right now instead of Sir Amis."

"Do you really think so?" She had never considered that her intervention might have actually saved the King's life.

"Yes, I really believe that. Now tell me, what was so important that the King would send in someone else to joust for him? And what did you mean when you said you should have trusted me more and long ago, and that you were sorry? Sorry for what?"

Vivienne looked down the corridor toward the King's chamber and then back to Zachariah. She owed the sheriff an explanation. Then again, she didn't want the King to leave before she could try to talk him into freeing Sir Guy and Lord Rowen.

"I'd like to talk to you, Zachariah, but can it wait until after I speak to the King?"

"Nay, it cannot wait," he snapped, sounding angry as well as hurt. "If you and I are going to be solving murders together, then you can't be keeping information from me. You said you should have trusted me, so start doing that right now."

"Oh, Zachariah, I'm sorry." She reached out and gently rested her hand over his. "Yes, you are right. I owe you an explanation, and I mean to give it to you right now."

"Well? Go ahead," he said with a nod, waiting to hear what she had to say.

Chambermaids brushed past them with their arms loaded down with pillows and blankets. Pages scurried up and down the stairs, while ladies and knights staying at the castle kept walking past, causing Vivienne and Zachariah to have to keep moving out of the way.

"Not here," she said, taking him by the arm and all but dragging him to her own chamber. "In here," she said, with a quick nod of her head. She started to push open the door but he hesitated.

"Nay, my lady. It is not proper for me to be alone with you inside your chamber."

"We won't be alone." Throwing open the door, they could both see Nairnie, Starah, and Martin sitting at a table. Grunt was lying on the bed. When the dog saw her, he jumped up and ran over to lick her hand. Then Grunt proceeded to do the same to Zachariah.

"Oh, I see. You want to talk with everyone in here?" he asked with a raised brow. "I thought it was private."

"It is," she told him, pulling him into the chamber and closing the door.

"Blethers, what are ye two doin' here?" asked Nairnie, pushing up from the table. She waddled her plump body across the room. "Are we goin' back to town, Sheriff?"

"Nay, I want to stay here," whined Starah. "And I want to visit Midnight, but Nairnie won't let me."

"The cat?" asked Zachariah. "Where is she? I thought she was in here."

"Nairnie put poor Midnight in our chamber, away from Grunt," said Starah.

"Good idea," he said, looking not at all pleased that Nairnie and the children were here. Of course, whenever Midnight was even mentioned, he seemed to get upset. He was slowly starting to accept the cat, but since she had once been the rat-catcher's pet, Vivienne thought that put a sour taste in the sheriff's mouth.

"Nairnie, I need to talk to the sheriff in private," said Vivienne.

"Are ye finally goin' to tell him, lass?"

"Tell me what?" asked Zachariah.

"Yes," she answered. "However, I'd like to do it without anyone else listening."

"I understand. I will take the children somewhere else."

"Nay, that is not what I mean," said Vivienne. "I think you should stay, so no one gets the wrong idea. I mean, if they should see me and the sheriff walking out of my chamber together."

"What wrong idea?" asked innocent little Starah. "What does she mean, Father?"

"They're talking about what they do together," said Martin, playing with the dog.

"Martin!" Vivienne was shocked to hear these words come out of her seven-year-old son's mouth. "How could you say such a thing?"

"What?" asked Martin. "Aren't you going to work together with the sheriff again, trying to solve the murder like you usually do?"

"Oh, that." Vivienne flashed a quick smile at the sheriff. "Yes, of course, Martin. After all, that is what we do together."

"I knew that. What did you think the boy meant?" Now it was the sheriff's turn to flash a quick smile back at her.

"Nairnie, keep the children occupied. I am going to be talking to the sheriff in the wardrobe," she said, talking about the adjoining small room that housed her clothing.

"Aye, my lady. Come on, wee ones, I'll tell ye a story about when I was on the pirate ship."

"Nay, not that," moaned Zachariah. "Anything but pirate stories, please."

"Oh, come on. One story isn't going to hurt them." Vivienne pulled Zachariah into the wardrobe, walking far into the hanging gowns, just to make sure the children couldn't hear them since the wardrobe had no door. It was dark in there and hard to see.

"All right. So, what is it you wanted to tell me?" asked the sheriff.

"I'll do better than just tell you. I'll show you," she said, reaching for her necklace under her bodice.

ZACHARIAH FROZE when he heard Vivienne say she was going to show him, and then looked as if she were undressing.

"Here, help me. It's stuck."

"Vivienne, not here," he whispered, looking back to the

entrance of the wardrobe. "The children are right out in the other room.

"What are you talking about?"

"I don't think you should be undressing at a time like this."

She started laughing. "I think we need some light." She walked back to the entrance of the wardrobe, and lit a candle that was kept there on a small table. The firelight lit up the inside of her storage space.

"Yes, that's better," said Zachariah, clearing his throat, glad to see she was still clothed.

"I am talking about this." Vivienne reached for her neckline again. "Oh, I have it, never mind." Then, to his surprise, instead of undressing, she pulled out a chain she wore under her clothes and around her neck. Dangling from the end of the chain was a gold ring ... with a very large ruby in the center.

"God's eyes, is that gold? Where did you get that, Vivienne?" He reached out and took it into his hand. "This looks to be very expensive."

"It should be. It's a ruby encased in solid gold."

"That's a real ruby?" he gasped, not believing the size of it. He had never seen anything like this before.

"Shhhh," she warned him, glancing back over her shoulder. Martin could be heard asking Nairnie where pirates pooped. Nairnie's loud cackle filled the air, while Grunt barked. Starah could be heard saying, "Eeeeew."

"Where did you get this, my lady? It looks a lot like the ring that King Edward was wearing, but the gemstone is different. Wait a minute. Is that the King's crest engraved on the gold?" Zachariah took a closer look.

"Yes, it is the King's ring, Zachariah, that's right. My mother gave it to me right before she died."

"She did?" He couldn't even imagine what this big secret was, but he hoped her mother hadn't stolen it from King

Elizabeth Rose

Edward. He would hate to think that anyone in Vivienne's family was a thief. "Where did she get it?"

"From the King, silly." Vivienne chuckled. "You see, my mother was once the King's mistress."

"What?" he said, quite loudly. But there was so much noise now in the other room since Martin was asking if pirates kissed girls and Nairnie found that funny, that no one heard him. "You have got to be jesting. I've known your mother my entire life. She was happily married to Abiathar."

"Nay, you misunderstood. She was the King's mistress before she ever married my father. I mean, before she married my stepfather."

Suddenly, things were starting to come together. But his mind often ran rampant and he wanted to hear the truth from Vivienne's mouth. "Continue," he said in a low voice, not exactly sure what was coming next, but he had a suspicion regarding what she was about to say.

"I am the King's bastard daughter, Zachariah. I've known since the day my mother died, but she told me to keep it a secret. Oh, I know I was wrong in not telling you. I am sorry that I never said a word about it to you."

"You? The King's bastard." He could barely wrap his head around the idea and had a hard time pushing the words from his mouth. She nodded but said nothing.

"No one else knows about this then?"

"Well, I was so upset and dismayed after the murders and losing my son and brother that I had to talk to someone. I admit, I did tell my aunt and uncle."

"You should have talked to me about it, Vivienne. As sheriff, investigating your parents' murders, I really needed to know that."

"I understand that now, yes. And like I said, I am sorry I

kept the information from you. I was only trying to follow my mother's dying wish."

Zachariah closed his eyes and slowly shook his head. "Had I known this bit of information seven years ago, I might have been able to catch your parents' killers by now. By keeping that from me, you doomed us both. Don't you see that?"

"I know. And I will never keep anything from you again, I promise." He wanted to be angry with her, but for some reason, he could not. He cared about her too much to ever hold a grudge against her.

"Is that why you were talking to the King in private? To tell him this?"

"Yes," she answered. "He had no idea I was his daughter."

"This changes everything, Vivienne. Nothing will ever be the same between us now."

"Don't say that." She took his hand in hers. "This changes absolutely nothing, Zachariah. I mean, I don't think the King even likes the fact I'm his daughter. I was hoping to use that information to my advantage, to talk him into stopping me from being offered up as a prize bride, but he won't change it."

"He won't?"

"Nay." Her eyes held incredible sadness. "I'm afraid he is as stubborn as my uncle when he's made a decision. I was hesitant to even tell him about me, since I heard that he wanted his bastard triplets killed at birth."

"Bid the devil, then Lords Rook, Rowen, and Reed are you half-brothers?"

She smiled and nodded. "Yes. And that is why I need to talk the King into changing his decision. I can't have my brother imprisoned. And Sir Guy doesn't deserve to die because I know he had nothing to do with any of this."

"I agree," said Zachariah. "We need to find the true killer

109

fast, because if the King so decides, he can have both Sir Guy and Lord Rowen hanged tomorrow, blamed as Sir Amis's killer."

"Lady Vivienne," came Nairnie's hoarse whisper from the entrance of the wardrobe.

"What is it, Nairnie?" asked Vivienne.

"Are ye done tellin' the sheriff about bein' the King's daughter?"

"Egads, Nairnie knew too?" Zachariah was starting to wonder just how truthful Vivienne was really being with him. Plus, he felt hurt that she'd tell the old woman whom she'd just recently met, and not tell him, when they'd been friends since childhood.

"I didn't tell her," said Vivienne. "She guessed. Nairnie is very observant. And no, Nairnie, I am not done yet. I still have more to tell the sheriff."

"I just wanted ye to ken that the King's men are movin' Edward out now."

"What?" both Vivienne and Zachariah said together.

"Nay, we have to stop them," said Zachariah. "For all we know, one of his own guards could be the killer. He might be in danger."

"Let's go," said Vivienne, stopping for just a second to blow out the candle, and then rushing to the door with Zachariah right behind her.

Chapter Eight

"Your Majesty," called out Vivienne, running down the corridor after the King and his guards. "Please wait."

"Nay, Lady Vivienne, I am leaving," said the King without turning around.

Rook was coming down the corridor, and caught up to her. "What's going on, Lady Vivienne?" he asked.

Vivienne leaned over and whispered to him. "Our stubborn father is leaving, and I've yet to convince him to release our brother and Sir Guy." It sounded odd saying *father* and *brother* to Rook, but in another way, part of Vivienne loved it, too. Someday, she hoped to actually get to know Rowen, Rook, and Reed, but for now it wouldn't happen. They didn't have a moment to spare, and they needed to move quickly regarding the King.

"My good king," said Zachariah, passing them up, and managing to get to Edward's side. "I'm afraid I cannot let you leave."

The King froze, then whipped around to face Zachariah. "You don't tell me what to do, Sheriff. I am king, in case you've forgotten."

"Forgive me, but I don't think it's safe," said the sheriff. "Until we find the true killer, everyone is a suspect and your life is in danger. Even one of your guards could be the murderer for all we know. I can't let you leave with them."

"Even my guards could be the killer?" The King looked from one guard to the other, seeming to consider this. None of the guards said a word. "I suppose I hadn't thought of that."

"It would be best if you went back to your chamber and stayed there under heavy guard until I ... until *we* find the killer." He looked over at Vivienne and smiled. It did her heart good to hear him include her. That meant that he'd forgiven her for keeping her secret for the past seven years. Too damned bad she hadn't been able to tell him about her parents being spies too. But the King made her promise not to say a word. She would have to think this over when she had some time alone, because it didn't feel right keeping things from Zachariah when she'd promised to always tell him everything from now on.

"I agree that you shouldn't leave yet," said Vivienne. "Your Majesty, our goal is to keep you safe by all means possible. You need to give us that chance."

"And to keep you alive," added Rook, stepping forward. "I will send for some of my men to come to Mablethorpe Castle anon."

"Your men?" The King scowled. "Whatever for?"

"My men weren't here at the time of the killing, so you will know they can be trusted," explained Rook.

"I think that is a great idea," broke in Zachariah. "Lord Rook, how soon can you have your men here?"

"Well, it'll be at least a few days to get word back to Naward Castle and to give them time to arrive," said Rook.

"Nay. That's too long without the King being guarded by someone trustworthy," said the sheriff. "We'll have to think of something else."

"Don't you have any other men closer by that could make it here by nightfall?" Vivienne asked her new brother.

Rook's hand went to his chin. "As a matter of fact ... yes, I do."

"Then get them here right away, Rook," the King commanded. "And by God, they better truly be trustworthy."

"Of course, they are. I wouldn't have it any other way, Father." Rook threw the King a nasty glance as he headed away at a near run. Vivienne had an odd feeling that mayhap Rook was still upset about not being chosen over Rowen to joust against his father. Or mayhap it was still a festering wound from his knowledge of the days when the King wanted him killed as a baby. She wasn't really sure. One thing she did realize was that Rook was as angry as she that the King had imprisoned Rowen.

"Well then, I guess I'll go back to my chamber for now, but I'm going to need to send Alice a missive that I'm not returning today," said Edward. "Sheriff, how long will this investigation take?"

"I'm not sure," said Zachariah. "Every investigation is different, My King. This one, with so many people around, and more arriving every day, makes it a true challenge."

"I think the tournament needs to be canceled," suggested Vivienne. "That way, we can at least keep more people from showing up, and focus on the ones that were here when the murder happened."

"It would perhaps be better," agreed Zachariah.

"Nay!" snapped the King. "I have paid good money for this damned tournament, although now I regret ever letting Lord Mablethorpe talk me into it. The tournament will continue as planned."

"It is going to be hard keeping the villagers and townsfolk here without telling them why," said Vivienne.

"We'll let them return to their homes," said Zachariah. "It

isn't likely they would have the means to do something like this, I think I can safely say."

"I agree," said Vivienne. "It has to be someone who can get close to the King. It wouldn't be a commoner. Besides, the commoners will all return tomorrow, not wanting to miss the events or the food."

"I'll keep my eyes open as well," said the King. "I need to get something for the money I paid for this to happen."

"Nay. I'm sorry, My King, but as sheriff, your safety is my responsibility," said Zachariah. "I cannot let you attend the tournament. It wouldn't be safe."

"I didn't say I wanted to attend the blasted thing!" Edward let out a deep breath of air and waved a hand through the air. "Back to my chamber," he told his guards. "So now I, too, will be imprisoned until the killer is found. Sheriff, you'd better do your work quickly, I warn you."

"I will do my best," said Zachariah with a respectful bow.

"King Edward, I am going to post some of my most trustworthy guards at your door," Vivienne told him.

"I don't know them. How can I believe they are trustworthy?" asked the King.

"You'll have to take my word on that," she said, looking around, realizing that the guards were at a far enough distance not to hear what she was about to say next. "Trust me ... Father."

"Don't call me that!" the King warned her, spinning on his heel to glare at her. "Do not ever call me that again." Then he left, storming back to his room.

Vivienne watched him go, feeling a huge hole in her chest. It was obvious King Edward didn't want her for a daughter, after all. Why had she thought that perhaps once he knew who she was, he'd take her in his arms and welcome her into his life? What a fool she'd been. He didn't want her for a daughter any more than she ever wanted him for a father. Abiathar was the only father she ever knew, and now she wanted it to stay that way. Holding back the tears, she ran down the corridor to get her guards. She wanted this investigation over with even more than getting out of being a prize bride, because she wanted to make as much distance between herself and King Edward as possible. She despised the King for saying that to her, and for locking away Rowen and Sir Guy. Nay, she decided. She wanted nothing to do with him ever again. Her mother had been too good for him, and now she wondered if the silver-haired ruler had ordered her mother to sleep with him against her will. No one, especially not her mother, could ever really love this arrogant, ruthless, despicable excuse of a man.

"We need to view the corpse," Zachariah told Vivienne a while later. Ever since the King seemed to shun her, Vivienne had not been in the best mood. Zachariah's heart went out to her, but her troubles would have to wait until later. They had other concerns that were more important to deal with first. The murder investigation needed to be their priority right now.

"Yes, I know," she told him, as they walked together to the dungeon.

"I'm sorry about the way things went with King Edward, but you need to focus on the matter at hand," he reminded her. "Someone is out to kill the King, and it is our responsibility to stop it before it happens."

"I thought that was what I already did. And why Sir Amis is now dead when it was supposed to be the King. Mayhap I never should have stopped him to talk to him, after all."

"Stop it, Vivienne," he said lowly, not using her title since they were alone and he was speaking to her as a friend. "You need to push any feelings about your relationship with Edward aside for now. I am sorry that it didn't turn out the way you wanted it to, but you need to accept it for what it is. There are some things in life that we just cannot change."

"Accept it?" Her head jerked upward in surprise. Then she grabbed his arm to stop him. No one else was in the corridor leading to the dungeon, but she still spoke softly. She meant to tell him what the King said about her parents. She opened her mouth to do so, but the words just would not come.

"What is it?" he asked her. "You seem as if you want to say something to me."

"I ... it's nothing," she said, cursing herself inwardly for not being brave enough to divulge such a private matter to the sheriff. She was so angry at Edward right now that she didn't care if she broke the promise to keep it a secret. Vivienne was tired of keeping things from Zachariah. She wanted to tell him everything, more than anything right now.

So, why then couldn't she do it?

"Well, we're here," he said, putting his hand on the dungeon door. "You don't have to come in there with me. I won't think less of you if you don't."

"I've already seen Sir Amis's gored body," she told him.

"I was talking about the fact that Sir Guy, as well as your new brother, are also in there. It's not going to be easy to see them behind bars."

"Nay, it's all right." She swallowed forcefully. "I am the lady of the castle ... behind my aunt, I mean. I should be there to comfort them. Especially since they were falsely accused of something that we both know they didn't do."

"All right, then. Let's go on in." Zachariah opened the door to the guard's room to find not only one of Mablethorpe's guards in the room, but also Vivienne's uncle. "Lord Mablethorpe. I didn't expect to see you here."

Lord Mablethorpe spun around. "Why not?" he grunted.

"After all, it is my castle. I don't need anyone's permission to go wherever I want."

"Uncle, don't take offense," said Vivienne. "The sheriff didn't mean anything by it. We just thought you'd be out at the tiltyard, that's all."

"Why? I've canceled any other jousts for now."

"The King said the tournament will continue," Vivienne reminded him.

"Yes, it will. However, not today. Right now, I need to find out what the hell happened out there. Guard, open the gate to the cells and make it fast."

"Yes, my lord," said the guard, pulling out his keys.

"Lord Mablethorpe, I am here now. There is no need to bother you with this," the sheriff told him.

"Yes, and I am here as well," said Vivienne. "We will find the murderer, just give us a chance to do so in our own way."

"Don't tell me what to do!" Lord Mablethorpe was once again acting riled. "Now open the damned gate, I said."

"Aye, my lord." The guard put the key in the lock and turned it. The gate that led to the main area with the cells, creaked open. Lord Mablethorpe went inside, followed by Vivienne, Zachariah, and then the guard.

"The corpse is in the first cell," Zachariah told Vivienne. "Unlock this cell," he instructed the guard.

"Yes, Sheriff Fitch." The guard did as ordered. All three of them went inside.

"Let us out of here," called out Sir Guy from the cell next to the corpse.

"Aye," agreed Lord Rowen from his cell, one more over. "This is absurd. We shouldn't be here. I demand to be released at once."

"Hush!" called out Lord Mablethorpe. "Your own father put you in here, Lord Rowen. Don't think I can go above the

King's head to let either of you out. You'll both stay there until the King decides to release you."

While Zachariah and her uncle perused the dead body of Sir Amis, Vivienne quietly stepped out of the cell and made her way past Sir Guy.

"Lady Vivienne, please," whispered Sir Guy, his fingers curling around the bars. "You know I am innocent. Can't you do something to help me?"

"We're working on it," she whispered back, keeping an eye on her uncle and the sheriff who were in deep conversation, looking over the corpse. The guard had gone back to his post. She continued on to the next cell, meeting Lord Rowen at the bars. "I'm so sorry, Brother," she whispered, so Sir Guy wouldn't hear her. "I will do everything possible to talk some sense into our father."

"There is no reasoning with King Edward. Unless you know how to play chess, he's not interested in anything you do or have to say."

"Play chess?" she asked, looking up at him. "I know how to play chess. What do you mean by that?"

"Edward prides himself on his skill at playing chess," explained Rowen. "No one can beat him except my brother, Reed." He looked down at her and smiled slightly. "*Our* brother."

"Reed is still in the Highlands?" she asked.

"Aye. He's never gotten along with Edward."

"How can I reach him? I'd like to send him a missive to tell him that you are in the dungeon."

"It doesn't matter. By the time he gets the missive, it'll be too late, because something will have happened to me and Sir Guy, one way or another. Your best bet is trying to talk some sense into Edward. The King is the only one who can get us out of here. Unless you and the sheriff can quickly discover the killer and bring him before the King, I don't know what would make my father change his mind."

"Yes. Yes, we can do that, I promise," she told Rowen, meaning what she said. "And thank you for the tip about chess. I will use that to my advantage to try to break down that wall between me and King Edward. Not for my own sake, but only to help you."

"Be careful," Rowen warned her.

"I'm not afraid of the King," she boldly answered.

Rowen chuckled. "My, you really are of the same blood," he said softly. "But I wasn't warning you about Edward. I am warning you about whoever tried to end the King's life. After all, weren't your parents murdered too?"

"Yes. Seven years ago. Do you think by any chance this could be the same killer?"

"I don't know. But I'd be willing to bet now, knowing your background, that it might just all be related somehow."

Vivienne thought about what the King had told her, that her mother and stepfather had been his spies. He'd warned her not to tell anyone, even though she'd almost told Zachariah. She wanted more than anything to tell Rowen about it right now, but didn't think it was the place or time. Sir Guy was staring over at her, and her uncle just realized she was missing.

"Vivienne, get away from the prisoners," bellowed her uncle.

"They are not real prisoners at all, Uncle Gilbert, and you know it. There is nothing for me to fear from them."

"Step away, I tell you, or I'll come over there and pull you away by the hair, if I have to."

"My, he's harsh," mumbled Rowen. "Is he always like that with you?"

Vivienne let out a deep sigh. "He didn't used to be so harsh when I was growing up. As a matter of fact, he used to be so calm and friendly that his knights often teased him about it. But ever since the murders of my parents and when he became my guardian, he's changed. I suppose it's because his children have all died, and now I'm the only one he's got left. He thinks of me as his daughter. Being so gruff, I guess, is his way of protecting and watching over me."

"If you say so."

"Vivienne, what did I say?" Her uncle walked up behind her.

"Lady Vivienne, it is time we leave now," Zachariah told her, joining them.

"Thank you for your help in this matter, Sheriff," said Rowen, showing his gratitude and his honorable ways of being a noble, even though he once used to be a pirate. He acted more like an honorable man than most of the nobles Vivienne knew. She liked that about her new brother.

"Lord Rowen, Sir Guy, I'm sorry that it has come to this, but I promise you we are working diligently to find the killer and thus release you both," Zachariah told them.

"We appreciate it, Sheriff," said Sir Guy. "Lady Vivienne, I am sorry that I've turned out to be such a bad influence on your son, when I am supposed to be mentoring him."

"You're not a bad influence," said Vivienne, hearing Grunt barking from the guard's post and Martin's voice telling the guard to let him in. "I'm afraid my son just has a little too much of my ways in him, that's all."

Chapter Nine

Vivienne slept restlessly that night, once again part of her real-life nightmare seeping out into her dreams. This one involved her missing brother, Adrian, as well as Vivienne stabbing the killer, and finding out about her true father.

Gripping the hilt of her father's sword with two hands, Vivienne slowly stepped around the front of the wagon, just in time to see a shadowy figure stab her mother with his sword and then throw her body to the ground. Too scared to even speak, she froze. Standing in the dark, fear consumed her, making her feel as if she were in hell.

"Someone's coming. Hurry, let's get out of here," came the voice of another shadowy form atop a horse. The man who stabbed her mother withdrew his sword and headed toward his waiting horse.

"Mother! Nay!" screamed her little brother. Vivienne's head snapped around to see Adrian standing in the hay in the back of the wagon, looking over the edge, terror on his face.

"Dammit. There's someone else," shouted the first bandit to the second.

"Kill him, too," commanded the ruffian's companion. *"Leave no witnesses."*

The first man rushed over, but Vivienne wasn't about to let him kill her brother too. Guilt already ate away at her that she wasn't able to save her parents. She stepped out in front of the attacker, wildly swinging her father's sword in the air. Mayhap it was her anger controlling her actions, but somehow she managed to stab the man on his right shoulder with her blade. The tip stuck into his flesh and she was sure she felt the blade meet his bone. Quickly, she pulled the blade back, seeing the blood oozing from the man's wound.

"Aaaaah!" the attacker screamed, one hand gripping at his bleeding shoulder from where Vivienne had struck him.

"Dammit, there's a girl here too," shouted the other man from his horse.

The fighting frightened the horses, causing them to rear up and paw at the air, whinnying loudly. The wagon jerked and her brother fell back in the hay with his feet in the air. Then the horses took off down the road at a run, pulling the wagon along with them. The sound from the bench seat of Vivienne's crying baby inside the basket caused her to panic and become furious all at the same time. Even in her weakened state from just having given birth, Vivienne's motherly instincts kicked in and she fought like a lion. She started swinging the sword wildly at her attacker as she lunged forward, stabbing at him over and over again. All the while, she gritted her teeth. No one was going to kill any of her family and get away with it! She was so angry right now, that she wasn't even scared. She wanted both of these bandits to die.

"You bastard! I'll kill you for what you've done," she shouted, causing him to actually back away from her now. His sword dangled from his fingers as he gripped his bleeding sword arm

which she had injured. *God's eyes, she wished she had severed his arm altogether.*

"Let's go," called out the man's friend from his steed. "Someone's coming."

The man she'd struck mumbled something under his breath that she couldn't decipher, but it sounded as if he'd said the words, 'too soon.' He then turned and ran, mounting his horse, taking off with his friend, leaving her stranded and all alone.

"Vivienne," came her mother's soft cry from the ground. Vivienne spun on her heel and ran to her mother, dropping the sword and falling to her knees at her mother's side.

"Mother!" she cried, cradling the woman's head atop her lap. "They killed Father. And the horses ran off with Adrian and my baby." Tears gushed from her eyes as she looked down at her mother bathed in the scant light of the partial moon that broke through the clouds. "Mother, please don't die too! Do not leave me, I beg you. I need you!" Vivienne said the words, but knew that all the wishing in the world wasn't going to change what happened here tonight. Blood covered her mother who clutched her abdomen and moaned in pain. There was no use denying that the woman was not going to live. Her mother lifted her hand, yanking at a chain around her neck until the chain released. Then she slowly held out her closed fist to Vivienne.

"Take ... this ... Daughter. For you ... and the baby."

"Mother, what are you doing? What do you mean?"

"Listen ... to ... me."

"I need to get you help. I think I hear horses coming down the road. I'll signal to the riders." She started to stand, but her mother's hand on her arm stopped her.

"Too ... late," came her mother's soft reply as her eyes started to close. "Go to ... your father. He ... will protect ... you ... and the ... babe."

"Mother, didn't you hear me? Father is dead!" she screamed.

"I can't go to him for help. It's too late! I need to find Adrian and my baby."

"Wait." The woman opened her fist, and Vivienne looked down to see a gold ring with a ruby gemstone embedded in it dangling from the chain. It was something her mother had been wearing around her neck, although Vivienne had never known it. "This is ... your father's."

"Mother, what are you saying?" Vivienne cried. "You are delirious from the pain. Father doesn't have a ring like this. He is only a poor foot soldier." She picked it up in two fingers, taking a better look at it in the moonlight. "This is gold. With a ruby! It must belong to a very rich noble, or mayhap even a king."

"Yes. King ... Edward. He's your ... father. Don't ... tell ... a ... soul."

"My lady, you need to wake up," came Maleine's sweet voice, and Vivienne felt the girl's gentle touch on her arm. Vivienne's eyes popped open. "The castle gates are open already and people are starting to arrive for the tournament."

"Oh, nay. I overslept once again," she mumbled, getting up off the pallet she had shared with her son. "Where is Martin?" She frantically looked around, still being half in her nightmare and for a moment believing her son was still lost.

"He's fine, lassie," came Nairnie's voice from the window. "Martin went with Milo to the front gate. He didn't want to miss all the excitement with all the competitors and onlookers arriving for the events today."

"Where's Grunt?" Vivienne looked about for her hound next.

"Martin asked if he could take Grunt with him," explained Maleine. "Since the hound needed to relieve himself, we didn't think it would matter."

"Nay, I suppose it's fine," said Vivienne with a yawn.

Next, there was a knock at the door.

"I wonder who that could be?" said Vivienne.

"Maleine, why dinna ye answer it, and I'll help Lady Vivienne dress," said Nairnie, taking Vivienne's hand and rushing her to the wardrobe.

"Slow down, Nairnie," said Vivienne. "What is your hurry this morning?"

Once they were inside the wardrobe, Nairnie whispered to her. "I didna want Maleine to hear me say this, but I think there is goin' to be trouble, my lady." She yanked off Vivienne's night rail and started pulling a gown over her head.

"What are you saying, Nairnie? Did something happen that I don't know about? Tell me if you've heard something, I need to know."

"No' yet, nothin' has happened, but it will happen soon," said the old woman, pulling Vivienne's gown in place, and shoving a pair of shoes at her. "All hell is goin' to cut loose once yer uncle and the King discover that Lord Rook brought back mercenaries to guard King Edward."

"What are you saying? Why would Lord Rook do a thing like that?" she asked, pushing her feet into her shoes.

"Because Lord Rook once led an entire army of mercenaries against King Edward, that's why." Nairnie picked up a brush and ran it over Vivienne's hair. It hit a snarl and yanked her head. Vivienne held back from crying out, knowing Nairnie was only trying to help her, although the woman wasn't gentle at all like Maleine.

"You don't really think Lord Rook would bring mercenaries into the castle walls, do you? Especially since he told the King he was going to bring his trusted men."

"Those mercenaries are Rook's trusted men, lassie. However, they are also the same men who helped the Legendary Bastards raid the King years ago."

"Oh, no. That's not good."

"My lady, Sheriff Fitch is here to see you," called out Maleine from the main room.

"I'll be right there, Sheriff," Vivienne called back. "Nairnie, please keep Starah and Martin close to you today. Whatever you do, don't let them out of your sight."

"I'll do that, my lady. Dinna ye worry. I'll go find Martin and keep him with me, ye can count on me."

Vivienne walked out of the wardrobe into the adjoining chamber to find Zachariah standing there holding his hand on Starah's shoulder. The little girl had her big, fluffy black cat in her arms.

"Where is Martin?" asked Starah, still sounding sleepy. "I'm sure he'll want to say good morning to Midnight."

"Oh, you brought the cat?" asked Vivienne, wondering why the sheriff let her do that.

"I'm sorry," said Zachariah. "She wouldn't leave the room without her, and we're already late. We need to get down to the courtyard and continue this investigation. As it is, it'll be hard to do anything once everyone arrives for the tournament."

"Are they still going to have the tournament jousting competition?" asked Maleine. "I mean, after what happened and all?"

"I'm not sure," said Zachariah. "I hope not, because I don't think it is safe to proceed in that direction right now, considering the circumstances."

"Oh, they'll have it," said Vivienne, sure that her uncle would never cancel the joust. "Remember, not everyone knows a man was killed yesterday while jousting. Therefore, no one would be wary of this event. Besides, it is the last event of the competition, and also the most important. It will help determine which man wins me as his bride."

She noticed the sheriff shifting from foot to foot. His gaze dropped to the ground. He didn't seem to like it when she mentioned that she was to be a prize bride. She couldn't blame him because she didn't like it at all either.

"Starah, be sure to stay close to Nairnie today," Zachariah told his daughter. "There will be a huge crowd and it'll be easy to get separated from her in all the commotion."

"Dinna worry, Sheriff. I willna let go of her hand," promised Nairnie.

"And leave that damned cat here in the room," added Zachariah. "Don't you dare take her out of here. Do you understand me?"

"I understand, Father." Starah kissed Midnight on the head. The cat mewed loudly, jumped out of her arms, and ran across the room. Then she jumped up to the window ledge and stared out into the courtyard.

"Oh, get her off of there," said Vivienne. "She's going to fall out the window if she's not careful."

"I'll get her," grumbled Zachariah. He went over to the window, pulled the cat down and tossed her to the floor. Midnight ran across the room before jumping up on the bed.

"You'd better close the shutters," suggested Vivienne. "Just to be safe. Midnight is a lively one who seems to have a mind of her own."

"You're right. Just like someone else I know," he answered with a chuckle. Zachariah started to close the shutters but stopped, gawking at something in the courtyard below. His jaw dropped and then his eyes narrowed. He tightly clenched his jaw. Slamming the shutters closed, he latched them and spun around. "I'm leaving now, with or without you, Lady Vivienne." He brushed past her and before she knew it he had left the room just like he'd warned her.

"I'll see you all later," said Vivienne, running after him. "Wait up," she called out, but Zachariah didn't slow down at all. When Vivienne finally got to his side he was in a horrible mood.

"Why can't you for once get up at a decent hour? You always oversleep," he complained to her.

"I'm sorry, but I'm here now," she answered. "What's the matter? I can tell something is upsetting you."

"It doesn't matter. We need to solve this case as quickly as possible, and then I'm returning to town."

"Yes, of course. That is the plan." Vivienne had no idea what was bothering the sheriff so much until they stepped outside into the courtyard. There stood Lord Rook with at least a dozen men, all armed to the hilt with an array of deadly-looking weapons. Rook was giving them instructions. "Oh, look. Lord Rook has brought some of his soldiers to help with protecting the King. How nice."

"They're not soldiers, Vivienne. They're goddamned mercenaries," he said with a grunt, stopping so quickly that she crashed into the back of him.

"Mercenaries? No, I'm sure you are wrong." Nairnie had just warned her about this, but Vivienne still didn't want to believe it. "Lord Rook said he would bring some of his most trusted men here to help. He said nothing about hiring mercenaries."

"I'm not wrong. And remember, Lord Rook as well as his brothers were once known as the Demon Thief. His mercenaries *are* his most trusted men."

"Sheriff, how can you be so sure?" she asked, seeing him raise his arm and point. A stoic expression covered his face. When she turned to look at where he pointed, she immediately understood why he was acting this way.

"Zachariah, isn't that your brother, Isaac?" she asked him.

"So it is." He said nothing more.

"You haven't spoken to Isaac in years, have you?"

"That would be the way of it."

"Well, I think this is a perfect time to make amends then.

"Isaac, over here," she called out, waving her arm in the air to get his brother's attention.

"Stop that!" commanded the sheriff, grabbing her arm and pulling it down, but it was too late. His brother already saw her and was heading across the courtyard to greet them.

"Zachariah!" Isaac smiled at the sheriff as he approached. "I thought I might find you here." Isaac was a few years younger than the sheriff and quite a bit taller too. He had that same dark hair and oaken eyes as his brother. Isaac had a short beard and mustache as well. "How are you, Brother? It's been a long time since I've seen you." Isaac held out his hand for a shake, but Zachariah didn't extend his arm to return the greeting. Instead, he purposely looked the other way.

"Isaac, I've got a job to do," he told him, sounding blunt and right to the point.

"Aye, I know," answered his brother. "Lord Rook explained about the murder during the joust. Hello, Lady Vivienne," he said, bowing and giving her his attention now. "It's been so long since I've seen you. Time has been good to you, I see. You are more beautiful now than ever." Isaac took her hand and kissed the back of it, being ever so proper. Vivienne appreciated his gesture and also rather liked the attention she was receiving from him.

"Why, thank you, Isaac. And I see that you've become even more charming in time. How are you?" she asked him with a smile.

"Vivienne, this is a murder investigation," grunted the sheriff under his breath. "We don't have time for idle pleasantries."

"We?" Isaac questioned the sheriff's choice of word.

"Yes, I now assist your brother in investigating murders," Vivienne explained to Isaac.

"You do?" Isaac broke out into a full-blown smile. "Somehow, that doesn't surprise me. You have always been a lady with a mind and will of your own, Lady Vivienne."

"Isaac, I've yet to assign you to your post." Lord Rook walked over to join them.

"Sorry, Lord Rook. I just needed to stop and say hello to Lady Vivienne and my brother," replied Isaac.

"Your brother?" Rook looked at Isaac and then over to Zachariah in question.

"Yes, that's right," said Vivienne. "Lord Rook, the sheriff and Isaac are brothers."

"Well, what a surprise. I can't believe I didn't know that after all these years," said Rook. "Then, I guess I'll assign you to stay with the sheriff, Isaac."

"All right. I'd like that," agreed Isaac.

"Nay! I don't need protecting," objected Zachariah, being in a very foul mood.

"Sheriff, I think it would be a good idea," broke in Vivienne.

"God's teeth, Lady Vivienne, I am the sheriff, unless you've forgotten!"

"Nay. Nay, I haven't forgotten at all."

"Pardon me, Sheriff, but are you saying that you don't want Isaac assigned to stay close to you?" asked Rook, seeming confused. "I thought since you were siblings, you'd like to catch up on things." He looked over at Vivienne when he said it, and it made her want to know her half-brother better. She wanted to catch up on things as well.

"Isaac and I have nothing to talk about. Now, if you'll excuse me, I have work to do." Zachariah stepped around them and headed toward the tiltyard.

"What was that all about?" asked Rook, shaking his head as he watched the sheriff walk away.

Isaac frowned as he watched Zachariah leave after dismissing him so easily. "My brother never forgave me for becoming a mercenary," Isaac told Rook. "He also thought I'd stay here in Mablethorpe and assist him when Father died, but I didn't."

"Why didn't you?" asked Vivienne. "I would think it was important to stay near your family."

"I don't know." Isaac shrugged. "I suppose I just felt that I needed to get out and see the world and not be tied down by responsibilities. Now, I have to admit, I regret my decision because I really do miss my family."

"Well, I guess I'll assign you to the battlements then," said Rook. "Unless Lord Mablethorpe objects. He seems to be furious about everything that's happened."

"I'll handle my uncle, don't worry about him," said Vivienne. "But I think it would be good if Isaac came with me. After all, I'd appreciate the extra security. Being lady of Mablethorpe Castle, I can't be too careful."

"I'd like that," said Isaac, with another of his handsome smiles.

"So be it," said Rook, going back to talk to the rest of his men.

"Isaac, the first place we'll head is to the tiltyard where the murder took place," Vivienne told him.

"Sounds good. I'm ready." Isaac nodded.

Together they walked to the tiltyard, making small talk along the way. Vivienne was going to do everything she could to reunite Zachariah and Isaac, since family was important. Besides, Zachariah needed to stop being so serious all the time.

"Isaac, did you know that your brother made amends with your sister, Magdalena?"

"I didn't. That is wonderful. I am guessing you had something to do with that?"

"Well, mayhap just a little." She felt the blush rising to her cheeks. Isaac knew her ways, and also that Zachariah was a stubborn man who didn't seem to like change. "Magdalena, or Sister Magdalena as I should say, was at the abbey in Maltby le Marsh, but now she is residing right here at Mablethorpe Abbey."

"Then I'll need to pay Magdalena a visit while I am in Mablethorpe."

"Yes. It is nice because now she and Zachariah, as well as Starah can visit whenever they want."

"Starah," repeated Isaac. "I haven't seen her since she was not more than a baby. Of course, I did see her at Margaret's funeral, but Zachariah wasn't speaking to me, and wouldn't let me see Starah because he said it would only upset the girl more."

"Zachariah is changing. Just be patient and give me a little more time to work with him," said Vivienne.

"Thank you, Vivienne. I mean, Lady Vivienne. You always did have a kind heart and seem to care about everyone. I appreciate that."

"Where do you live now, Isaac?"

"Here and there," he answered in a nonchalant manner. "Anywhere I can get work, actually. I travel around a lot."

"So you are a soldier of fortune, then."

Isaac's face darkened. "I don't like to be called that, but I suppose it's true. I hire out my sword to whoever will pay me the most. I know it is far from an honorable profession, such as being the town sheriff, which my brother decided to pursue. I often stop and wonder what my life would be like if I'd never gone away and had just stayed here and worked with Zachariah, after all."

"Do you think you'd enjoy working with your brother?" she asked.

He shrugged. "It wouldn't be the worst job I've had. But I

don't think Zachariah would ever consider it now, so it doesn't really matter."

Vivienne's heart went out to Isaac. She couldn't imagine what a lonely life a mercenary led. Hearing his story only made her want to try harder to reunite Zachariah and Isaac. The sheriff might not know he needed his brother back in his life, but Vivienne knew it. She saw how happy both Zachariah and Magdalena were now that they'd made amends. Determination filled her, making her want to rejoin these two brothers more than anything now.

They approached the weapon tent that was being watched by the King's guard, Geoffrey. Vivienne could see that Zachariah was inside. No one else was there at this time.

"Where is everyone?" she asked the guard.

"The sheriff wanted to look around inside by himself, so he asked me to have the competitors step out for now," reported Geoffrey. He nodded to an area between the tent and tiltyard. Vivienne looked over to see a bunch of anxious knights and their squires. The events were about to start, and they wanted to be prepared and were not happy about being separated from their weapons. She couldn't blame them, at all.

"Stay out here and keep watch with Geoffrey," she told Isaac, slipping into the tent and walking to the sheriff's side. "Sheriff Fitch, did you find anything?"

"I'm not sure," he answered, picking up one lance after the other. "These seem to be the rest of Lord Rowen's lances, but I don't see anything suspicious about them. However, I did find footprints behind the rack holding the lances. That seems like an odd place for anyone to be."

"I see." Vivienne stuck her head around to see the footprints the sheriff mentioned. They looked large enough to be from a man, but there were no discreet markings from the bottom of the shoes or boots. That wasn't going to help them in the least.

"Perhaps someone was hiding in here until everyone left. Then they sabotaged one of the lances."

"My thoughts exactly," he answered. "Do you have any idea when Lord Rowen had his equipment brought in?"

"I believe he brought his things with him when he and Lord Rook arrived just yesterday."

"Then the killer must have had to act quickly to conceal the blade on the end of the lance," said the sheriff. "That means he or she was here waiting for Rook and Rowen to arrive, knowing ahead of time that the King planned on jousting with at least one of them."

"Yes. He or she must have known exactly what they were doing. Plus, the killer was skilled enough to be able to conceal a blade on the end of the lance under the coronel."

"They also had to have known which brother the King was going to joust against, and be able to make sure the right lance was taken from the rack. Who would have that type of information?"

"Someone who is close to the King?" she asked.

He nodded. "Yes. I am thinking the same thing."

"Since it seems King Edward didn't even decide until yesterday which of the brothers he was going to joust against, the killer had to be close enough to be listening," Vivienne surmised. "I heard the King talking up on the dais to Lords Rowen and Rook about it."

"Then the killer must have been close enough to the platform to have heard it, as well."

"Or, he or she received the information from someone who was," she added.

"Yes. That is a possibility too."

"Sheriff, do you really believe someone was trying to murder the King?"

"I do. Unless you think this was meant for Sir Amis all

along. We haven't even considered that possibility. Although, that seems unlikely to me. Pulling off something like this with so many people around was a challenge. I'm not sure anyone would risk being caught unless the results were huge. Like killing the King."

"Yes, that makes sense," agreed Vivienne.

"And if you hadn't stopped King Edward to talk to him, Vivienne, then he'd be dead right now."

"So I saved the King's life, then."

"Yes. Indirectly, I guess you did. Since the switch happened at the last second and the King's armor and Lord Rowen's lances were being borrowed, the killer didn't have time to remove what he'd already set in place.

"What's our next step?" she asked him. "I mean, with the tournament still in progress, and all the people arriving, I don't see how we'll ever catch the killer now."

"I agree that it won't be easy," said Zachariah, still inspecting the lances. "But for the sake of Sir Amis and the safety of King Edward, we have no choice but to find answers. And to catch the murderer quickly."

"Mayhap the killer has already left the castle grounds, knowing his plan has been foiled."

"Perhaps. However, something tells me that is not the case, at all. It is my guess that the killer will use the tournament and all the confusion and commotion to his advantage. I believe there is going to be another attempt on the King's life before the end of the competitions."

"Then it's a good thing Lord Rook brought in more soldiers for reinforcement." She watched for his reaction from the corner of her eyes.

Zachariah's face tightened at hearing her say that. He didn't look at all happy. "They're damned mercenaries," he snarled. "Any one of them wouldn't hesitate to try to kill the King himself if he was being paid enough. Mercenaries will kill anyone for enough money, Vivienne."

"It's Lady Vivienne, as we've agreed to call each other using our titles." She raised her chin in the air. "And mayhap at one time the mercenaries were paid to help Lord Rook raid against the King, but you need to remember that Lord Rook made amends with his father in the end. He now serves the King. His mercenaries will protect King Edward, since that is what they're being paid to do."

"Hired swords have no morals, my dear. You can't trust them any farther than you can throw them."

"You sure seem to have your mind made up about this."

"I represent the law, Lady Vivienne. Mercenaries break the law any chance they get."

"But I'm sure if a mercenary wanted to change, he could. I am sure it happens all the time."

"What are you saying?" He looked at her in suspicion now. As so often, it was hard to make Zachariah consider a differing view. "Don't even think of trying to fix things between me and my brother, because it is not going to happen. I do not want you getting involved, regarding Isaac."

The tent flap was pushed aside and Isaac stuck his head into the tent. "Did I hear my name mentioned?"

"Isaac? What are you doing here?" snapped the sheriff. "I told you, I don't need your protection."

"Calm down. I'm not here protecting you."

"Then who?" Zachariah watched his brother's gaze flit over to Vivienne. "Oh, hell no."

"I asked him to protect me," admitted Vivienne. "I don't feel safe after that murder."

"Like hell you don't. I know exactly what you are trying to do and I warn you that it's not going to work. So stop trying!" Zachariah headed toward the exit. "The tournament is about to start. I'm going to watch each event closely, just in case we were wrong and the King wasn't the intended target after all. Someone else's life might be in danger, since I am almost certain that Sir Amis was not supposed to die."

"Whose life do you think is in danger?" she asked, seeing him stop in front of his brother and turn back to glare at her.

"Yours, if you don't stop interfering in my affairs. I won't warn you again to mind your own business."

"I was only trying to help. That is what I do," she protested.

"Well, stop trying to help. I will have Constable Dorson assist me for the rest of the day, so your help won't be needed regarding any matter." With that, he stormed from the tent, leaving Vivienne and Isaac standing there, shaking their heads in disbelief at how obstinate and stubborn Zachariah could really be.

Chapter Ten

"Let's go, Isaac," Vivienne turned to leave, bumping into one of the King's knights.

"Oh, excuse me, Lady Vivienne. I didn't see you there."

"It's all right," she said, brushing off her gown. "Who are you?"

"I am one of King Edward's knights, my lady. My name is Sir Barclay. I am happy to have run into you because I wanted you to know that I will be the one winning your hand in marriage."

"Oh, really?" She found this man pompous and so sure of his skills. He was not at all handsome like Zachariah or Isaac. This knight was overweight, had a hook nose, and pock marks covered his face. His hair looked greasy and thinning strands were brushed over the top of his head. She was sure he was trying to hide a bald spot. "What makes you so sure that you'll win, Sir Barclay?"

"I am the King's best knight, that's why." He straightened his back and stood upright, even though he wasn't much taller than her.

"That's funny. I heard that Sir Amis was King Edward's

best knight." Vivienne started to wonder if Sir Barclay had a reason for killing Sir Amis, after all.

The knight's face changed upon hearing what she'd said. He seemed insulted, wrinkling his nose as he spoke. "Not anymore he's not, now that Sir Amis is dead. I will be the grand winner of this tournament, and when I claim you as my prize bride, you'll not be walking around in the company of mercenaries, I can promise you that!" He sniffed and glared at Isaac before spinning on his heel and walking away.

"Lady Vivienne, mayhap I shouldn't have come to Mablethorpe Castle, after all," said Isaac. "I seem to be causing you nothing but trouble."

"Don't be silly," she told him. "You are here for a reason, so don't let Sir Barclay or even your brother make you feel less than wanted."

"I'm used to being shunned. It is your reputation that concerns me."

"My reputation?" She laughed.

"Yes. I don't want it ruined because of me."

"Believe me, Isaac, when I tell you that I don't think you or anyone could do much to tarnish my reputation. I do a good enough job of that myself."

Vivienne heard a dog bark and looked over to see Grunt heading toward her through the crowd. "Grunt," she said, hunkering down to pet him. Martin and Maleine came running up behind him.

"Grunt, get back here!" shouted Martin, waving his wooden sword in the air.

"Martin, don't do that!" she scolded her son. "You're going to hit someone with your sword waving it around like that in this crowd."

"Sorry, Mother. But I was trying to find you." Martin slowly lowered his wooden sword to his side.

"Grunt led us right to you," said Maleine.

"I'm surprised you two aren't over watching the sword fighting that is about to begin."

"My lady, we were going there when I saw something that seemed suspicious," Maleine told her.

"Really? What was that?"

Maleine looked over at Isaac and seemed hesitant to say anything.

"Oh, I'm sorry. This is Isaac," she introduced him. "Isaac, this is my handmaid, Maleine, and my son, Martin."

"And her dog, Grunt," Martin quickly added.

"Nice to meet all of you," said Isaac, having very good manners for a mercenary.

Still, Maleine didn't say a word.

"Isaac can be trusted. He is the sheriff's brother," Vivienne told the girl.

"Oh, I see." Maleine's stiff body loosened up and she became relaxed. "My lady, I was outside earlier and I saw that cook named Gisela in the stables."

"In the stables?" Vivienne asked. "She is the King's food taster. She is supposed to be in the kitchens. What was she doing in the stables?"

"I don't know for sure. She wasn't carrying any food or wine. As a matter of fact, she was whispering to the King's blacksmith. They saw me coming and suddenly stopped whispering and went back to their work. That is when Gisela darted away."

"Well, I'm not sure that seems too suspicious, Maleine. After all, it is a secret that the King is still here. Most people think he's already left. Mayhap they didn't want others to hear them talking about the King."

"Oh. I guess you're right. I probably just overreacted," said Maleine with a shrug. "Well, come on Martin. Nairnie and

Starah are waiting for us to join them. The hand-to-hand combat competition is about to begin."

"Martin, you should see if Milo needs you to do anything," said Vivienne. "After all, Sir Guy is in the dungeon, and his squire might need your help since you are a page."

"I will, Mother," said Martin, sliding his wooden sword back into his belt. "Come on, Grunt." He tried to pull at Grunt's collar but the dog used his legs to pull back, then sat down at Vivienne's feet.

"I don't think that dog wants to go anywhere," said Isaac with a chuckle.

"Perhaps it is best he stays with me," said Vivienne. "I don't want you two taking off in the crowd chasing him again. It isn't safe."

"Fruit hand pies," called a servant, carrying a tray on her shoulder. "Bilberry and strawberry today."

"Red wine. Who wants red wine?" cried a young servant boy, walking through the crowd with a full pitcher and a bag of wooden cups attached to his side. The crowd was becoming more dense, making it almost hard to move now.

"Isaac, come with me," said Vivienne. "I want you posted outside of the King's door."

"My brother won't like that, my lady," said Isaac, following her through the crowd. Grunt stayed at her side.

"I don't care. I would feel better if one of our people were posted there to watch over the King during the competitions."

Vivienne finally made it into the keep with Isaac right behind her. Grunt followed on their heels.

She saw John, the castle steward, and walked over and spoke to him softly.

"Now, my lady?" asked John.

"Yes," she said. "I will be waiting for you."

"Of course," said the steward, bowing and hurrying away.

"What did you tell him?" asked Isaac.

"I am trying to find a way to reach the King with my words and I think I might have found it."

They went up the stairs and down the corridor to the King's chamber. One of the King's guards was at the door.

"Halt," he commanded, as she reached out to knock. "No one goes in there, Lady Vivienne, you know that."

"What is your name?" she asked the guard.

"My name is Herman."

"Herman, this is Isaac. He will be guarding the door with you until I say otherwise."

"You don't look like a guard," said Herman, eyeing him up and down.

"He is not from around this area." Vivienne didn't want Herman finding out that Isaac hired out his sword. It wouldn't bode well with the King if anyone knew.

She quickly knocked on the door.

"Who goes there?" came Edward's gruff voice from inside the room.

"It is Lady Vivienne, my good King." She didn't wait for him to grant her entrance. She pushed open the door and entered, stopping suddenly when she saw Gisela inside the room, putting down a tray of food in front of the King.

"Oh. I didn't know it was time for a meal." Vivienne closed the door and headed over to the King's chair. He was about to reach out for the food, but Vivienne pushed the tray to the other side of the table.

"What did you do that for?" growled the King. "I'm hungry."

"Did Gisela already taste your food?" she asked.

"Of course, I did. I always do," was Gisela's answer.

"Did you see her taste it, Your Majesty?" asked Vivienne, getting a nasty glance from both Gisela and the King.

143

"Well ... nay. She said she tasted it in the kitchens," answered the King.

"You need to have her taste it right in front of you," Vivienne told him.

"Are you telling me how to do my job, my lady?" was Gisela's bold question.

"Of course not. I am just concerned for the King's safety." She watched their reactions closely.

"Gisela, take the tray of food away." Edward waved his hand through the air.

"But, My King. You've yet to even take a bite. You need to eat to keep up your strength," the woman insisted.

"I've decided I'm not hungry right now. Mayhap later. Take it down to the kitchens. Now."

"Yes, Your Majesty." Gisela didn't look happy as she picked up the tray and headed to the door. When she opened the door, John was standing there about ready to knock. He had a wooden box in his arms.

"Your Majesty, the castle steward is here to see you," announced Isaac.

"Who is that man?" The King squinted, looking at the door.

"That is John. The castle steward," she told him. "I requested an item and he's brought it to me." She walked over and took the box from him. "Thank you, John. That is all for now."

"Yes, my lady. Your Majesty," said John, bowing first to Edward and then to her before he backed up and left the room, leaving the door open.

"Nay, I mean the guard," said the King. "I know my guard, Herman, but who is that other guard? I have never seen him before."

"Oh, this is Isaac, Your Majesty. He is the sheriff's brother," explained Vivienne. "Isaac, please step in here and meet King Edward," she said, introducing him.

"Your Majesty, it is an honor and a pleasure," said Isaac, bowing to the King from out in the corridor, not daring to enter into the room. "If there is anything you need, please let me know and I will get it for you at once."

"You can get me the hell out of here," complained the King, pushing back a long strand of hair from his eyes. "I feel like I am the prisoner, restricted to this godforsaken room."

Vivienne nodded her thanks to Isaac and quietly closed the door. "I thought it would be better protection to have someone as honorable as Isaac, the sheriff's brother, posted at your door, My King."

"Hmph," snorted the King. "Well, I suppose I see your point."

"May I talk with you ... Father?" she asked, watching his eyes snap with annoyance. She expected him to chastise her or throw her out. Instead, he silently nodded. She gently put the box upon the table and opened it up.

"It's a chess game!" The grouchy king's mood suddenly lightened. "I love the game," he said, reaching for the board and pieces. "Do you play, Lady Vivienne?" Before she could even answer, he was already setting up the game.

"I do," she told him, feeling as if her plan was working after all. Thank goodness her half-brother Rook told her that chess was Edward's weakness.

"Then sit. Sit, please," he said, almost seeming anxious to prove his skill to anyone, even if she was a woman. "Play a game against me."

"Of course." Vivienne smiled. She figured while the King was distracted with the game, she would talk to him about releasing Sir Guy and Lord Rowen from the dungeon. And also convince him to get her out of her prize bride agreement.

"I'll move first," he told her, pushing one of his white pawns forward. The pieces were far from being ornate enough for a king, but they were still nice enough for a noble. Her uncle had this set constructed years ago when Vivienne was just a child. She'd learned to play the game from her Uncle Gilbert, even though usually only men learned the skill. Carved from wood, half the pieces were painted in black, and the other half in white. The board was also made from wood, the light squares being made from inlaid oak, while the dark squares were crafted from walnut. A skilled carpenter had created this, and wasn't happy when Vivienne, at a young age, painted the chess pieces without asking for permission.

Vivienne followed the King's move by doing the same, moving a pawn.

"We haven't been able to find any clues yet about who tried to kill you," she told him.

"I thought the sheriff was better than that." The King kept his eyes on the board and moved again.

Vivienne purposely pushed a pawn in the way so he'd have to capture it on his next move. She wanted him to be in a good mood when she asked him her questions. For that to happen, the King had to be winning.

"Silly girl, that wasn't a smart move at all." He chuckled and pushed his pawn forward and snapped up her piece, enclosing it in his big hand.

"Oh, how careless of me." She tried to look upset about it. Continuing to make small talk with him, she purposely let him think he was getting the upper hand by knowingly sacrificing her pieces, playing to the man's pride. Then, when she decided the King was happy and that this had gone on long enough, she started in with her questions. "I really don't wish to marry the winner of the tournament, Father," she added, thinking mayhap that would soften his heart to hear her call him that. Of course, he'd warned her not to ever call him that again, but she had to risk it. If nothing else, it was reminding him that she was his daughter.

"Vivienne, I told you, that cannot be changed." He took her bishop next, smiling from ear to ear.

"Why not?" She carelessly moved a piece, not caring if she won or lost. Getting him to agree and bend to her will was all that mattered.

"Why not? Because, it is already done, that's why. You will be a prize bride just as planned." He smiled again, moving his rook, setting it up to take out her queen.

"Hrmph," she said with a sniff, moving her queen and capturing his knight, putting his queen in jeopardy now.

"Damn," he ground out, his gaze focused on the board, his attention no longer on her.

The game of cat-and-mouse went on for a while. Every time he gave her an answer she didn't like, she was sure to snatch up one of his pieces. He didn't seem to like that at all. Then it came time to ask him to free Lord Rowen and Sir Guy. She took a deep breath and released it slowly. "Sir Guy and Lord Rowen are missing the entire tournament that has already started." She moved her knight, but kept her eyes focused on his face.

He stroked his long beard in thought, surveying the situation. "Yes, well, I'm missing it too, sitting here in my prison," he mumbled. He wavered above several of his pieces but he finally moved his queen.

"I don't feel as if you've treated them fairly." Her queen closed in on his king now.

His angry blue eyes flashed up at her and then lowered to the board once again. She was upsetting him, she could see that. She was also breaking his concentration. "Your opinion doesn't matter. I needed someone to pay for the attempt on my life and the death of Sir Amis. I did what needed to be done." He stupidly moved his bishop right into danger and she took it without a second thought. The distraction was working. "Damn, how did you do that?" he ground out.

"Don't you think it would be good to free the men?" She slid a pawn forward.

"Nay. Not until the killer is caught."

Every time one of them spoke, they moved a piece with a little more force.

"Then what about at least freeing Lord Rowen so he can help find your true killer?"

"I thought that's what you and the sheriff were doing."

Several more pieces were pushed around the board, the air in the room becoming thick between them.

"Rowen is your son! He forgave you for ordering his death when he was born, and he now pays fealty to you."

"That's right, he did. So, what of it?" His eyes remained on the board, his hand wavering over one piece and then another as he studied her face now.

"You cannot lock up someone who has given up his life to pay fealty to you."

"He was a damned pirate! He had no life before paying fealty to me." He angrily moved anything haphazardly, barely looking at the board when he did it.

"I am asking you to release Rowen. My half-brother. I am asking you to please trust that your own flesh and blood never did a thing to try to hurt you, and neither would he even consider it."

"My own flesh and blood and his brothers raided from me for years," snapped the King, his voice getting much louder as his anger grew.

"But your triplet sons never hurt you or tried to kill you. Did they?"

"Nay. But what the hell does that matter? They tried to steal me blind. That is just as bad in my opinion."

"Your Majesty, if I win this game, will you at least release Rowen? If I lose, I'll stop asking you and he'll stay imprisoned."

"You won't win, you silly thing. You are a woman! God's teeth, everyone knows I am king of the game and that women cannot play chess and certainly never win! I always win. You should know that."

"More likely, everyone lets you win because you are king."

"Not true."

"Then take my challenge."

"You are being a fool. You'll lose, my dear."

"That is a chance I am willing to take. So, do you accept my challenge? If I win, Rowen is released? Besides, it won't look good for you to keep him imprisoned. He has a lot of alliances and a castle of his own. It could be beneficial to you not to keep him behind bars. It'll also only anger his brothers."

"I'm not afraid of what anyone will think, and I certainly am not scared of Rowen's brothers. However, I think you are a brash young woman who needs to learn her lesson. So, yes, I accept your challenge. Rowen can be released if you win, but not Sir Guy. But you won't win, so after this game I want you to stop asking me about it."

"For now, I'll take that." Vivienne quickly moved her piece and he counter-moved one of his own. She had kept him so distracted that he hadn't even noticed what was going on right in front of his nose. One more move of her queen and she knew she had him. "Checkmate! I win." Vivienne jumped up out of her chair and hurried to the door, leaving the King sitting there with his mouth hanging open, staring aimlessly at the board.

"Have a wonderful day ... Father. I'll be off to the dungeon now to release my brother." She pulled the door open and when she left, she smiled, knowing Edward sat there scratching his head, not saying a word. She was certain that he couldn't believe he'd just been beaten at his favorite game ... by a woman!

Chapter Eleven

"Constable, are the suspects ready to be questioned?" asked Zachariah near the end of the day. After having watched the hand-to-hand combat with swords, the archery challenge, and the quarterstaff, which was basically fighting with wooden poles, he hadn't noticed anything suspicious or out of the ordinary at all. The competition part of the tournament was over for the day, and now the feast and celebration with entertainment would begin and probably last throughout the night.

"Aye, Sheriff." The constable walked with him to the chamber the sheriff had been given to use while he stayed at Mablcthorpe Castle. "I've had Milo and Martin go with Mablethorpe's trusted guard, Richard, and gather them up. The potential suspects are waiting outside your chamber as we speak."

"Good, good," he said, lowering his voice as people passed them by. "Even though at this point, we have very little to go on and everyone is a suspect." Zachariah hadn't seen Vivienne or his brother the entire day, and he couldn't really say it upset him in the least. Vivienne was meddling in his affairs again, and that wasn't what she was supposed to be doing. This murder investigation should be taking her attention, but instead she was trying to get him to accept his mercenary brother when he had no intention of doing such a thing. Isaac had made his decision to leave Mablethorpe and become a mercenary, and now he could just live with that decision for the rest of his life. Zachariah didn't agree with his brother, and Isaac had never listened to him while growing up, so he was sure the man would never change.

"Sheriff, what is this all about?" asked Frederick, the King's valet, as Zachariah approached his room, striding by those standing in the corridor, waiting for him.

"Are we going to be here long?" complained the food-taster, Gisela. "I need to prepare the King's food tray before the meal starts."

"And I need to get back out to the stables to check on the horses' shoes," complained the King's blacksmith, Theodoric. "I also have to sharpen Sir Barclay's weapons for tomorrow's events."

"Quiet down, all of you," commanded the sheriff, halting to look over at Mablethorpe's guard. "Richard, where are Sir Barclay and the King's squire, Peter?"

"Milo is fetching them now," Richard reported.

"And how about the juggler? What was his name?" Zachariah couldn't remember.

"His name is Alvin," said the constable. "Martin went with Grunt to get him."

"All right, then. The constable and I will talk to you all as quickly as possible, and you'll soon be on your way. Richard, send them in one at a time, please."

Zachariah pushed open his chamber door and stepped into the room, stopping when he saw his brother Isaac lying on Zachariah's bed, munching on an apple. He was fully clothed and had his legs crossed, his dirty boots soiling the covers. "What the hell are you doing here, Isaac?"

"I told him he could share your chamber with you during his stay at Mablethorpe," came a very familiar voice from across the room, causing him to cringe.

"Vivienne," he said in a low voice, seeing her sitting on his chair. Why was she getting involved in his personal life once again? Wasn't it bad enough that she had interfered with his sister, Magdalena, during their last investigation? This woman would never stop!

"I'm sure you meant to say *Lady* Vivienne, Sheriff Fitch." Vivienne got up and strolled across the floor toward him. "Didn't you?"

So, they were playing this game again, were they? If he hadn't been angry before about not being able to find a clue, he was certainly angry now. Vivienne was up to old her tricks again. He knew damned well what she was doing. She wanted him to reconcile with Isaac, and that is why she told Isaac he could share Zachariah's chamber. Well, it wasn't going to happen if he had anything to say about it. His brother had made wrong choices in his life that just happened to affect Zachariah and the entire family. Zachariah had no intention of forgiving Isaac for whoring himself out as a hired killer to the highest bidder. That wasn't what Fitch men did. Their father worked for little pay, but he always thought of the people of the town's safety over his own. That was what Zachariah was trying to do as well. Too damned bad his younger brother only seemed to think of himself. He was about to explode with anger when he heard a slight knock behind him and he turned to see both Lord Rook and Lord Rowen standing in the doorway.

"May we join you for the questioning, Sheriff?" asked Rowen.

"Lord Rowen? I thought you were locked up in the

dungeon." Zachariah didn't know what was going on. "Please don't tell me your brother helped you escape."

"Nay, it was all my s—Lady Vivienne's doing," said Rowen. Zachariah realized Rowen almost called Vivienne his sister in front of everyone, but stopped himself at the last second. Good thing. That didn't need to be common knowledge at a time like this.

"Please, come in," said Zachariah, with a nod and a wave of his hand.

The two men entered.

"How did Lady Vivienne help you escape?" Constable Dorson questioned Lord Rowen.

"Lady Vivienne didn't help my brother escape—she changed our father's mind is what she did," Rook answered for him.

"She did? How?" asked Zachariah, his gaze darting over to Vivienne and then back to her bastard brothers.

"She played chess with our father and won Rowen's freedom," Rook explained with a big smile. Dear old Dad never saw it coming." He chuckled as if this amused him.

"She played chess with the King and won? Really?" When Zachariah looked back over to Vivienne she was smiling smugly from ear to ear. Zachariah and Vivienne had both learned how to play the game of chess when they were just children; however Zachariah had usually beaten her. As Vivienne grew up, she became sly enough to do and say things during the game to distract him. Hence, she ended up winning the game by more or less cheating. Or at least, that is the way he saw it. He was sure she used her same tricks on the King. "Yes, I'm sure she did," he mumbled.

"Shall I send in the first person for questioning?" asked Richard from the door.

"Yes, bring in the food-taster first," instructed Zachariah. "Then she can get back to work."

"Aye, Sheriff." Richard disappeared for a second to get her.

"Isaac, off my bed," said Zachariah, snapping his fingers.

"You mean *our* bed." Isaac got up, still munching on the apple.

"You can't stay here with me. I've got my daughter, Starah, sharing my room. It wouldn't be proper for you to be here too."

"I've already taken care of that," interrupted Vivienne. "Starah will be staying with me. She'll share the bed with Nairnie and Maleine, while I sleep on the floor with Martin and Grunt."

"You thought of everything, didn't you?" he said with an exasperated sigh.

"See, Brother? Now we'll have plenty of time to catch up on everything." Isaac seemed amused by the entire situation, even though he could see how upset Zachariah was by it.

"You can leave for now, Isaac. I've got work to do and you can't be here."

"Leave?" he asked. "Where am I supposed to go?"

"Isaac, your break time is over," said Vivienne in a sweet voice. "Will you please take Geoffrey's place guarding the King's door? You can send Geoffrey here to be questioned as well."

"Of course, my lady. For you, I'd be happy to do it." Isaac bowed. and then quickly left the room.

Zachariah looked over at Vivienne, giving her his most disapproving glance, although she barely noticed. "We'll talk about this later," he told her in a low voice.

"Sir Amis's body that is being kept in the dungeon is starting to smell," announced Rowen. "You'll have to get him out of there soon. Sir Guy is already starting to retch from the stench."

"Yes, I agree. I'm sure my uncle will be complaining about

155

that, so mayhap we can find a more suitable place to put the corpse," said Vivienne.

"Buried is where he should be," said Zachariah. "However, I am sure the King and his entourage will want to take Sir Amis's body back to his family. Mayhap we can at least get a coffin to contain him in until the tournament and joust are over."

"I'll speak to the undertaker about that," Constable Dorson offered.

"Here is the food-taster," announced Richard, bringing the small woman into the room.

"I don't know why I'm here," said Gisela, seeming confused as well as worried.

"You are here for questioning regarding the murder of Sir Amis," Zachariah told her.

"You don't suspect me of murdering Sir Amis, do you, Sheriff?" Her eyes opened wide in surprise. "I barely even knew him."

"We make no judgments until we have collected all the facts and evidence first," stated Zachariah.

"We're questioning anyone who might have had access to the weapon tent," explained Vivienne.

"Then I shouldn't be here." The woman shook her head. "I wasn't anywhere near the tent. I was in the kitchens the entire time."

"Nay, you weren't. You were out there by the tent, ready to watch the joust just like the rest of us," came the voice of the blacksmith from the door.

"I said one at a time," Zachariah said in aggravation. "Richard, can you please close the door?"

"Nay, wait. Let Theodoric in as well," said Vivienne. "We can question them both at the same time."

"Lady Vivienne? What are you doing?" he asked through clenched teeth.

156

"Sheriff, I am sure all these people are anxious to get to the feast," she answered. "Let's just hear what they have to say, and then let them go celebrate with the rest, as is proper."

Vivienne could tell Zachariah didn't like her suggestion, but she had a feeling there was something between Gisela and Theodoric and mayhap they were somehow involved in the murder together. By questioning them at the same time, there was a chance they would rat each other out. On the other hand, they could be totally innocent, but this was still worth trying.

"Please tell us your names and your positions in the King's household," said the constable, sitting down at a table with quill and paper to record the information.

"You already know I'm Gisela, and the King's food-taster," said the woman. She was small but still comely, even at her age. It was hard to tell too much about her since she wore her hair covered by a wimple and was dressed in a plain gown.

"I'm Theodoric, his blacksmith," answered the man.

"How long have each of you been in the King's service?" asked Vivienne.

"I've worked for the King for about five years now," said Gisela.

"How did you become the King's food-taster?" asked Zachariah. "After all, it is an odd job for a woman to hold."

"How is a woman risking her life every day any different than a man doing it?" Vivienne challenged him, making him realize he should have perhaps worded that differently.

"My father held the position before me," answered Gisela. "Therefore, I grew up living in the King's castle. When Father died, to honor him, I decided to approach the King about keeping the profession in our family and he agreed."

"How did your father die?" The constable stopped writing and looked up in surprise. "Was it by poison?"

"Nay, of course not," Gisela answered. "He unfortunately caught the great white plague."

"I see," said Zachariah, knowing she was talking about consumption that killed many by affecting the lungs. Eventually, the ill just wasted away.

"What about you?" The constable asked Theodoric. "How long have you held your position in the King's household?"

"I've only been the King's blacksmith for about a year now," said the man. "But my family has served in the King's smithy since I was a child."

"One year? That's all?" Rowen spoke up.

"Lord Rowen, if you and Lord Rook are staying, I'll have to ask you to refrain from talking," warned Zachariah.

"Sorry," said Rowen, crossing his arms over his chest and looking at the floor. His long blond hair fell over his eyes.

"Theodoric, can you tell us what type of work you did before you were in service for the King?" asked Vivienne. "Were you a blacksmith at another castle, or in a town perhaps?"

"Aye," said the man, at the same time Gisela said "nay." Theodoric glared at Gisela from the side of his eye.

"Well, which is it?" asked the constable in confusion, holding his inked quill in the air. "Yes or no, then?"

Theodoric answered. "Yes, I was a blacksmith in Northumbria for a while."

"Northumbria?" asked the sheriff. "I thought you said your family worked in the King's smithy since you were a child. What were you doing so far north?"

"I lived with an estranged uncle who lived up north. I was also a guard for a while too, since my uncle was friends with the lord of the castle and got me the job."

"Which lord?" asked Rook.

"Lord Rook, please, stay silent," said the sheriff. "Continue, Theodoric."

The blacksmith nodded and continued his story. "I just wanted to say that my family comes from a long line of smithies. You see, my family was always in the blacksmith business and that is how I learned the trade. After my father died, I came back home and started helping out more, and even learned the trade of being an armorer."

"You said you were a guard. Where exactly did you serve as a guard?" asked Rook. "Because you look familiar to me but I can't quite place where I've seen you before."

"Lord Rook, please," grunted Zachariah, releasing a puff of air from his mouth, obviously not liking the fact Rook and his brother were asking questions when it was his job, not theirs.

"My lords, mayhap it would be best if you waited for us in the great hall," suggested Vivienne, but in a kind and thoughtful manner. She didn't want Zachariah snapping at her brothers anymore.

"I wouldn't mind." Rowen shrugged. "After all, I didn't get anything but crusts of stale bread to eat in the dungeon. I am famished and thirsty and could go for a tankard of ale as well. I just hope someone sends food and ale to Sir Guy or he's going to die down in that hell hole."

"I'm sure he'll be taken care of," said the sheriff, walking over and opening the door for them to leave.

"I'll see to Sir Guy, don't worry," Vivienne promised her brothers.

"Thank you, once again, Lady Vivienne, for helping to get me released," said Rowen. "How can I ever repay you?"

"I'll think of something and let you know." She waggled her fingers, waving as they left, noticing Zachariah rolling his eyes now. The sheriff closed the door and came back into the room.

· · ·

ZACHARIAH WASN'T happy with the way this questioning was going. He needed answers and didn't seem to be getting a single clue. "Theodoric, as a skilled blacksmith, I am sure you can make a lot of things in the forge, can't you?" he asked the man.

"Well ... yes. I suppose so," answered the blacksmith.

"How about something like this?" Zachariah reached down and picked up the sharp knife that had been concealed on the end of Lord Rowen's lance.

"I didn't make that, if it is what you are asking."

"That blade took an innocent man's life," snarled the constable. "We will catch the killer, and I promise, he or she will pay for what they did."

"I didn't have anything to do with the murder." Theodoric held up his palms and when he did, Zachariah noticed they looked a shade of orange. Most likely rust from handling metal in the smithy.

"I didn't have anything to do with the murder either," said Gisela. "Can we go now, Sheriff? The King will be impatient, wanting to eat and wondering why I am not there."

"Not yet." Vivienne stopped them. "My handmaid said she saw the two of you whispering in the stables. Tell us what that was all about, please."

"Can't two people have a private moment together?" asked Gisela.

"Oh. Do you mean you two are lovers, then?" asked Vivienne. Zachariah had never considered that.

"Aye," said Gisela at the same time Theodoric said "nay." This time Gisela glared at the blacksmith.

There was a quick knock at the door and the guard stuck his head inside the room. "Excuse me, my lady and Sheriff, but the valet says he needs to leave to help the King dress. I told him he can't go until you question him first."

"He what?" asked Zachariah. "Isn't King Edward already

dressed? It's not like he's going anywhere, so why would he need to change his clothes?"

"Excuse me, Sheriff." Frederick looked into the room from around Richard. "The King has sent word to me that he will be dressing and joining the feast this evening in the great hall. I need to go to him at once. It is my duty."

"He said what?" Zachariah almost exploded with anger and frustration now. "The King is in seclusion for a reason. God's teeth, he was almost killed yesterday. We cannot take the chance that the killer might try again. He needs to stay put for his own safety."

"Sheriff, it's true," said Geoffrey, the door guard that Isaac had replaced. "The King just decided that he was tired of sitting alone in his small chamber while the tournament is taking place outside. He said he wants to eat at the feast tonight, since he's paying for the food, drink, and celebration. He also said that he is king, and no one is going to stop him from doing whatever he likes."

"I'll have to talk with him." Zachariah started toward the door.

VIVIENNE REALIZED that Zachariah confronting the King was not a good idea. Especially since King Edward was probably still furious that she beat him at chess.

"Sheriff, you cannot tell a king what to do," she told him. "Please, have respect and do not even try."

"Me? Tell a king what to do?" asked Zachariah, his palm slapping against his chest. "What about you?"

"She's right, Sheriff," agreed the constable. "It wouldn't be proper to be giving orders to our ruler."

"Nor would it be proper if he's killed at the feast, either," snapped Zachariah. "It is my job to provide security for him, and that is what I intend to do."

"Let him join the feast, the people will love it," said Vivienne. "Besides, I'll have my uncle post extra guards throughout the great hall and even in the kitchen. It'll be fine," she assured him, not wanting any trouble.

The sheriff shook his head, but stopped protesting and instead took his seat. "Guard, bring in the next two," he ordered. "Let's move this along."

Gisela and Theodoric left, and Frederick and Geoffrey came into the room next.

"Each of you please state your name and position and how long you've worked for King Edward," said the constable.

"I'm Frederick, and I am the King's valet." Frederick had a medium build, was shaven except for his mustache, and was completely bald. "I have been the King's valet for the last twenty years."

"And what about you?" Zachariah nodded to the guard.

"I am Geoffrey, the King's head guard." Geoffrey was a big man, tall and with lots of bulging muscles. He wore the attire of the King's guards, which consisted of a scarlet coat with gold trimmings. "I have been in the service of the King for ten years now."

"Did the two of you arrive here at Mablethorpe Castle before the King's arrival?" asked Vivienne.

"Nay, I arrived with the King and was at his side the entire time," stated Geoffrey.

"What about you?" Vivienne asked Frederick.

"I arrived the same day as the King as well," said the man. "It is my job to travel with him, and of course, to bring his clothes and tend to dressing him."

"Yes, I remember you arriving then," said Vivienne. "I also remember the pages who carried the King's trunk."

"One of the pages was from Mablethorpe, I believe," said Frederick. "That was not proper and never should have happened."

"You're right, and I'm sorry. That boy was my son. I'll see to it that he doesn't interfere again," said Vivienne.

"Were the two of you near the weapons tent when the joust with the King was supposed to happen? Or for that matter, were you near or in the tent ahead of time?" asked the sheriff.

"I believe the King's entire household was there by the tent, preparing to watch him joust," said Frederick.

"Yes, we were there, just like everyone else," added Geoffrey. "Many people went in and out of the tent that day."

"Thank you. That'll be all." Zachariah dismissed them.

"Sheriff, Sir Barclay, the squire, and the juggler are all here now," Richard reported from the door.

"Send them in, Richard," Vivienne spoke up.

"Aye, my lady." Richard opened the door wider as the last two suspects left and three new ones entered.

"What is this all about?" Sir Barclay demanded to know. "I don't like being pulled away from the other knights in the great hall."

"Thank you for coming, Sir Barclay. We'll only take a few minutes of your time," Vivienne told him.

The knight's head snapped around when he heard Vivienne. He smiled, showing his dirty and chipped teeth. "Oh, it's you, my bride-to-be. I'm happy to be here for you. Anything for you."

"I am no one's bride-to-be," Vivienne retorted.

"After I win the entire tournament tomorrow, you'll be mine. In every way." He chuckled, and Vivienne shuddered. She noticed a look from Zachariah like he wanted to strike the man. Vivienne couldn't blame him. She wanted to get Sir Barclay far away from her as soon as she could.

"I am Peter, one of the squires to the King," said the lanky young man standing next to the knight. "Are we suspects in Sir Amis's murder?"

"We are only questioning people at this time," said the sheriff.

"I'm Alvin," said the juggler, tossing eggs in the air, juggling four of them at once.

"Stop that," commanded Zachariah.

"All right." Alvin stopped, catching two of the eggs, letting the other two fall to the ground at his feet. They splattered as they broke.

"Clean that up," ordered Zachariah, but Grunt ran in and licked up the eggs for him.

"Good girl," said Alvin, patting Grunt hard on the head. Grunt looked up at him and gave a low growl.

"Grunt, come here," said Vivienne, calling the hound to her. "Come here, *boy*."

"Ooooh, Grunt's a boy," said the juggler with a chuckle. "No wonder he growled at me."

Vivienne looked up to see Martin peeking around the door, probably looking for Grunt. He mouthed the words to her that he wanted to enter, but she shook her head, telling him no. Then she pointed and mouthed the words to meet her in the great hall."

"Lady Vivienne? Are we disturbing you?" the sheriff asked snidely. "Because if you have more important things to attend to, don't let us stop you from leaving."

"Nay, of course not," she said.

"Richard, close the door," Zachariah called out, solving the problem.

"Did we do something wrong?" asked the juggler.

"Why don't you tell us," was Zachariah's reply. Vivienne didn't like the sheriff's sour attitude that seemed to come about once his brother showed up here at the castle. She really had to try to do something to help them make amends, because she didn't like seeing Zachariah so on edge. This couldn't continue. They had a murder to investigate and Zachariah seemed to be far off his usual sharpness. She could see that Isaac's presence was also affecting the sheriff's ability to do his job. They'd never catch the killer if his mind was elsewhere.

"We saw you at the castle the day before the King arrived," said the constable.

"Yes. That's right," said Alvin, putting the eggs in his pouch and pulling out a coin. He did something with his hand and kept making the coin disappear and reappear again with the way he twisted his fingers."

"Wow, you're good at that," said the squire, being fascinated by Alvin's movements.

"It's my job. To entertain people," the juggler replied.

"You know sleight of hand," said Zachariah.

"Aye, he said, showing his empty hands and then reaching out and pulling the coin from Peter's ear.

"It's my skill," said Alvin proudly.

"So, you like deceiving people, and you're good at it, then." Zachariah almost sounded as if he were accusing the man of something.

Alvin stopped and frowned. "What does that mean?"

"He doesn't mean anything by that." Vivienne pushed forward, leaving Grunt sniffing around the floor.

"What about you, Sir Barclay?" the sheriff asked next. "You were here a day early, is that correct?"

"Of course. We all show up early to prepare."

"To prepare what?" asked Zachariah.

"Sheriff, please," said Vivienne, deciding it was time for her to do the questioning since Zachariah's foul mood was getting in the way. "Sir Barclay, do you usually prepare your own lances for the joust?"

"Nay, I do that," said Peter.

"What about the coronels on your lances?" she asked. "Where do those come from?"

"Why, the blacksmith makes them, of course."

"Do you mean Theodoric?" asked the constable.

"Yes, that's right," said the knight. "Theodoric makes the coronels for everyone who resides at the King's dwellings."

"Then you don't even know how to apply one to the lance?" asked Zachariah.

Sir Barclay chuckled. "Of course, I know. I'm not stupid. Every knight and squire knows how to do that, and even some pages have the knowledge. What does this have to do with anything?"

Vivienne decided to come out and just tell him. "There was a sharp blade concealed beneath the coronel of Lord Rowen's lance," she told him.

"Oh," said the knight. "I heard that but thought it was only gossip. Either way, why are you questioning me? My lances are fine. Check them if you don't believe me."

"That won't be necessary," said Zachariah.

"Why don't you question that bastard of the King?" continued Sir Barclay. "After all, everyone knows how those triplets ganged up on King Edward and robbed him every chance they got."

"Lord Rowen was a pirate, wasn't he?" asked Peter.

"He most certainly was," growled Sir Barclay. "Why did I see him out of the dungeon? He's a cutthroat and has the most reason to want to kill our king. He needs to be locked up with the key thrown away, if you ask me."

"No one asked you," said Zachariah, holding his head. "That'll be all. You can all leave now, thank you."

"Do you think Lord Rowen will try to murder the King again at the feast?" Vivienne heard Alvin ask Sir Barclay as they headed out the door.

Once the door was closed, Zachariah plopped down on his bed and let out a big sigh.

"That didn't go very well, did it?" asked Vivienne.

"Nay," said the sheriff. "Not at all."

"We're not any closer to finding the killer now than we were before," said the constable. "And it seems that even though we tried to keep things hushed, everyone knows what happened and that a man was murdered."

"Yes, there are no secrets around here." Zachariah rested on his back, staring at the ceiling.

Grunt jumped up on the bed next to Zachariah, and started licking his face.

"Stop that, Grunt. I don't have egg on my face," said the sheriff, pushing the dog away.

"He is just trying to comfort you," explained Vivienne. "He wants you to pet him."

"I don't need comforting," he said, looking away from the hound.

"Constable, will you give me and the sheriff a moment alone?" Vivienne asked Constable Dorson.

"What? Why?" The constable looked over at Zachariah in question.

"It's all right," the sheriff told him.

"But it's not proper to be alone in your chamber with a lady, Sheriff," said the constable in a half whisper.

"We're not alone," said Zachariah. "We have Grunt here to chaperone. If we get too close, I guarantee he'll push between us begging for attention." Just as Zachariah said that, Grunt sidled up close to him on the bed, sniffing the sheriff's ear.

"If you're sure, Sheriff." The constable collected up his

things. "I could go for a bite to eat. My wife and children are here, so it would be nice to spend time with them as well."

"Before you do that," said Zachariah, "please see to ordering a coffin for Sir Amis's body."

"Aye, of course, Sheriff." The disappointment on the constable's face was evident. "Would you like me to feed the prisoner too?"

"Nay, I'll see to that," said Vivienne. "And Sir Guy is not a prisoner. Well, not really. My heart goes out to him, since it seems as if he was framed for a murder he didn't commit."

"My lady, he *did* commit the murder," the constable reminded her. "He was the one to shove the knife right through Sir Amis's heart. You can't think the King won't sentence him for that, even if he wasn't the one who originally planned it."

"What do you mean?" she asked.

"Sir Guy will hang for the crime, whether it was really his fault or not," the constable told her.

"Nay! Is that true?" she asked Zachariah, who only pushed the dog away from him and put his face in his hands, trying to get away from Grunt's tongue.

"Yes, it is most likely true, Lady Vivienne," Zachariah told her, his voice muffled from behind his hands. "I am sorry to say that it doesn't look like a promising future for Sir Guy."

"Nay, that can't be. They can't kill him for it! It was someone else's ploy, not his. He had nothing to do with it."

"He did volunteer to joust against Sir Amis," the constable pointed out. "I mean, no one forced him to do it."

"That doesn't mean anything," she told him. "Now, please leave and do not be talking this way around anyone. There is enough gossip floating about and we don't need more."

"Yes, my lady," the constable softly answered. Then, with a quick bow, he turned and left the room, closing the door behind him.

"Zachariah, do something," Vivienne said as soon as they were alone.

Zachariah slowly removed his hands from his face, making sure Grunt wasn't there waiting to lick him again. His eyes traveled upward until they interlocked with hers. "Did you mean to say *Sheriff*, by any chance? After all, we don't want to start sounding too familiar with each other, do we?"

"I'm sorry that I corrected you before, but I was angry with you."

He abruptly sat up on the bed. Grunt was instantly at his side. "So, every time you become angry or don't agree with me, I'm Sheriff or Sheriff Fitch? But once things are pleasant between us and we are alone, I am your good old friend Zachariah again? Is that how it goes?"

"Well ... you know I have to keep up appearances. We both do."

"*Lady* Vivienne," he stressed her title, which told her he was still upset with her. "You had no right to tell Isaac he could stay in my chamber. You know better than anyone the way I feel about him."

"You felt the same way about your sister, if I must remind you," she answered. "Yet, now you and Magdalena are the best of friends."

"Mayhap so. But I am telling you right now, that will never happen with my other siblings so please stop meddling where you don't belong.

There came a small knock on the door, and Richard popped his head inside. "My lady, your handmaid is here to see you."

"Tell her I'm busy," said Vivienne.

"She said it's important."

"Go on," said Zachariah with a flick of his fingers.

"But we haven't even had a moment to discuss the interviews or what we think," she told him.

"I need to gather my thoughts. We'll discuss things later."

"Oh. All right," she said, slowly heading to the door. She didn't like being pushed away by Zachariah. Mayhap her intervening in his relationship with his brother did more damage than good. Now, it seemed as if there was a wall between them, and she didn't like that at all.

"And take your damned dog with you," he ground out, getting up off the bed.

"Come on, Grunt. The sheriff wants to be alone."

The dog whined and jumped off the bed, running after Vivienne.

Vivienne walked out into the corridor to find Maleine seeming very anxious about something.

"What is it, Maleine?"

"Can we talk in private?" The handmaid's gaze traveled over to Richard, who was still standing post at the door.

"Richard, will you please relieve Isaac and take his post at the King's bedchamber?" she asked.

"Of course, my lady." Richard bowed and hurried down the corridor toward the King's chamber.

"Now, what is so important?" she asked the girl.

"My lady, I saw that food-taster and she was delivering food," said Maleine.

"Yes, that's her job to bring the King his food. But it is odd that she is doing so," commented Vivienne. "I thought the King was coming to the feast."

"She wasn't headed to the King's chamber, my lady." Maleine seemed excited, as if she'd discovered a secret.

"She wasn't? Well, then, I wonder where she was taking the food?"

"I am not exactly sure, but I think she was headed to the dungeon."

170

"The dungeon? Whatever for? The only prisoner in there is Sir Guy right now."

"Do you think she is going to try to poison Sir Guy?" asked Maleine.

"Now, stop it, Maleine," Vivienne scolded. "I swear sometimes you let your imagination run away with you. Why would she do a thing like that?"

"Mayhap you are right. Perhaps it was nothing," said the girl with a shrug, looking like she thought she did something wrong.

"Thank you for reporting it to me," said Vivienne, not wanting the girl to feel bad. "I promise to look into the matter."

"Aye, my lady."

"Why don't you go to the great hall for the feast? I am sure Wymond is there waiting for you," she said, speaking of the boy who was about Maleine's age, and who clearly had eyes for her.

"Do you think so?" Maleine slowly looked up and grinned.

"I'll bet on it," said Vivienne. "And when you see him, make sure he didn't bring Chomp and Snuff to the great hall with him, or there is bound to be trouble." She spoke of the former assistant rat-catcher's ferrets.

"I will, my lady. Thank you," she said with a curtsy before hurrying away.

Grunt let out a whimper and scratched behind one ear with his back leg. Vivienne started thinking about what Maleine had said. It was odd that the King's food-taster would be headed to the dungeon instead of going to the great hall when the feast was about to start, and she knew the King would be present. Perhaps it would be best if Vivienne checked on Sir Guy for herself.

"Come on, Grunt. Let's take a little walk," she said, meaning to investigate and hopefully be able to stop any trouble from happening before it started.

Chapter Twelve

Vivienne headed to the dungeon with Grunt at her side. She pushed open the door to the guard's room, seeing Gisela talking to the man. The tray of food was on the table.

"Hello," she said, almost seeming to startle them.

"Lady Vivienne. What are you doing here?" asked the guard with wide eyes. She recognized him as one of her own guards. "I thought you'd be at the King's feast."

"Yes, Gregory, I will be going to the feast. But I came to make sure Sir Guy was all right first."

"He's a prisoner," Gregory reminded her.

"I understand that, but he is being held under false pretense, I am sure. Is that food for Sir Guy, Gisela?"

"Yes," said the woman.

"Why isn't one of Mablethorpe's servants bringing it?"

"They are all busy. Preparing the feast for the King," she answered. "So, I said I'd be happy to bring Sir Guy his food."

Vivienne supposed it sounded plausible, but still, she wasn't sure she could trust the woman.

"I see."

"I was just going to bring it to him, and was asking the guard to open the cell door for me." Gisela picked up the tray of food.

"Wait," said Vivienne, with her hand raised. "Did you taste it first?"

"My lady?" asked the girl in confusion. "I am food-taster for the King only."

"Taste it. Now. I want to see you eat the food before you give it to Sir Guy."

"But, I don't understand," said Gisela, seeming alarmed by this suggestion. "I am not a food-taster for prisoners. That is not part of my job."

"You are food-taster for anyone you bring food to, as long as you are at my castle. Especially since you are bringing my prisoner a meal, when that is certainly not your job. Now, take a bite. Go on," she coaxed the woman, wanting to see how she'd react.

"Fine," she said, throwing Vivienne a daggered glance. Gisela picked up a piece of cheese and took a bite, chewing and swallowing it down. Then she did the same with some bread and salted herring. "Satisfied?" she asked, snidely.

"What about the ale?" Vivienne nodded toward the drink on the tray.

The woman's eyes interlocked with Vivienne's. Slowly, Gisela picked up the cup and swallowed down some ale. "Will there be anything else you'd like me to taste?" asked Gisela. For some reason, her tone of voice must have made Grunt bark at her. "Perhaps you'd like me to gnaw on your hound's bone for a while too?"

"Talk like that will get you thrown into the dungeon next if you're not careful. Now, leave the food and go back to the great hall and take care of the King's needs like you are supposed to be doing."

"Aye, my lady." Gisela nodded and curtsied and quickly left the room. Grunt growled once more as he watched her go.

"Would you like me to bring this food to the prisoner then?" asked the guard.

"Nay, that won't be necessary, Gregory," said Vivienne, knowing this guard and how much he liked to eat. Vivienne wasn't sure the guard wouldn't keep the food for himself. "From now on, no one goes in to see the prisoner or to bring him food unless it is Cook or Maria from the kitchen, or the sheriff or myself. Do you understand?" Vivienne wasn't a hundred percent certain that this murder wasn't really done to frame Sir Guy. She needed to be cautious in every step they took.

"Yes, my lady," said Gregory. "Did you really think that food-taster was going to try to poison Sir Guy?"

"Anything is possible," said Vivienne. "And until the sheriff and I have caught the killer, everyone is a suspect."

"Everyone? Even me?" asked the guard in surprise.

"Until proven innocent, everyone is considered to be possibly guilty, like I said. Now open the door for me. I'll bring Sir Guy his food myself." She picked up the tray as Gregory put the key in the lock and opened the door. Then she followed him to Sir Guy's cell, already smelling the putrid stench of Sir Amis's corpse from the other cell. Water dripped from the ceiling, hitting her on the head and making her cringe. This whole place was damp and smelled moldy. A green sheet of mildew covered the walls. Her stomach already started to churn and she wasn't at all certain that she wouldn't retch. If Zachariah knew she was in the dungeon, he'd be more upset with her than ever.

"Just hold up the food and tell him to grab it through the bars," said Gregory. "That's the way we feed prisoners."

"Nay, I won't do that," she answered, thinking how crude and demeaning this was. Especially toward a knight. "Open the door, Gregory. I am going in."

"Nay, my lady. He is a killer! It's not safe."

"I said, open the door. Now."

"Yes, my lady." Gregory did as told. Sir Guy was crumpled up in a ball, sitting on the cold floor holding his knees at the back of the cell. His head was down and he didn't even look up as she entered.

"Thank you," she said, stepping into the cell. Now leave us," she instructed the guard.

"Leave you? Nay, I can't do that," protested Gregory. "Lord Mablethorpe would have my head if he found out."

"Let me worry about Lord Mablethorpe. Now leave, and don't return until I summon you. Understand?"

"Yes, Lady Vivienne." Gregory reluctantly did as told.

Grunt bolted into the cell, running right over to Sir Guy, licking his face. Slowly, the man's head came up and Vivienne could see his sunken eyes on his pale face. "Grunt?" he asked in a feeble voice. "Is that you, boy?" His hand slowly reached out to pet the dog's head.

"Sir Guy, I am here too," she announced, bringing the food tray into the cell. There was a chamber pot on the floor at one end, and an old bench at the other side, but nothing else. It was frigidly cold in there, yet the poor man had no bed or blanket or anything for comfort.

"Lady ... Vivienne?" he asked, seeming almost too weak to talk.

"I brought you some food, Sir Guy. When is the last time you ate?"

"No one has brought me ... food or ale ... or anything since they put me in here."

"That is preposterous! I will have a word to my uncle about your barbaric treatment. This isn't right. Now come here and have something to eat."

"I'm afraid, I can't ... stand."

"God's eyes, what is happening here?" Vivienne took the tray to him, putting it right in front of him on the floor. Then she went back and got the bench and dragged it over and sat atop it to talk to him. "I am so sorry," she apologized to him. She watched as he tried to reach for the bread, but his hand shook so badly that he couldn't grab it. Grunt started sniffing the food. "Stop that, Grunt! This food is for Sir Guy, not you." She picked up the bread and tore off a piece and dunked it into the ale and brought it to his mouth. "I will feed you. Don't worry."

"Nay, my lady. It is not right."

"Neither is the fact that you are being blamed for a murderer's failed attempt to kill the King. Now eat."

He opened his mouth and closed his eyes as he chewed.

"Take your time," she told him, feeding him by hand until the food and ale was just about gone. "I promise you that one way or another, I will get you out of here."

"We both will," came a deep voice from behind her.

Her head snapped around in surprise to see Zachariah standing at the door to the cell. He looked tired and weary. His one arm was up as he leaned against the cold, iron bars.

"Sheriff? What are you doing here?" she asked, surprised but at the same time pleased to see him. So, he must have cared enough about Sir Guy to want to check on him, after all.

"Lady Vivienne, I think the real question is what are *you* doing here?" Zachariah answered. "This is no place for a lady."

"Neither is it a place for an innocent man, which Sir Guy is, I am sure."

"I know," said the sheriff slowly walking into the cell. "Sir Guy, I am sorry for your ending up in this situation."

"It's not ... your fault," said the man, seeming a bit better now that he had eaten a little. Grunt lay next to him with his chin on Sir Guy's lap, begging for food as always.

"I know this isn't the best time," said the sheriff. "But I need to ask you exactly what happened on the jousting field."

"Sheriff, please, not now," scolded Vivienne. "Sir Guy is so weak he is barely able to speak. He is in no condition to answer questions."

"Nay, it's all right." Sir Guy reached out and put his hand on her arm. Vivienne covered his cold hand with her own, meaning to comfort him. "I took ... Lord Rowen's place in the joust, as you know."

"Yes," said the sheriff. "And you used his armor and shield and lance?"

"Aye," Sir Guy answered softly. "I hadn't planned on jousting that soon so my squire didn't have my things there and ready for me."

"Did you notice anything different at all when you held the lance?" asked Zachariah.

"Nay. Yes. Now that you mention it, the lance did seem a little heavier than I was used to. However, I didn't think anything of it. After all, I didn't know anything about Lord Rowen's lances and I thought mayhap the extra bit of weight was his preference."

"Did you notice anyone else in the weapon tent when you prepared to joust?" asked Vivienne.

"Anyone else?" asked the knight. "Well, yes, there were many people in there, including Lord Rowen, my squire, Martin, and others.

"Were any of them the people who came here to the castle with the King?" asked the sheriff.

"Yes, I believe so."

"Who?" asked Vivienne.

"Let me see." He closed his eyes to think. "There was Sir Amis, of course, being assisted by the King's squire, Peter, and being overlooked by the King's valet. Frederick, I think is his name."

"Anyone else?" asked the sheriff.

"Let me think." Sir Guy put his hand to his head. "The King's guard, Harold. And that stupid juggler was there distracting everyone with tossing around knives and catching them."

"He what?" Zachariah's body jerked at hearing this.

"I guess he thought he was being entertaining, but he was actually just being a pest."

"He had no right being inside the weapon tent," said Vivienne. "Zachariah, we need to look into this. Especially since he was juggling knives."

"We will, at once," the sheriff answered. "Thank you, Sir Guy. This might help us to find the killer faster. "Lady Vivienne, come on. I don't want you in here any longer than you have to be." He held out his arm to escort her.

"Sir Guy, I'll have Milo bring you a sleeping pallet, as well as fresh clothing and a pillow and blanket," said Vivienne, getting to her feet.

"Thank you, my lady, but I hope not to be here so long that I'll even need it."

Vivienne picked up the empty food tray. "If it were up to me, I'd release you right now. Unfortunately, King Edward believes someone should be held responsible, and that is why you are here." She headed to the door and Grunt followed.

"My lady?" came Sir Guy's voice from behind her. "Will I be executed for the murder if the true killer isn't found?"

"Nay, of course not," she told him, even though that was exactly what would probably happen.

"Oh, I just remembered, there was one more person in the tent as well."

"Who was that?" asked Zachariah.

179

"It was the King's blacksmith. He was checking over the King's weapons, making sure they were sharpened and polished, I think."

"But this was a joust. No swords or other weapons were needed. Just lances."

"That's true," said Sir Guy with a shrug. "I guess he was just doing as he was told."

A rat ran over Vivienne's foot and she jumped and screamed, gripping on to Zachariah's arm even tighter. Grunt took off in a hurry to chase it.

"I'm getting you out of here right now," said the sheriff, guiding her back to the guard's room where she found the constable and two other guards hauling a wooden coffin into the room.

"What's that for?" she asked, for a moment thinking they were preparing to collect Sir Guy's dead body as soon as he perished from hunger and the cold.

"We're collecting the corpse of Sir Amis," Zachariah told her. "He'll be moved out of here."

"Where are you taking him?" asked Vivienne, as Grunt ran past chasing another rat, and almost knocking the constable over.

"God's teeth, that dog is a pest," complained the constable.

"The body will be moved to a shed located near the gong pit for now," said Zachariah. "When the King and his entourage leave, they'll take Sir Amis's body home to his family to be buried there."

"I understand," she answered, feeling sick and sad at the same time. Poor Sir Amis had been doing the King a favor, trying to be the best knight he could be, and ended up paying for it with his life. Now, instead of sitting by a warm fire with other competitors, drinking wine and eating the best food, his body would be at the gong pit, rotting away and stinking as much as the excrement that fell from the castle's garderobe high above. There was no excuse for what happened, and it only made her more determined than ever to find the murderer quickly. Justice would be paid. She would make certain of this. No one was going to get away with murder if she had anything to do with it.

A HALF HOUR LATER, Vivienne sat up on the dais, watching in awe as the procession of servers carrying food paraded sumptuously-filled trays past the King. King Edward sat in the center of the noble's table, using her uncle's chair. Sitting at one of the King's sides were her uncle, and her aunt. Next to her aunt was Lord Rowen. Lord Rook was at the King's other side, then her, and, to her dismay, the seat next to her had been claimed by one of the King's knights, Sir Barclay, who seemed to be in the lead for winning the entire tournament so far.

"What a wonderful tournament, don't you agree, Lady Vivienne?" Sir Barclay looked over at her and smiled. She almost retched when she noticed something green between his teeth.

"I would hardly call it a good tournament, Sir Barclay. After all, an innocent man died, another is imprisoned, and there is a killer on the loose that we've yet to catch."

"Oh, that. Yes." Sir Barclay picked up his cup and took a drink, suddenly but thankfully becoming quiet.

The musicians played a noble tune while a new round of servants arrived with even more elaborate food on their trays, this procession's lavish display clearly intended to impress everyone catching a glimpse of the delicacies Mablethorpe's kitchens had prepared for the King. There were swan and peacock, both cooked, stuffed, and re-dressed in their plumage, creating a fantastical display. The wild roasted boar was on a silver platter with an apple stuffed into its mouth. Around it was an array of spiced, cooked apples with raisins and almonds. Drizzled over that was a black sauce made from wine and cherries. There was roasted duck accompanied by a relish of small cranberries that grew wild in the bogs and marshes. Venison in a savory gravy followed, and mutton with mint sauce had also been prepared, the delicious aroma filling the air. After the meat dishes came the fish selections. Poached salmon and trout encrusted with breadcrumbs soaked in vinegar and pepper, parsley, and white wine was one of Vivienne's favorites.

"I'm so hungry, I could eat a horse," said Rook from next to her, already devouring the offerings with just his eyes.

"There is so much food here, that I wouldn't be surprised if horse is the next thing we see on a platter," mumbled Vivienne, thinking that she'd never seen such an extraordinary feast in her life. They'd all be too stuffed to stand before they finished, while poor Sir Guy was eating nothing but bread and cheese and a few salted herring—all she could manage to have slipped to him.

"Lady Vivienne, what do you think of the feast so far?" The King leaned over Rook to talk to her. "It is quite a display, don't you agree?" He chuckled, seeming proud of what he'd ordered.

"Yes. It looks delicious, Your Majesty," she replied, still sore at the King for keeping Sir Guy in the dungeon when it was obvious the man was innocent. She had no doubt now that he'd also execute Sir Guy if she and Zachariah couldn't find the murderer by the time the tournament ended tomorrow.

"Look at that," said Rook in awe, pointing to a tray on Maria's shoulder that contained deep-fried hand pies filled with dates and figs, almonds and walnuts, and many exotic spices. The sweet aroma of cinnamon, cloves, and ginger wafted through the air, making Vivienne's mouth water. Right behind Maria was Leif, Mablethorpe's jongleur, helping out the kitchen servers by carrying a pie that was just about as big as himself.

"It's the blackbird pie," said Rook excitedly. "Oh, I love this part. It is so fascinating. I know it's only blackbirds, but they remind me of my pet raven in a way." Rook had lived in the catacombs for years when he and his brothers were the Demon Thief, raiding the King. He had a big black raven that was always on his shoulder. Rook was sometimes referred to as lord of the crypt. She'd heard that he'd changed a lot now that he was a knight, married, and even had children.

"I don't like this part," mumbled Vivienne, even though she realized that the birds weren't harmed and not actually cooked in the pie, but put in after the crust was done. Still, she found it cruel and senseless.

Two other servants helped Leif to lift the gigantic pie up to the dais table, placing it right in front of King Edward.

"Your Majesty." Leif handed him the handle of a long pie knife over his arm, and waited.

"Go on, Father," Rook urged him. "Break the crust and release the birds."

"Nay. You do it," said Edward, nodding to Rook.

"Me? Really? Thank you, I'd love to have that honor." Rook took the long knife from Leif, gently tapping the top of the crust of the pie. The crust broke open and out flew a dozen blackbirds, or collie birds, as they were called. They were most likely escaping for their lives, thought Vivienne. It made a wonderfully entertaining show, and everyone oohed and aahed and clapped their hands in admiration. Even the King laughed in a jolly manner. The birds flew up to the high beams of the great hall, settling there, out of arm's reach, safe for the moment. "Wasn't that a wonderful show?" Rook asked her, seeming too excited over a damned pie that had imprisoned birds. Vivienne didn't like anyone or anything to be imprisoned. Then one of the blackbirds roosting on the rafters above Rook's head, decided to let loose with some excitement of his own. Excrement fell, spilling onto Rook's head, making him curse. Vivienne found it funny and laughed aloud.

"Oh, yes, that is a wonderful sight, Lord Rook," she told him. "I am sure everyone enjoyed it. Except mayhap, you." Rowen saw what happened from the other end of the long trestle table and started laughing heartily.

"Dammit, I need to wash this off." Rook got up and stormed away, leaving an empty seat between her and King Edward now. The food procession continued, with roasted root vegetables, and fresh white bread that was molded and baked into the forms of ducks, frogs, and rabbits. Cook had outdone himself, and Vivienne would have to make sure to point this out to her uncle, to win the man some favors. Mayhap her uncle would be so impressed with Cook by the end of the tournament that he'd grant Cook and Maria the favor of letting them be married, and celebrate their wedding right here at the castle soon.

"Isn't Lord Rowen supposed to be in prison?" asked Sir Barclay, eying up Rowen at the other end of the long table. "Why is he even allowed up at the dais at all, after framing the poor man in the dungeon for his attempt to murder the King?"

Vivienne's anger rose. "Sir Barclay, there is no evidence at all that Lord Rowen tried to do any such thing."

"Isn't there?" he asked. "After all, it was his lance with the concealed knife on the end. And he let someone joust in his place at the last minute. Plus, he and his bastard brothers are known to be the Demon Thief who raided their own father for years."

"I know Lord Rowen is innocent and saw to having him released," she answered.

"Then you must be in on the planned murder too, if you let him walk free after that."

Vivienne was about to give this man a piece of her mind, when her father ... the King ... came to her defense.

"Sir Barclay, I ordered Lord Rowen to be released from the dungeon," said the King. "And if you question it again, it'll be *you* taking my son's place behind those bars."

"So sorry, My King," said Sir Barclay, seeming startled to have been overheard. "I won't let it happen again."

"You'd better not," said Vivienne softly.

Then Lord Barclay leaned over and sneered at her, his face much too close to hers for comfort.

"Once you're my wife, you won't be speaking so brashly and acting with such disrespect."

"I'll never be your wife," she told him. "I'd rather die first."

"Watch what you wish for, Lady Vivienne. Especially since we both know there is still a killer on the loose."

She was about to ask him what that meant, and tell him that it sounded like a threat. But before she could say anything, Lord Rook returned.

"What did I miss?" he asked, sitting down, smoothing back his wet, black hair.

"Nothing but that little streak of white," said Vivienne, pointing to the hair at the top of his head.

"Really?" Rook grabbed a hand cloth and started dabbing at his head. "Did I get it? Is it still there?"

She couldn't keep a straight face anymore and burst out laughing. "I was just jesting ... Brother." She had called him brother very softly, leaning over and almost whispering it into his ear, not wanting anyone else to hear her.

"What did you just call him?"

Vivienne looked up in surprise to see Gisela standing directly behind her. She hadn't even known the woman was there.

"Gisela? How long have you been standing there?" The chaotic music, talking, and the procession of the food dishes continued. It was amazing anyone could hear anything at all.

"Long enough, my lady, to hear you call Lord Rook your brother."

"Nay, she didn't. You heard wrong," said Rook quickly.

"I know what I heard," said the woman.

"Did you say Lady Vivienne is the bastard lord's sister?" asked Sir Barclay now, already having had too much wine.

Vivienne panicked. Because of her, the secret was now out. She had to stop this gossip from going any further but didn't know how to do that.

"Silence," commanded the King, rising from his seat, holding his hand in the air. The music suddenly stopped and the voices died down quickly. The procession of dishes slowed, and all the servants looked up at the King as he spoke. "Before anyone says another word about it, I announce that it is true."

"True? What is true?" came a voice from the crowd.

"Your Majesty?" asked Lord Mablethorpe. "I'm sorry, but we don't understand what you mean."

"Lady Vivienne," said King Edward, holding out his arm.

"My King," said Vivienne jumping to her feet, shaking her head, silently telling him not to announce their secret. Her hand went to her chest to cover the King's hidden ring that she wore.

"What about Lady Vivienne?" asked Lord Rowen, leaning over to look down to the end of the trestle table. The crowd stirred with a soft lull of commotion.

"Lady Vivienne. She is … she is my bastard daughter."

The crowd gasped in surprise, and there was a lot of talking amongst them now.

Vivienne's eyes closed as she slowly lowered herself onto her chair. Her stomach churned, her heart beat wildly, and a heat engulfed her that felt so hot that she thought she was about to combust.

"Lady Vivienne is a bastard?" said Sir Barclay, so loud that everyone, even in the kitchen, had to have heard.

"She's the King's bastard?" spat Gisela, almost sounding angry to discover this.

"Lord Rook," she whispered, not able to catch her breath. "I can't breathe. I think I'm going to ..." Before she could even finish her sentence, everything went black all around her and she collapsed atop the table.

Chapter Thirteen

Zachariah watched and listened from the other side of the great hall, unable to believe that the King just announced to everyone that Vivienne was his bastard daughter. Even though Zachariah wasn't happy that Vivienne had kept this information from him for so long and only just recently revealed the truth to him, he surely didn't think that she deserved this kind of humiliation. Or was it considered an honor? He wasn't even sure what to think anymore.

"Sheriff, I think somethin' is wrong with Lady Vivienne," said Nairnie, pushing through the frenzied crowd, holding on to the hand of his daughter.

"What do you mean?" he asked.

"Look at her. She's slumped over on the table."

Zachariah stretched his neck, peering over the heads of the people filling the great hall. Sure enough, just as Nairnie said, something seemed wrong with Vivienne. All he could see was the top of her head, and her face seemed to be down on the table.

"Father, what is a bastard?" his daughter asked him at this very inopportune moment.

"Don't worry about it, Starah," he mumbled, not having time to explain things to her right now.

"Being a bastard is a good thing," said Martin from behind him. Zachariah hadn't even known the boy was there.

"It's good?" asked the innocent little girl.

"Aye, it means you're special," continued Martin, sounding confident that he really knew. "Just like the Legendary Bastards of the Crown."

"Oh," said Starah, still seeming confused.

"I wonder. If my mother is a bastard then does that mean I'm a bastard too?" asked Martin.

"Hush, child," scolded Nairnie. "Enough of this talk about bastards. Somethin' is wrong with yer mother and we need to help her."

"What? I can't see," said Martin, jumping up and down, trying to get a glimpse of the dais. Even though it was a raised platform, there were so many people around him, and being so short, Martin couldn't see the dais or his mother at all.

"God's eyes, I think Lady Vivienne has fainted," announced Zachariah, pushing through the crowd, quickly making his way to the dais. Grunt barked furiously from Vivienne's side, as if he knew something was wrong. "Let me through. Move aside, I tell you." Zachariah got to the dais and ignored the guard, bolting right up the steps and quickly making his way over to Vivienne's side.

"I don't know what's wrong with her," Lord Rook told him, his arm over Vivienne's back, his face down near hers.

"We need to get her out of this crowd. She needs some air." Without asking permission, Zachariah scooped Vivienne up into his arms and carried her off the raised platform. Her head fell back over his arm, her long, blonde braid swinging back and forth as he walked. Her arms dangled like a rag doll's at her sides.

"Sheriff, where are you taking my niece?" Lord Mablethorpe demanded to know. He stood up and rested his hands on his hips, looking down from the other end of the table.

"I'm taking Lady Vivienne to my chamber, my lord. She has fainted and needs help immediately. Someone, please call for the healer."

"He's taking her to his room?" he heard a snide comment from the crowd.

"She must be a whore as well as a bastard," said someone else.

If he hadn't had his hands filled with Vivienne, he would have stopped and hauled out and punched the people who dared to voice such slurs about her.

"Clear the way! Move aside," shouted a man who Zachariah realized was his brother, Isaac.

Zachariah froze. "Isaac? What are you doing?"

"I'm helping," Isaac answered.

"I don't need your help," he grunted.

"Yes, you do. Now shut up and follow me. Lady Vivienne's well-being depends upon it." Isaac cleared the way with the tip of his sword, people jumping aside so they wouldn't get hurt.

"Let the feast continue," announced the King from the dais, and once again the music started and the talking grew louder again. It seemed as if Lady Vivienne's condition didn't matter to most. The feast would continue as planned.

Zachariah followed Isaac up the staircase and to his chamber. Isaac opened the door and held out an arm, waiting for him to enter first.

Zachariah stopped in the doorway, looking up at his brother. "Thank you," he said softly, feeling a little remorseful now that he'd treated Isaac so poorly. It seemed at the moment as if his brother was the only one he could count on for support.

"At your service, Sheriff," said Isaac with nod. "And anything for Lady Vivienne."

"Of course," said Zachariah, clearing his throat. "We wouldn't want anything to happen to her." He walked over and laid Vivienne down on his bed. Her long braid fell over her shoulder, resting on her chest. She wore a crimson velvet gown with a thick leather girdle, or belt, around her waist. The contrast of her light hair against the vibrant gown made her look so beautiful that it was breathtaking. Even though she was unconscious, Zachariah couldn't help admiring her beauty. Her little mouth looked heart-shaped, and her big eyes, even closed, seemed mysterious, like she was a fae of the earth.

"Vivienne? Vivienne, wake up, sweetheart," he said, gently rocking her by the shoulders. Her head lolled to the side and he heard a slight moan, but she did not open her eyes. Her breathing seemed faint and shallow.

"Is she all right?" asked Isaac, leaving the door open and running over to the bed to join them.

"I don't know. She won't wake up and that concerns me. I think you'd better go find a healer, Isaac. Hurry."

"Right away," said Isaac, slipping his sword back into his belt and rushing out the door.

"Vivienne, can you hear me?" Zachariah gently pushed a stray stand of her hair behind her ear and then cupped her cheek in his palm. "Please wake up, sweetheart. I would never forgive myself if something bad has happened to you."

He brushed his thumb across her lips, feeling her faint breath against his hand. Still, she remained unmoving and silent. Emotion welled up within him. His emotions rose to the surface and he started to reminisce about a time four years ago when he was in a similar situation. He saw in his mind his dead wife, Margaret, lying on his bed, looking a lot like this. Tears started to form in his eyes. He never truly accepted the demise of his wife, and Vivienne was his only saving grace to pull him out of his depression. Now, he couldn't imagine life without his best friend Vivienne at his side. They'd always been there for each other since they were children. He'd confided his hopes and dreams to her through the years, and she had told him her innermost secrets as well. Or almost all her secrets, he thought, pulling the King's ring out from under her clothes, laying it atop her chest.

"Well, I guess you don't need to hide this anymore," he told her, even though he wasn't sure if she could even hear him. Damn, why did this have to be happening? When the King announced her being his bastard right out loud in front of everyone, it had to have been too much for her to handle. She'd lived with this secret for so long, being careful not to let anyone see the King's ring that she wore. Her mother had warned her not to tell anyone. It wasn't safe. And now ... now she could be just as much a potential victim as the King, since the secret was out. For all he knew, the murderer was still lurking inside the castle walls, waiting to make another kill. Would Vivienne be the killer's next mark? God's eyes, the thought terrified him, and he hoped it wasn't true.

"Vivienne, you are special to me," he whispered, his hand still cupping her cheek. "I am sorry I never told you how much you mean to me." Why did he feel as if he were saying goodbye to her? Goodbye ... forever. His feelings for her bundled up inside him, and Zachariah could not stop himself from leaning over and gently placing his lips against hers in a soft and gentle kiss. She stirred a little and let out a slight moan.

"Sheriff, move aside. Let me see her." Nairnie burst into the room and hurried across the floor, all but tossing him to the side in her rush to administer aid to Vivienne.

"Nairnie," he said, jumping up, feeling embarrassed that she'd caught him giving Vivienne a kiss. Or at least he thought she saw him, but he wasn't really sure. The old woman didn't say a word about it, and for that he was glad. Zachariah's tongue shot out to lick his lips, savoring the sweet honeyed essence of Vivienne, the taste of her sweet lips being engraved upon his mind now forever. "Will she be all right?" he asked Nairnie, not knowing how he would handle it if the old woman said no.

"I dinna ken yet, Sheriff. It's still too early to tell."

"Zachariah, I'm sorry, I couldn't find a healer in that noisy crowd." Isaac ran into the room, out of breath. "Nairnie said she used to be a healer and thought she could help."

"Thank you, Nairnie. But if you're here, who is watching my daughter?" asked Zachariah, not wanting Starah to be at risk now.

"Dinna worry yer head about her, Sheriff. Maleine is with her and Martin," Nairnie informed him.

There came the sound of a barking dog next. Zachariah turned and looked over to the open door to see Grunt run into the chamber. Maleine, Starah, Martin, and even Wymond were right behind the dog. Thank goodness he didn't see those damned weasels with the boy.

"God's eyes, not all of you," grumbled Zachariah, not wanting everyone in the room at a time like this. He still didn't know if Vivienne would live or die. This was no place for children.

"She's still breathin' and her heart is pumpin'," announced Nairnie, her ear to Vivienne's chest. "I think she just passed out from the excitement. I'll have to get some herbs to administer to her."

"Excuse me," came a girl's voice. Maria, the kitchen maid, and Cook, the head chef, rushed into the room and hurried straight over to the bed. Cook had a bowl of what looked like herbs cradled in the crook of one big arm. With them was the jongleur named Leif, his lute strapped on and thrown over his back. The room was becoming quite crowded now.

"What is all this? Why are you all here?" asked Zachariah. "Everyone needs to leave. Cook, Maria, you should be down in the great hall seeing to the King's feast."

"We saw what happened," cried Maria. "We want to help Lady Vivienne."

"Aye," said Cook. "She's always been there for us in our times of need. We want nothing more than to repay the favor."

"That is kind of you, but there is nothing any of you can do," Zachariah told them. "Nairnie is seeing to her."

"I told Cook to bring those herbs." Leif stepped forward. "When I was unconscious for so long, Lady Vivienne had the healer wake me by putting strong smelling herbs under my nose. Don't you remember, Sheriff?"

"Well, yes," he said, now that he thought about it. "I suppose it wouldn't hurt to give it a try."

"Give me those herbs," commanded Nairnie, holding out her hands for the bowl.

"I grabbed a bunch of mint from the kitchen too," said Martin crawling up atop the bed next to his mother. Grunt jumped up next to him, sniffing Vivienne from head to toe. "My mother told me mint has good smells."

"Hold the herbs under her nose," instructed Maria. "She needs to breathe them in."

"Really close to her," added Cook. "I added some strong onions and garlic to the herbs."

"Yes, I can tell," said Zachariah, waving a hand in front of his face. His eyes were already burning.

"Wave the herbs around," said Leif. "That might help."

Nairnie did as they said, and even Martin stuck his handful of strong mint under Vivienne's nose, but still she did not awaken.

"Thank you all, but it doesn't seem to be working," Zachariah told them. "We'll just have to wait until someone finds the healer to tell us what to do."

Grunt barked and then barked some more.

"Quiet down," Zachariah scolded the dog. "Martin, get that hound out of here. He is causing too much havoc."

Before Martin could do so, Grunt started licking Vivienne's face. The hound licked her nose, her eyes, her ears, and even her mouth. Vivienne's eyes slowly opened and she bolted upright in the bed. Her hand was on her mouth and her tongue shot out to moisten her lips. "Where am I? What's going on?"

"Mother! You're alive," cried little Martin, throwing himself into her arms, giving her a big hug.

Vivienne returned her son's hug, suddenly noticing all the rest of the people standing there. The last thing she remembered was hearing King Edward announcing aloud to everyone that she was his bastard daughter. Then she remembered not being able to breathe, her heart beating in her ears, and then everything going dark.

"Vivienne, I mean Lady Vivienne, are you all right?" asked Zachariah with deep concern to his tone. His dark, caring eyes drank her in.

She suddenly remembered the sheriff carrying her off the dais, or so she thought. "Yes. Yes, I think so," she answered.

"Oh, thank goodness, my lady," said Maria, sounding filled with relief.

"We were all so worried about you," Maleine told her next.

"Well, I'm fine now, so no one needs to be concerned," she said, swinging her feet off the side of the bed, meaning to stand. But her head dizzied and the room started to spin. She quickly reached out to grab on to Zachariah's arm to steady herself.

"Get back in bed. Ye need to rest, lassie," ordered Nairnie. "Sheriff, it would be good to send everyone out of here."

"Yes, I agree. Everyone, go back to your duties or to the great hall for the feast," said Zachariah. "Lady Vivienne is fine now, but thank you all for your help and concern."

"We woke you up with herbs," said Martin, sniffing the bunch of mint he still had clutched in his hand.

"Cook, take the bowl. Please." Zachariah reached out and collected the bowl, giving it to Cook, wanting the odor of onions and garlic gone.

Everyone slowly headed out the door while talking softly amongst them.

"Come on, Grunt," said Martin. "Cook said he has a nice big bone for you in the kitchen."

"Does Cook have something for Midnight too?" asked Starah, speaking about her cat. She followed Martin to the door.

"We have plenty of rats around here for that cat of yours to catch and eat," she heard Cook saying as they walked out into the corridor.

"Midnight doesn't like rats," said Wymond. "Cook, do you have some scraps of food for my ferrets as well?"

"What is this?" grumbled Cook, his voice getting fainter as they walked down the corridor. "Isn't it bad enough I have to work by the sweat of my brow to make these blasted fancy dishes for the King? I don't need to feed animals too."

"Cook, I'm sure we could find some scraps for the animals," Maria told him.

"There is so much food I prepared that there is no way it'll all be eaten," Cook told her. "Don't worry, even the rats and the pigs will have a good meal or two once this feast is finally over."

"Nairnie, you and Isaac can leave too," said Zachariah, making Vivienne feel as if he wanted to be alone with her.

"Fine bunch of thanks I get," complained Nairnie, pushing up from the side of the bed. "Come on, Isaac, let's go to the kitchen and get some of that extra food Cook mentioned."

"I'm so hungry that I'd even be happy with that collie bird pie right now," said Isaac with a chuckle, heading out of the room and closing the door behind them.

"Zachariah?" asked Vivienne, once they had all left. "I get the feeling you wanted to be alone with me for some reason?" She distinctly remembered Zachariah kissing her. And saying that he had feelings for her ... or so she thought. Mayhap that's why he wanted to be alone with her. To tell her this.

"Yes, I wanted to be alone so we could talk."

"Talk? About what?"

"Something very important."

"Really. All right, what is it?"

He sat down on the side of the bed next to her. And just when she thought he was going to say he had romantic feelings for her, he surprised her by saying something else entirely.

"I think now that the King announced you are his daughter, that your life is in danger."

"What?" She blinked, taking a minute to try to understand what he meant. He was back to being all business again, when she was sure that just moments ago he had bared his heart to her. And that he'd kissed her! She could still taste the rugged essence of his lips on hers.

"If your mother was the King's mistress at one time and someone killed her, what is saying they won't come after you too?"

Well, now Vivienne started wondering if being kissed by Zachariah was naught but a dream, after all. Because, how could anyone who had said all those sweet things that she thought he said to her, suddenly kill the moment by talking about another possible murder. Especially since he was saying she could be the next victim.

"Why would anyone come after me?" she asked. "I mean, I was right there the night my parents died. The murderers could have killed me easily then, but they didn't. As a matter of fact, I wounded one of them pretty bad on his right shoulder."

"Yes, I know. You told me that," said Zachariah, seeming to suddenly become quite impatient with her. "But what is it that you didn't tell me, Vivienne?"

"I don't know what you mean."

"I think you do, sweetheart. There is more to this story, and you need to tell me all of it and hold nothing back. If I'm going to be able to help you, I need all the facts."

Vivienne thought back about when she'd told Zachariah she was the King's bastard. She hadn't had time to tell him more before they'd been interrupted.

"Vivienne?" he said, staring at her with those sexy brown eyes. "Please, trust me enough to let me into your life. Tell me why your parents were killed that night. I have the feeling that since you spoke to the King, you now know the reason."

"I ... think perhaps I do," she admitted, taking a deep breath and slowly releasing it, trying to gain the courage to tell him the what she'd learned.

"Go on," he said, not rushing her in the least. The man was being very patient and this wasn't a common trait for him.

"Well, I don't know much. Not really." She twisted her hands on her lap as she relayed the information. "King Edward ... my father ... told me that my mother, as well as my stepfather, were both spies in his service." It felt so odd to call the King her father, and she still wasn't sure she really believed it was true. But if the King announced it to everyone, then it must be so. Even if Edward had told her never to call him Father, he must have had a change of heart. If not, he never would have announced to everyone that she was his daughter.

"Your parents were spies?" A look of astonishment washed over the sheriff's face. "Well, I didn't expect to hear that at all."

"I know. Neither did I. I felt just as shocked as you do right now when the King told me."

"If they were spies, then were they killed for some knowledge they might have held regarding the King?"

"Yes, I think so, Zachariah. King Edward said they had information about someone who was deceiving everyone and possibly wanted to kill him. My parents ... I mean my mother and stepfather, were coming to tell the King the information in person the night we were ambushed on the road and they were killed."

"Then whoever murdered them was the person or persons that they had information on," surmised the sheriff.

"It seems so. I mean, it certainly would make sense, I guess."

"Damn, I wish I had known all this seven years ago, Vivienne."

"So do I."

"Do you realize that this basically reopens the case of your parents' murders? Even though it was never really closed in the first place."

"Do you think this information could bring us closer to their killer?"

"Anything is possible. And I thank you for telling me this."

"The King made me promise not to tell anyone, but I made a promise to you as well, Zachariah. I told you I wouldn't keep secrets from you anymore. and I plan on always upholding that promise for as long as I live." Her stomach twisted in a knot. She needed answers about her parents' murders, but now that they seemed to be getting a little closer to the truth, she wasn't sure she really wanted to know.

Zachariah reached out and gently cupped her cheek. "Thank you for that, sweetheart. And continue to have faith that we'll solve this mystery soon, because I promise you, I will never stop trying to solve their murder. You just need to have faith for a little longer. After all, you found Martin after so many years, and now you are a mother again. That alone proves that anything can happen."

"I suppose you're right. Will you help me think more on this matter after we solve Sir Amis's murder?"

"Yes, you know I will. But for now, I have to ask you to keep your mind on this murder only. We need to move fast, and only have a very short time to solve it. Sir Guy's life is on the line, not to mention the King's life could still be in danger."

"Or mine," she said, feeling very nervous.

"Have faith, Vivienne. Things will work out, I promise."

"Thank you. I know you're right."

"Vivienne, I have a feeling this killer at the joust might be the same person or persons who killed your parents."

"What?" She blinked. "Why would you say that?" Her body stiffened. It made her sick, just thinking that the men who murdered her parents in cold blood could be right here at her home.

"I don't know." He shrugged. "It's just a feeling I have, although I have no proof that it's true. But somehow ... somehow I think it might all be related."

"Then we'd better hurry up and start getting some answers really fast." She stood up, and this time he jumped up to grab her arm and steady her when she got a little lightheaded.

"You're not going anywhere, sweetheart."

"Of course I am. We have a killer to find. We have work to do! If we don't find him or her before the end of the tournament tomorrow, Sir Guy is going to be executed for a crime he didn't commit."

"Now, calm down."

"It's true, and you know it. You said it yourself. Besides, you saw the way they were treating Sir Guy in the dungeon. I can't let an innocent man go to his death for a crime he didn't commit. Justice must be served."

"I agree," said the sheriff, releasing a deep puff of air from his mouth.

"Then let's go. What are we waiting for? Time is wasting."

"Vivienne, I'm not going to let you out of my sight until I find and convict that killer."

She slowly smiled. "Really. Then, you'll look pretty silly sitting next to me in the garderobe, or lying with me on the pallet on the floor of my chamber."

"You know what I mean. I'll be outside your door at all times."

"And how are you going to find a killer if you're playing guardian outside my door?"

"You're right. I'll get a trusted guard posted at your door instead. Now, sit down and I'll have some food sent up to you."

"Nay, don't leave me here locked up like a prisoner, because you know I won't stay here. It's not right."

"It's just for now," he told her. "I want you well-guarded and feeling better. You've been through a lot today." He reached out and cupped her cheek in his hand once again. She thought he was going to tell her now how he really felt about her. That made her nervous. If he did, she wasn't sure how to respond. She was attracted to the sheriff, but they'd both agreed that they'd stay friends and nothing more. It was too casual between them already with them not using their titles behind closed doors. She supposed it would be better for both of them to keep things the same as they were.

"I think I hear someone out in the corridor." She ran to the door and pulled it open before Zachariah could stop her.

"My lady?" It was her guard Richard passing by.

"Egads, Vivienne, don't do that!" Zachariah ran after her. "Oh, Richard. Just the person I want to see."

"About what?" asked the guard.

"I need you to guard the door for Lady Vivienne until I return," he told him.

"Why? Is she is some kind of danger, Sheriff?" asked Richard, looking very confused.

Zachariah shook his head. "We don't know yet for sure, but I am playing it safe. I'm going to have food sent to her room by the kitchen maid, Maria. Don't let anyone else into her chamber, do you understand me?"

"Aye, Sheriff." Richard didn't look happy about it, but followed orders, since it had to do with Lady Vivienne.

"I'll be back soon," he told them. "There are just a few things I need to do first." The sheriff turned and hurried away.

"My lady," said Richard with a nod, standing at attention outside her door.

"You cannot stand there all night, Richard. Here." She went back into the room and returned with a chair. "Sit down, please."

"Thank you, my lady."

"I suppose you didn't get a chance to eat any of that sumptuous food at the King's feast, did you?"

"Nay, my lady. But I'm ... fine." Richard's stomach growled as he sat down atop the chair and stretched out his long legs.

"I'll be sure to share any food I get with you."

"That is too kind of you, my lady."

"It's the least I can do. Or should I say, all the sheriff will allow me to do." Vivienne had half a mind to leave the room anyway and go out on her own investigation. But since she was still feeling lightheaded, and with the sheriff putting the thought in her mind that someone might be out to kill her now, too, she decided to stay here at least until after she had some food in her belly. "I'm going to lie down for a few minutes, Richard, until the food arrives." She slowly turned around and closed the door, heading over to the bed, wondering how her life had changed so drastically in just a few minutes. She also wondered what would happen to her now that everyone knew she was a bastard of the King. Her stomach twisted into a knot, telling her that whatever it was, it wasn't going to be good.

"CONSTABLE, we need to step up the investigation," Zachariah told Constable Dorson once he returned to the great hall. Lively music was being played by the musicians in the gallery. The meal was underway, and everyone was eating and drinking and laughing merrily. No one seemed to have a care in the world about Vivienne or any potential murderers right now.

"Aye, Sheriff." The constable was sitting down at a trestle table, holding on to the end of a chicken leg, chewing as he talked. His wife Agatha, his young children, Archibald and Anabel, and even his baby boy Aaron, were all there enjoying the feast with him.

"Did you get some food, Sheriff?" asked Agatha, feeding baby Aaron, who was sitting on her lap. "It is so delicious you won't even believe it. It is the best food I've ever tasted in my life."

"I like the sweetmeats," said little Anabel, picking up a dried apricot and popping the whole thing into her mouth at once.

"Eat your meat, Anabel," the constable told her.

"I didn't have any food, but I'll eat something later," said Zachariah. "Right now we have work to do. Are you coming, Constable?"

"Yes," said the man, throwing down the chicken bone and standing up, wiping his hands on his trews.

"Father, you're coming home tonight, aren't you?" asked Archibald.

"I don't know," said the constable.

"Emery, you promised to spend some time with the children this evening," complained Agatha. "They are so excited from being at the tournament all day that I'll never get them to go to sleep on my own."

"Agatha, I have a job to do," said Emery. "You know it is sometimes demanding."

"I'll help the sheriff, you go on home tonight with your family, Constable Dorson." Isaac stepped forward, in his hand a big piece of fresh bread with a slab of boar's meat on it.

"Why, thank you so much, Isaac," said Agatha with a smile. "That is truly appreciated."

"Yay! Father will be home tonight so we can feel safe," said Anabel clapping her hands together, still chewing on the sweet-meat, or candied fruit.

The constable sheepishly looked over at Zachariah. "The children are still feeling nervous at night. Since their ordeal with the Pied Piper, they frighten easily, you see."

"Oh, the Pied Piper. Yes, I've heard all about him," said Isaac. "It is understandable that the children would be scared. You need to be there for your family, constable. Right, Zachariah? Isn't family the most important thing of all?"

Zachariah felt like strangling Isaac for suggesting the constable spend the night at home in town. Here is where he needed help. Then again, Isaac's comment about family being the most important thing of all, had him thinking about Starah and how he'd like to be spending time with his daughter. She was still frightened after her encounter with the Pied Piper as well. His only saving grace was that Maleine and Nairnie were watching after her. He supposed taking the constable away from his family overnight wasn't a good thing to do. Mayhap accepting Isaac's help wouldn't be that bad, after all. At least he was trained with a sword, and it would be nice to have his brother covering his back.

"Yes, go home tonight with your family, Emery," he told the constable. "Isaac will be here to assist me until you arrive back at the castle in the morning."

"Why, thank you, Sheriff. That is very kind of you. Thank you, too, Isaac." The constable sat back down and continued eating. His daughter giggled and climbed atop his lap, giving him a big, wet kiss on the cheek.

"Yes, kind of me," muttered Zachariah, thinking about Vivienne and how she accused him of locking her up like she was in prison. Mayhap he wasn't so kind, after all.

Chapter Fourteen

Vivienne felt as good as new when she awoke the next morning. After eating the scrumptious food Maria had brought her, she'd fallen asleep atop Zachariah's bed and hadn't awoken again until morning. She sat up and stretched and yawned, then quickly dressed in her crimson gown and pushed her feet into her shoes. Getting up, she walked over and pulled open the shutters.

"Oh. I overslept again," she said to herself, seeing the hustle and bustle of activity down in the courtyard. Today was the last day of the tournament, which would finish up with the joust. To her surprise, the hammer throw and the strength contests dealing with physical prowess already seemed to be over. She could see the knights lining up to joust in the final event that would determine which of these men she would have to marry. The joust.

The thought of being a prize bride made her want to slam the shutters closed once again and hide her head under a pillow. But she couldn't. She needed to get out there and help Zachariah find the killer before everyone left the castle. Her own problems would have to wait. Once the tournament was over, there would be no real chance of ever finding whoever tried to murder the King. Not to mention, Sir Guy would die for a crime that he didn't really commit.

She hurried over to the door and pulled it open, but stilled when she saw Gisela with a tray of food in her hand and one fist raised, ready to knock.

"Gisela? What are you doing here?" asked Vivienne.

"I am bringing you food since you missed the main meal," said the food-taster.

"Where is Richard?" Vivienne looked up and down the corridor for her guard, but his chair was empty.

"Oh, he went to the garderobe, but said he'd be right back. He told me not to wait, but to bring you the food since it was already so late. I honestly think he wanted to go watch the jousting with everyone else."

"Yes. He shouldn't have to stay on watch here and miss the entire tournament. That's not right. I'll tell him so when he returns. Actually, I'll just go find him, since I was about to leave anyway."

"Nay, my lady," said the girl. "The sheriff told me not to let you leave your chamber."

"The sheriff said that? To you?" Vivienne found it odd that the sheriff was saying anything to Gisela at all.

"Yes, I saw him just now, down in the kitchens. He said that you had to eat something if you wanted to regain your strength. To help him with the murder investigation, of course."

"Of course," she said, feeling suspicious of the woman. "And why isn't Maria bringing my food?"

"Maria was having some pain from the baby, and asked me to bring this tray up to you so she could sit down and rest."

"That doesn't sound like Maria at all. She hasn't had pain before from her pregnancy. I hope she is all right."

"She'll be fine, my lady. She just needs to rest. Like you do, too. Now come and eat or the sheriff will have my head." She pushed her way into the room with the food tray in her hands.

Vivienne looked up and down the corridor but saw no one at all to ask about this. She realized everyone was outside enjoying the remaining event of the tournament. That is where she should be too.

"My lady, please eat so the sheriff won't be angry with you." The girl's back was toward Vivienne as she put the food tray down on the table.

"Well, all right, I guess." Vivienne slowly closed the door, knowing that Zachariah would be furious if she didn't eat. He was probably already upset that she'd overslept once again. Since he wasn't letting her out of the chamber, she decided she'd use that to her advantage and interrogate Gisela once again while she was here. Perhaps she could try to find out more information. Something that they'd missed before. At least this way, Vivienne would feel helpful.

"Come, eat," said Gisela, motioning to the food. Vivienne sat down in a chair, looking up at the girl just standing there watching her.

"Gisela, why don't you have something to eat, too. Please, sit and join me."

"I already ate, my lady, but thank you."

"I insist."

The woman's face darkened, her smile instantly disappearing. "Oh, I see. You still don't trust me, do you?"

"I didn't say that. I am just being cautious and careful. Just like the sheriff wants me to be."

"I understand. Since you're the King's bastard, I suppose that is a good idea." Gisela sat down and picked up a hard-boiled egg, taking a bite, followed by a piece of bread and some cheese. "I'm sorry I didn't bring you something more suitable for nobles, but I was lucky to even get this. Cook is in a foul mood this morning, and he seems to hate me for some reason. He wasn't at all happy that I was even in his kitchen."

Satisfied that the food wasn't poisoned now, Vivienne picked up a piece of cheese between two fingers. "Tell me, Gisela. Have you ever been married?"

"Nay. Have you?"

"I have," she said. "However, I am a widow."

"So sorry to hear that."

"Do you have children? I have a son."

"Yes, I know. The page boy, Martin, right?" asked the woman.

"Uh huh." Vivienne took a bite of crusty bread. "You've had a baby too, am I right?" Vivienne was just guessing, to see what Gisela would say. After all, a woman close to her age should have been married with children by now. If not, it would be odd. When the woman became fidgety and her mood seemed to sour, Vivienne realized she'd stuck gold.

"I ... I did have a baby. At one time," said the girl, looking down to the ground. "Actually, they were twins."

"Twins, really? How exciting. Were they girls or boys?"

"One of each, my lady." Gisela looked to the table and pushed away some crumbs.

"They are no longer alive, are they?" Vivienne could tell that look anywhere. It was the same look she probably had for the past seven years when she'd thought her son was dead.

"Nay. They ... died."

"Oh, I am sorry."

"Have some wine, my lady." There was already one goblet of wine poured and on the tray. Gisela picked up a second goblet, poured wine into it from a decanter, and took a drink. "See? The wine is not poisoned either, so you don't need to worry." She pushed the other goblet closer to Vivienne. "Go on. I know that bread is a little dry and you need to wash it down."

She forced a laugh. "I wouldn't mention it to Cook though, or he'll get angry. Go on. Drink up."

"Yes, the bread is a little dry," said Vivienne, picking up the goblet of wine nearest to her.

Just then, there was a lot of cheering from out in the courtyard.

"I wonder what that is all about," said Vivienne, putting down the goblet and starting to rise. "I'll take a look."

"Nay, I'll do it, my lady." Gisela held out her hand. "You just finish eating and drinking. It's what the sheriff wants you to do." Gisela got up and ran over to the window, peering out. Then a huge smile crossed her face.

"What is it, Gisela? What is everyone cheering about?" Vivienne picked up her goblet once again.

"Didn't you hear, my lady? The King decided to partake in the tournament, after all. He is going to joust today. He is about to do so, and that is why everyone is cheering."

Vivienne brought the cup to her mouth, but stopped. "He did what? That isn't safe. I wonder why he changed his mind." Once again she raised the goblet to her mouth.

"Who cares? We wanted him to joust and now we'll get what we want, and he'll get what he deserves."

Vivienne stopped in midmotion. Did she just really hear Gisela say what she thought she heard? Suddenly, Vivienne realized that this was all just a little too odd. And convenient. Richard missing from her door, Gisela bringing her food instead of Maria or Maleine, and now the woman saying the King would get what he deserved. Vivienne's stomach clenched hard. Something bad, very bad was about to happen. She looked down at Gisela's goblet of wine, the fact finally dawning on her that the girl had brought two cups instead of one. Strange that a servant would do that. It was as if she expected them both to be drinking wine together, even though she was only a servant. But even so, why wouldn't she just have brought one goblet to share, instead of two? Vivienne got a bad feeling about this. Now that she thought about it, she never actually saw Gisela pour the wine into her cup because she'd been at the door and Gisela's back was toward her.

"Well, I guess things are going just as planned." Gisela started to turn around. Before she did, Vivienne quickly switched the goblets of wine, taking the one that Gisela had drank from, and giving the girl hers. "How is the wine?" asked Gisela, sitting back down across from Vivienne.

"I don't know. I haven't had any yet."

"Why not?"

"I don't like to drink alone. Won't you have some wine with me?" Vivienne raised her cup.

"Of course. I'd be more than happy to do that, my lady." Gisela picked up the goblet and took a sip, smiling all the while. Vivienne drank as well.

"Gisela, I get the feeling someone killed your babies," said Vivienne, taking another gamble and it paid off.

"Yes," said Gisela, taking another drink of wine as she looked over the edge of her goblet at Vivienne.

"Tell me about it." Vivienne took a big drink now, getting a huge satisfied smile from Gisela.

"It was ... the King."

"King Edward? He killed your babies? Why?"

"Because I had twins and he was sure they were spawned by the devil. He is superstitious."

"Yes, I know."

"He said he didn't want to be cursed, and so the babies had to die."

"Oh, I see. Just like Rook, Rowen, and Reed." Suddenly, Vivienne understood all too well what was going on. "You were ... you were the King's mistress at one time, weren't you?"

"I was," the woman admitted with a scowl, downing even more wine. "Until the King brushed me off like I was nothing. He wanted naught to do with me once I birthed the twins."

"But you are his food-taster. Surely that can't be true."

"It took me quite a few years to get back in his graces. I had to pretend I adored the man even after he killed my babies."

"But you don't, do you?"

"Of course not! I hate the King and everything about him." She started swaying a little and holding her stomach.

"I agree, that is an awful thing for him to do. How long ago did he kill your babies, if I might ask?"

"Seven years ago."

"Seven," said Vivienne taking another sip of wine, getting a really bad feeling about this. "That is when my parents' lives were taken by cutthroats on the road."

"Yes. That's right." The girl stared right through her.

"Gisela, did you have anything to do with my parents' murders?"

"Nay, I didn't. I never even knew them."

"Did you have something to do with the attempt to murder the King right here at the joust?"

Gisela finished off the wine and moaned and held her stomach. "Mayhap I did. And still will."

"What do you mean?" Vivienne's heart jumped into her throat.

"When the King jousts today, I will finally have my revenge. He will be dead, just like my babies. He will get exactly what he deserves."

"I don't understand why you're telling me this. You know I am working with the sheriff to find the killer. You just confessed, and will end up behind bars for what you did."

"I wasn't the one who took action, that is someone else. I just devised the plan, that's all."

"So there is another working with you?"

"Yes," she said, making a face and holding her throat now.

"You're not worried about me knowing all this?"

"You won't tell anyone." She made another face.

"Why not? Because you think I'll be dead as well? Why did you poison my wine?"

"What?" Gisela's voice rose and her eyes opened wide. "You know?"

"Of course, I know. I am not stupid. But the jest is on you, because I switched our goblets while you were looking out the window and gloating about how the King will get what he deserves."

"Nay!" cried the girl, dropping her cup in fear. The goblet clattered to the floor, rolling in a half circle. She clutched her throat now, seeming to have trouble breathing.

"Tell me, why did you want me dead? Was it just because you found out I was the King's bastard daughter?"

"Yes," she said, struggling to talk. "I wanted to punish King Edward for what he did to me and my children. It took me seven years to see this through. But I never gave up hope to find the perfect moment. When I heard of this tournament, I knew my time had come. Revenge would finally be mine." She wheezed and coughed and wheezed some more.

"You wanted Lord Rowen to kill his father, didn't you? And then he would be killed himself for doing the deed," Vivienne continued. "You were on a mission to kill any of the King's children that you possibly could."

"It would have worked, too, if you hadn't ... distracted the King. From his first ... joust." Her eyes started closing.

"Yes, King Edward would be dead right now, just like Sir Amis, if I hadn't detained him. Tell me, do you really think killing people is the answer?"

"I would ... do anything ... to get my revenge."

"And so your revenge has made its mark, killing an innocent man and framing another. These men had nothing to do with the death of your babies. You should be ashamed of yourself."

"Help me," she cried, reaching out for Vivienne as her face started to turn blue.

"Help you? Nay. Never." Vivienne got up and shook out her gown. "You said the King will get what he deserves, but in the end, you're getting what you deserve, Gisela."

"This wasn't ... supposed to ... happen."

"Tell me who you are working with. Tell me, who is it? Give me a name." Vivienne had to try to find out the answer before the girl died. If not, she might never know.

"My lady?" Richard opened the door and poked his head inside the room. "My lady!" He jerked in surprise. "What is she doing here?" He took a few steps into the room and stopped.

"Come in, Richard. Gisela is here because she tried to poison me," explained Vivienne.

"God's eyes, nay! I never should have left my post to use the garderobe. I'm so sorry, but the King's guard, Harold, said he'd stay posted at the door until I returned. I don't know why he left."

"Well, he wasn't there when I opened the door, but Gisela was," said Vivienne, wondering if Harold and Gisela were the ones working together.

"Are you all right, my lady?"

"I'm fine. Come in, Richard." Vivienne looked down at Gisela and sighed. The woman's eyes were opened wide in fear, but her head was back on the chair and she wasn't moving. A foam could be seen on her mouth. It was too late to get the information from her that Vivienne so desperately needed.

"Is she ..." asked Richard, stopping in midsentence, staring down at the woman.

"Yes, she's dead." Vivienne walked over and stuck her hand

inside the woman's pouch that was attached to her belt. She pulled out a small flask, uncorked it and took a sniff and coughed. "Whatever she used to poison the wine, she poured from this flask." Vivienne recorked it and put the small flask back, but in her own pouch this time. "I'll have to give this to the sheriff as evidence. Plus, you'll vouch for me, won't you, Richard?"

"Of course, my lady. This woman was no good from the start." He shook his head. "I cannot believe that because of my stupidity, you were almost killed."

"It's not your fault." Vivienne headed to the door. "Murderers are very sneaky. Stay here with her body. I'll send back the constable as soon as I find him."

"Where are you going, Lady Vivienne?"

"I have to stop the King's joust before he's really killed this time." Vivienne picked up the hem of her skirts and ran like the wind down the corridor, only hoping she wouldn't be too late to stop another death.

Chapter Fifteen

"Are you sure about this idea?" asked Isaac, as he walked with Zachariah toward the weapon tent. "I mean, the killer still hasn't been caught, and yet the King is going to joust? That doesn't sound very safe to me."

"That's right," said Zachariah. "The constable and I decided this would be the best way to lure out the killer. King Edward agreed to it."

"So, you think the killer will try to strike again?"

"I'm hoping he will. That is why we purposely announced it last night, to give the killer time to prepare."

"But what about the King's safety? Aren't you worried about him?"

"Nay. Lord Rook and Rowen are with him. Also, I promised the King I'd protect him if he helped us out. He was happy to do it. Here he comes now. I'm just glad Vivienne isn't going to be here to distract him again."

The King walked out from the keep with his guards and entourage surrounding him. The crowd cheered and waved items of clothing, trying to get the King's attention. Along with the King's people which consisted of his valet, his blacksmith,

Sir Barclay, his squire, two of his guards, and his juggler, were Lord Rowen and Lord Rook as well.

"I can't help but think that the killer is one of the King's own people and that he waited for this tournament to carry out the plan and make it harder for anyone to catch him. Or her. I wonder where that food-taster girl is, because I don't see her," said Zachariah, stretching his neck to see.

"I don't know, but you're probably right, Brother." As the little entourage arrived, Isaac cocked his head, staring at one of them, making an odd expression.

"What is it?" asked Zachariah.

"I don't know. I can't help thinking I've seen that blacksmith before, but I just can't put my finger on where I've seen him."

"Sheriff," came a voice, and Zachariah turned around to see Sir Guy's squire, Milo. Martin and Grunt were with him.

"Milo. Do you have information for me?" asked Zachariah.

"Yes," he said, coming closer and speaking softly. "Martin and I watched the weapon tent all night like you asked us to do."

"And did anyone enter it? Any of the King's people, I mean."

"Yes. All of them," said Milo in a low voice.

"All of them?" This wasn't what Zachariah wanted to hear.

"Sir Barclay was in there, as well as the squire, Peter, both the guards, Harold and Geoffrey, and the blacksmith, Theodoric. Because of Grunt sniffing around, we even saw the juggler, Alvin, and the valet, Frederick, sneaking out during the night."

"Well, that's no help to us," said Zachariah with a sigh. "Did you see any of them over by Lord Rook's lances?" Zachariah had announced that Lord Rook would be jousting against the King this time, at Rook's insistence that he wanted to do this.

"Just Sir Barclay, the squire, and the blacksmith, but they had reason to be there."

"Yes, I suppose so. Thank you," said Zachariah.

"Sheriff, I see my mother," said Martin excitedly.

"What?" Zachariah turned around so quickly that he almost fell over Grunt. Sure enough, Vivienne was running toward the King and his entourage, and was about to ruin all their plans. In order for the killer to strike again, the King and Lord Rook needed to joust. "Damn it, she must have sneaked out of the room. She's going to ruin all our plans. Isaac, can you stop her?"

"Me?" asked Isaac. "How am I going to stop a noblewoman?"

"I don't care how you do it. Throw her over your shoulder if you have to, just don't let her near the King until after he jousts."

"All right, if you say so. But she's not going to like it." Isaac hurried off to do as told.

"Sheriff, everything's in place," announced Constable Dorson as he hurried to Zachariah's side.

"Good," he answered. "And you told Lord and Lady Mablethorpe about the plan so they can help if need be, as well?"

"I did. Here they come now."

"Sheriff, if this goes wrong, you'll pay for anything that happens," growled Lord Mablethorpe walking up with his wife.

"Gilbert, the sheriff knows what he's doing," said Lady Mablethorpe. "Just work with him and let him do what he knows best."

"Hrmph," sniffed Lord Mablethorpe. "Well, I suppose we should get up to the platform to watch this unfold. Come along, Ellen." Lord Mablethorpe led the way with his wife following at his heels.

"Sheriff, is that Lady Vivienne struggling with your brother?" asked the constable.

"Yes," answered Zachariah with a groan. He kept his gaze

on Vivienne, thrown over Isaac's shoulder, kicking her arms and legs, attempting to get free. "He's trying to keep her away from the King until after the joust. Not an easy feat."

Grunt started barking, seeing that Vivienne was struggling against Isaac's hold. The dog ran to her, and Martin ran after the hound.

"Well, let's get on with this," said the King as he approached. "Peter, is my armor ready?"

"Yes, Your Majesty," said Peter.

"On second thought, I'm not going to wear armor," said King Edward.

"My King, you must," insisted Frederick.

"Yes. It's for your protection," Theodoric spoke up.

"I'm the King and I'll do whatever the hell I want. No armor, I say."

"That's fine. I won't wear armor either then," said Rook. "Milo, will you come with me as my squire for this?"

"Yes, Lord Rook," said Milo. "I'd be happy to do whatever I can to help out. Especially if I can help Sir Guy be released from the dungeon."

"Sir Guy is going to hang for killing Sir Amis," ground out Sir Barclay. "He'll get what he deserves."

"Enough!" The King held up his hand. "I'm going to joust now. Peter, bring my horse."

"Yes, Your Majesty." Peter ran to collect the King's horse and help the King mount.

"Get my lance. Quickly," commanded the King, as the herald announced the joust that was about to take place between the King and Lord Rook.

Zachariah could hear Lady Vivienne protesting, and when he looked over to her again, he saw her break free from Isaac, hitting the ground, and then start running. Grunt barked at

Isaac, jumping on him, keeping him from following after Vivienne.

"God's eyes, nay," mumbled Zachariah, seeing that his whole plan was about to be spoiled.

"It's time to get in place, Your Majesty," said the blacksmith, taking the reins of the King's horse and leading him to the starting spot. The horse acted strangely, snorting and stomping his feet in an odd manner.

"Sheriff, stop the joust!" cried Vivienne, running to his side. Isaac followed, pushing Grunt away as he ran after her.

"Lady Vivienne, not now," he ground out.

"I tried to stop her, Zachariah, but you need to hear what she has to say," called out Isaac as he finally caught up to Vivienne. Grunt continued to bark, still trying to protect Vivienne.

"Whatever it is, it'll have to wait until after the joust. And stop that dog from barking," commanded Zachariah.

"Nay. You don't understand. The King's life is in danger," cried Vivienne.

"I know that," he told her. "We have a plan set in motion, but you seem to be doing your best to try to ruin it."

"What in the world does that mean?" she asked, struggling to regain her breath.

He leaned in and told her. "We're trying to draw out the killer by having King Edward joust. We figure the murderer will try another attempt to kill the King."

"You're doing this on purpose?" she snapped. "That is a crazy idea. You need to protect the King, not help him be killed. God's eyes, Sheriff, he's not even wearing armor!"

"Don't worry, he doesn't need it," said Zachariah with a chuckle. "Rook and the King are not really going to hit each other with their lances. They're going to pull back at the last moment."

"Well, I certainly hope they do." Vivienne shook her head.

They were about to start the joust when Isaac stretched his neck, looking over at the King and the blacksmith who was holding back the unruly horse. "Bid the devil, I just remembered where I've seen that blacksmith before," said Isaac.

"What?" Zachariah looked over at his brother.

"He used to be a mercenary at one time. That is, before he became an assassin."

"An assassin?" cried Vivienne. "Zachariah, do something!"

The blacksmith let go of the horse's reins, and suddenly it dawned on Zachariah why the horse was acting so odd. It all made sense now.

"Wait! Stop, Your Majesty," called out Zachariah, rushing over and grabbing the horse's reins just as the King was about to charge down the lists to joust against Rook.

"What now?" complained the King. "I just want this over with and am tired of distractions."

"Peter, help the King off this horse at once," instructed Zachariah.

"But he's about to joust," protested the squire.

"Do it," snapped the sheriff.

Once the King was off the horse, Zachariah handed the reins to Vivienne and checked the horse's feet. "Just as I thought. The horse's shoes have been altered. One pass down the jousting field and the horse shoes would have fallen off and it would have probably tripped the animal, causing the King and the horse both to take a bad fall."

"What?" The King looked over to Theodoric. "Blacksmith, you assured me this horse was ready for the joust."

"I'm not sure how that happened, My King," said Theodoric with a bow. "I checked the shoes myself last night and they were fine. Someone must have tampered with them. I'm sorry I didn't notice."

"He's lying," said Isaac. "And he's not a blacksmith like he says, either."

"What's going on here?" Rook rode up on his horse. "Are we going to joust or not?"

"Nay. It's over," said Zachariah.

"Damn, I never get to joust against my father." Rook threw his lance to the ground in frustration. The end broke off to reveal another knife mounted there, just like last time.

"Look." Zachariah pointed to the lance. "The killer attempted once more to kill you, Your Majesty."

"Well, who is it?" asked the King. "Where is this murderer?"

"Constable, arrest Theodoric for attempting to murder the King," said Zachariah.

"Aye, Sheriff." The constable headed toward the blacksmith.

"Nay! I'm not guilty," cried out Theodoric, as Lord and Lady Mablethorpe walked up to join them. "I am the King's trusted blacksmith. I didn't do anything. Let me go."

"I recognize you," Isaac spoke up. "You were once a mercenary I worked with, but your name was different back then."

"He's mistaken," shouted Theodoric, as the constable held onto his arm and he struggled to get free.

"Nay, I'm not mistaken," said Isaac. "And let me point out that you weren't just a mercenary, but also a paid assassin."

"An assassin?" bellowed the King.

"He's lying," shouted the blacksmith. "Don't believe him."

"Nay, he's not lying," Vivienne spoke up, stepping closer to Theodoric. "You see, your accomplice, Gisela, tried to poison me earlier, and she admitted you were working with her." The girl never admitted such a thing, but Vivienne was trying to get the man to confess since it was obvious that he was guilty.

"What?" said the King. "My food-taster did that?"

"Vivienne, is this true?" asked Zachariah in shock.

"It's true," said Vivienne, looking over at Zachariah. "I was trying to warn you."

"Where is this food-taster now?" asked Zachariah. "She needs to be apprehended."

"No need for that," Vivienne told him. "Gisela is lying dead in your chamber, Sheriff. I outsmarted her, and she drank the poison in the wine that was meant for me."

"I told that bitch this wouldn't work," snarled Theodoric, now struggling harder against the constable's hold. "She hired me to kill the King," he finally admitted.

"Well, she might have done that, but now you'll hang for it all," said the sheriff. "An attempt to kill the King, as well as the death of Sir Amis are both on *your* shoulders now, blacksmith."

"Nay!" Theodoric, broke away from the constable and pulled out a dagger from his boot, holding it out, waving it in the air. "I will not die because of the King's mistress. I was only doing the job I was paid for. And not just by her. If you are looking for murderers, then look all around, because I have been hired many times, and was only doing my job is all."

"Get back here," shouted the constable, grabbing for the blacksmith and pulling out his sword. Theodoric pulled away as he struggled, falling to the ground.

Vivienne looked down at the man's torn tunic, seeing a large, long scar on his right shoulder, running down his chest.

"My God, you are the man who killed my parents," she said in disbelief. "I gave you that scar on that horrible night, seven years ago."

"That's right," said Theodoric. I killed your parents, but I was only doing the job I was hired to do," snarled the man, hurriedly getting to his feet, holding his blade out again.

"Who hired you?" asked Vivienne. "Tell me now, I need to know. Who wanted my parents killed?"

"Apprehend him, Constable," called out Zachariah. But this time, when the constable reached for Theodoric, the blacksmith rushed forward, knocking into Vivienne and pushing her to the ground. She landed hard, knocking the air from her lungs. Grunt barked at the man, trying to protect her.

"Someone stop him," shouted the sheriff, as Theodoric wove his way through the crowd." When Vivienne got back to her feet and turned around, she saw her uncle running his sword through Theodoric and pushing the man's dead body to the ground.

"No one will hurt my niece and kill her parents and get away with it," bellowed her uncle.

"Nay!" cried Vivienne, hurrying over to Theodoric, but seeing all the blood and the man's stoic expression, realizing that he was dead.

"I got him, Vivienne. He paid for what he did to you. I wasn't going to let him get away."

"Thank you, Uncle, but why did you have to kill him?"

"What the hell do you mean? I heard the sheriff yell to stop him, and he came at me with a knife. Plus, he tried to murder the King. Twice," said Lord Mablethorpe. "He confessed to killing your parents, and I saw him push you down and hurt you. I wasn't about to let him get away."

"He didn't hurt me," she said, rubbing her arm and feeling as if her last hope was gone. "I wanted to find out who hired him to kill my parents, but now I'll never know."

"Oh," said her uncle. "I'm sorry about that. I just became so enraged when I heard he killed your parents, that I reacted, not thinking it through, I suppose. I couldn't let him get away."

"Gilbert, that man killed my sister," cried Vivienne's aunt, clinging to her husband, gazing down at the dead assassin. "I am glad you killed him."

"So am I," said the King. "That man tried to kill me. Twice.

Mablethorpe, you did the right thing. I wouldn't want to have taken the chance that he would have gotten away."

"Thank you, Your Majesty," said Vivienne's uncle, seeming to beam with pride. Vivienne knew that all he was probably thinking about was looking good in the King's eyes.

"Lord Mablethorpe, you valiantly protected my daughter as well as me," came King Edward's next words. "I will make sure that you are rewarded for your brave and honorable actions."

"Thank you, My King," said Lord Mablethorpe with a deep bow.

"I've had enough of this, and will leave and go back home now," announced King Edward. "Someone bring me a horse that is shoed properly."

"You're leaving?" asked Zachariah.

"Unless there is another killer to catch, Sheriff?" said the King.

"Nay, I think that's it," said Zachariah, looking over to Vivienne. "For now, Your Majesty," he quickly added.

Vivienne felt her body shaking and wrapped her arms around herself.

Maleine and Nairnie ran up with Starah in tow.

"My lady, are you all right?" asked Maleine, running over and putting her arm around Vivienne's shoulders.

"God's eyes, another dead body. Does this ever end?" grumbled Nairnie, holding tightly to Starah's hand.

"It's over. The tournament is over," shouted Lord Mablethorpe, loud enough so all the participants as well as the onlookers could hear him. Shouts and protests went up from the crowd.

"But we haven't had our turn to joust," complained Sir Barclay. "And the winner of the prize bride needs to be chosen yet, as well."

"There will be no winner, and all of the entry fees will be returned," announced the King.

"Returned?" Lord Mablethorpe looked up in shock. "You want me to return the entrance fees?"

"You heard me, Mablethorpe. I've paid for the food and wine, so you're still coming out ahead," growled the King.

"But who is going to marry Lady Vivienne?" asked Sir Barclay.

"There will be no prize bride either," announced the King.

"What?" Vivienne looked up, thinking she'd heard him wrong, hoping she hadn't. "Then, I don't have to marry anyone? Really?"

"Nay, Daughter," said the King, getting gasps from the crowd once more at hearing him call her 'Daughter' aloud. "You almost died today, and I think your bravery deserves at least that. You can marry whom you want and when you want. I won't be the one telling you otherwise and neither will your uncle from now on. Here that, Mablethorpe?"

"Yes, Your Majesty," said Vivienne's uncle with a scowl.

"All right, let's move on out," the King told his people, hoisting himself atop a fresh horse that his guard brought him.

"Your Majesty, we'll get Sir Amis's body as well as Gisela's and Theodoric's and have them sent back with you," offered the sheriff.

"Yes, that's fine. I suppose. I shouldn't leave them here cluttering up the place, even though I am not pleased to be hauling killers home with me, even if they are dead."

"My King?" asked Vivienne.

"Yes, Vivienne? What is it?"

"What will happen to Sir Guy?"

"Bid the devil, let the man out of the dungeon," said the King. "And give him this." The King removed a pouch of coins

227

from his waistbelt and tossed it to Vivienne. "For all his discomfort and humiliation."

"Thank you," said Vivienne, feeling the weight of the coin pouch, realizing it was a good amount that would have Sir Guy living in comfort for a long time to come."

"What about my reward?" asked her uncle, eying up the pouch of money. "You said I'd be rewarded for stopping the assassin from getting away?"

"Aye, I suppose I did say that." He removed another pouch of coins and tossed it to her uncle. "For your loyalty, Mablethorpe."

"Thank you, Your Majesty." Her uncle smiled widely.

"Just make sure to give half of it to the sheriff for his services," said the King, causing her uncle's smile to quickly fade. Then the King turned toward Zachariah. "Sheriff Fitch, I thank you and your constable ... as well as my daughter, for catching the killers before they did away with me. I am sure Alice will be grateful as well."

"Our pleasure," said Zachariah, with a quick bow and nod of his head. "Anything to serve you, My King."

"King Edward?" asked Vivienne. "I would like to talk to you more. About my mother."

"Yes, but at a different time, my dear," said Edward. "Alice will be wondering what happened to me and I really need to leave. But feel free to come see me any time you want."

"Thank you, My King," said Vivienne, still not feeling comfortable to call him Father in public. Still, it felt good to know that the man at least didn't want her dead!

The crowd started to dissipate, and Lord Mablethorpe ordered his steward to set up a table for the contestants to reclaim their entry fees. Vivienne was sure that her uncle would be complaining about this for years to come.

"Vivienne," said her uncle, wiping the blood from his sword

with a rag and putting his sword back into his sheath. "I am sorry. I reacted in anger when I heard what the assassin said. Plus, I was frightened for your safety. Now, I wish I would have just injured him enough to try to get information from him, like you wanted to do."

"You did what you had to do," she told him, feeling as if she had been so close to finding answers, and now she was so far from it once again."

"The sheriff will help you find your answers. And, of course, I'll do anything I can to help as well," he told her.

"I know," she said, still feeling let down, and also angry at her uncle.

"My lady, can I accompany you back to your solar?" asked Maleine.

"Nay, Maleine, but there is somewhere else you can accompany me."

"Of course. Where to, my lady?"

"There is someone I feel a need to visit."

Chapter Sixteen

Zachariah entered the graveyard in town, seeing Maleine and Vivienne by her parents' graves. It had been three days now since the tournament ended and the King left, but Vivienne just still wasn't herself and had been coming here every day. Seeing the scar on Theodoric's shoulder had seemed to bring back all her old grief and worries.

"Lady Vivienne?" Zachariah walked up to the graves, seeing Vivienne on the ground, placing more flowers atop the resting places of her parents. Grunt was there, lying down next to her.

"I'm not in the mood for visiting and don't want to talk to anyone, Sheriff," she answered without turning to look.

"Maleine, will you give us a few minutes?" he quietly asked the handmaid.

Maleine nodded and walked back down the hill to wait for them.

"I know how hard all this must be for you."

"It's like reliving it all over again," she said with a sigh, reaching out to pet her hound. "When I think that the assassin whom I saw murder my parents was right there in my home and I was even talking to him without knowing who he was, it makes me so sick that I want to vomit. And the fact that he killed them for money, and didn't care a bit who they even were, but just thought of it as another job, is so unsettling to me that I want to scream aloud. Their lives meant nothing to the bastard. Nothing at all." Her body began to shake.

Zachariah sat on the grass next to her. "Good thing you don't want to talk," he said, trying to ease the moment, but she didn't even smile. They sat in silence for a few minutes because he didn't really know what to say. Vivienne had almost died, and then she'd come face-to-face with the man she'd seen kill both of her parents. She had to really be hurting inside. Plus, she'd missed the first seven years of her son's life, and still didn't know what happened to her younger brother. How could he do anything that would make her feel any better?

"I'm here for you," he said, slowly reaching out and putting his arm around her shoulders.

"I know. Thank you," she said with a sniffle, leaning over and resting her head on his shoulder, crying softly.

"Is there anything I can do to help?"

"Not really. Not now. Nothing besides finding that bastard who hired the assassin in the first place. Or the man's accomplice. He is still on the loose too."

"Well, at least one of them is dead," he told her. "And like I promised, I will never stop searching for answers."

"Thank you. That means the world to me, Zachariah." Then, just as he thought they'd sit there in silence, she started to pour out more of her feelings to him. It was like a dam breaking and water rushing through.

"I was so frightened as well as angry when I saw that scar on Theodoric. The scar I gave him."

"Yes, I know."

"I watched him slaughter my parents as if they were naught but sides of beef."

"You don't need to relive that night, Vivienne. Take a deep breath and let it go. For now."

"Nay, I can't," she said, looking up at him with tear-stained cheeks. "I have so many questions that have yet to be answered. I want to know more."

"Sometimes not knowing is easier."

"Zachariah, I have to know who hired him to kill my parents. I understand he was just the assassin, but there were two men there that night. Someone else, mayhap more than one person, is still out there."

"I'll protect you."

"That's not what I mean." She sat up straight and rolled her eyes. "I'm not afraid someone will come after me."

"Well, mayhap you should be. Or at least be cautious. After all this happened, it proves sometimes the killers can be right under our noses and we don't even know it."

"I thought of that." She sniffled again, and wiped away her tears with the back of her hand. "But now that Theodoric is dead, we'll never know. I am so angry with my uncle for killing him."

"Now stop it, Vivienne. Your uncle is your guardian and was only trying to protect you, as well as to defend himself. The man ran toward him with his knife drawn, and in your uncle's defense, I'd shouted for someone to stop him. He was only trying to help."

"Trying to help? How is killing off my only lead helping me at all?"

"He is your guardian, he was trying to help you, even if you don't believe it. You are like a daughter to the man. Did you ever think that he might feel helpless in this whole situation involving your parents? It was his wife's sister who was murdered, although she was your mother. Your uncle has a great sense of pride. How do you think he felt when they died that night, and your brother and son went missing and he couldn't do anything to fix things? I am sure he is angry and hurting, too. He was only making sure the murderer didn't escape. Remember, his wife was standing right next to him, and the assassin had just pushed you down. He was doing what any good father or uncle or husband would do. He was protecting you and your aunt."

"I didn't think of that. I'm sure you're right. Ever since that awful night seven years ago, he has seemed so angry all the time. I never considered it was because he was feeling so helpless about what happened. Then again, it is never easy to tell what a man is thinking."

"Because a man never gets a chance to say a word around a woman?" jested Zachariah.

"You know what I mean." She hit him playfully on the arm.

"Mayhap the fact that you aren't really talking to your uncle has him just as upset right now as you are."

"Perhaps," she said with another sniffle. "He did apologize to me, and I am sure anyone would have reacted the same way if they'd been in his situation."

"So, am I doing a good job trying to get you and your uncle to make amends, just like you've been doing with me and Isaac? Of course, you've had a lot more practice at this than I have."

She giggled. "Zachariah, you always know how to make me smile."

"Let's go back to the castle."

"Nay. I don't want to go there. Not yet. I'm not sure I am ready to answer questions when everyone comes up to me asking me about being the King's daughter, now that everyone knows."

"I understand. Then give it some time. Come home with me, instead. Nairnie is there, and she's whipping up a mean meal."

"She is?"

"Yes. Ever since she saw the food served at the King's feast during the tournament, she has been determined to make her cooking fancier and tastier. Of course, I think she is just trying to outdo Cook. There is a little competition going on there, whether you realize it or not."

"I think I'd love to join you," she said, as he helped her to her feet. "But I want to get Martin first. I need to spend more time with him. I've been very selfish since the tournament, only thinking about myself. He should be here with me right now. After all, these are his grandparents."

"I'm here, Mother," said Martin, walking up with Maleine. "I didn't think you wanted to be around me."

Vivienne looked over to see her son, and he seemed so sad that it made her heart hurt. Grunt jumped up and ran over to Martin with his tail wagging. That got Martin to smile a little as he bent down and hugged the dog, burying his face in the dog's fur.

"Nay, Martin. Never think that I don't want to be around you, because that is the furthest thing from the truth! Come here, sweetheart." She held out her arms and Martin ran to her. She scooped him up and held him to her in a big hug. "These graves are where your grandmother and grandfather are buried," she told him.

"I don't know them," said Martin, peeking over her shoulder.

"Nay, but they know you."

"They do?"

"Yes. They saw you the day you were born. Your grandmother put you in a basket and held you on her lap while we traveled."

"I fit in a basket? Really?"

"You sure did. Of course, you were much smaller then."

"They were murdered, weren't they?" asked the boy. "By that man who tried to kill the King."

"Yes, that's right," she told him. "And I am going to tell you all about your grandparents, because I want you to know everything about them. I am also going to tell you all about your missing uncle Adrian, too. You would have loved him."

"I have an uncle? Like you have your Uncle Gilbert?"

"Yes. Something like that, I suppose."

Zachariah cleared his throat. "Nairnie won't like us coming late to supper."

"Oh, that's true. Martin, I'll tell you all about them, but right now we are going to the sheriff's house because Nairnie is cooking up a storm, I hear."

"Yay! I want to see Starah." Martin wiggled out of her arms and took off at a run. "Come on, Grunt. You can visit with Midnight."

"Oh, good, this'll be nice and relaxing," said Zachariah in a sarcastic manner. When the dog and cat got together, there was always excitement as well as chaos.

"Come along, Maleine, you're going to join us too," said Vivienne.

"Oh, thank you, my lady, but Wymond's leg is finally healing, and he wanted to spend time with me now that he can walk without using a crutch. We were going to go for a walk and take Chomp and Snuff down to the river," she said, talking about the boy's ferrets.

"Nonsense," said Vivienne. "Invite Wymond to join us as well, and we'll share a fun feast and some laughs together. You two can go walking tomorrow."

"He's not bringing the ferrets along, is he?" mumbled Zachariah.

"Don't worry, they don't eat much," said Vivienne, feeling a new life surging through her, being around the people that she loved.

Maleine ran ahead of them, eager to invite Wymond to the sheriff's house for some of Nairnie's cooking. Martin and Grunt went with her, and that left Vivienne and Zachariah to walk alone together.

"I hope you don't mind that there will be a few extra guests at your dinner table," she told him, realizing that she'd never asked if she could invite all these people.

"And a few extra animals too?" he asked, giving her a look of helpless surrender.

"Sorry about that," she said with a little giggle. "But these people are all like family to me. Or should I say, my new family, since I lost my old one. All but Martin." She started thinking about her younger brother Adrian and became sad once again.

"What is it, Vivienne? You can tell me."

"I was just thinking about Adrian and wondering what ever happened to him. I miss him so much, and dream about him often. Sometimes, we're just children in the dream, running through a field, chasing butterflies. He's always happy and smiling. Except for in the nightmare, of course."

"I know you miss him. I do too."

"I also can't help thinking that if I had done things differently that awful night, then mayhap he'd still be here with me today."

"How so?"

"Well, I told him to stay in the wagon, when my family was attacked on the road. I thought he'd be protected there. But now I know that if I would have let him get out, he'd still be with me."

"You don't know that for certain. Adrian was a lot younger than you, and unable to defend himself. If he would have gotten out of that wagon, Theodoric might have killed him as well."

"Possibly. But even so, at least then I'd know what happened to my brother, and if he were alive or dead right now. The not-knowing is the hardest part."

"Don't give up hope, Vivienne. Mayhap Adrian will show up again in your life, the same way Martin did. Unexpectedly."

"I would love if that were true, but I sincerely doubt it." They left the graveyard, walking side by side even though she felt like holding his hand. She wouldn't. If so, it would only complicate things between them.

"Why do you doubt it? After all, we both know miracles exist. Martin is living proof of that."

"I know. But if Adrian were still alive, I am sure he would have contacted me by now. It's been seven years and I haven't heard a word from him. He was old enough to know how to ask for help getting to Mablethorpe Castle. He probably could have even found his way there on his own. But he didn't. And that tells me that he is no longer around."

"Have faith, Vivienne. We will find answers, but you need to be strong in the meantime."

"I know. You're right. Well, let's go have a good time eating Nairnie's cooking."

"Yes, let's. But do me a favor, will you?"

"What's that?"

"No matter what she cooked or how it tastes, just tell her it is better than the food Cook made for the King."

"Sheriff?" She looked at him and smiled. "Are you afraid of Nairnie by any chance? Because it sure sounds that way to me."

"Afraid of a little old woman, nay. Afraid of being hit by her flying ladle, hell yes, I am." He rubbed the back of his neck as she laughed. "It's not funny. That ladle feels like it is made of iron, and she wallops a good punch. It hurts!"

"Well, how do you think those pirates she lived with felt? It sounds to me that even they watched what they did and said around her."

"Oh, please, Vivienne. Enough with the pirate talk. You know she's making up all those stories just to be entertaining around the children."

"Do you really think so?"

"Yes. I know so. Because no one could really have lived through the things she claims to have experienced. God's eyes, she said she fell off a ship in a storm and survived. At her advanced age? That is ridiculous, to think she wouldn't have drowned immediately."

"You're probably right, but at least her stories are harmless, and they help occupy the children. Now I'll race you back to the stable to get our horses, because I am so hungry, I could eat whatever vile dish even *you* might have cooked up."

She teased him and ran, with Zachariah chasing after her in the warm sunshine. That instantly brought back memories to her of when she and Zachariah were children and played together and spent the summer days carefree and filled with happiness and life.

Vivienne wanted more than anything to feel that way again. She felt happy when she was around Zachariah, and was thankful that Martin was back in her life. But at the same time, she missed her parents, and there was a big hole in her heart for Adrian. If miracles really did come true, and Martin was proof they did, then she wished for Adrian back in her life as well.

Chapter Seventeen

W hen Zachariah opened the door to his house, he and Vivienne saw Nairnie standing there with her hands on her hips.

"Where have ye been, Sheriff?" huffed the old woman. "I told ye no' to be late. The food was ready an hour ago, and I have been havin' a hell of a time keepin' it hot."

"Sorry, Nairnie, it's my fault," said Vivienne, entering the house with the sheriff. "I hope you don't mind that there will be a few more people for dinner."

"Few more?" Nairnie cocked her head and squinted one eye. "How many more? I dinna make an over-abundance of food. It was hell tryin' to make it look ornate. I hope you appreciate it."

"We will. And don't worry because we'll all share whatever food you have, Nairnie," said Zachariah, going over to the washbasin to clean his hands.

Martin ran into the room, followed by Grunt.

"Martin! Grunt!" Starah stood on the bench with her cat cradled in her arms.

"Starah, sit down before you fall and get hurt," warned Zachariah over his shoulder.

"Och, it's just Martin, that's fine," said Nairnie with a wave of her hand in the air. "He doesna eat much."

"And us," said Maleine, entering the room with Wymond walking slowly but straight and tall and without a crutch, now that his leg was healing. They each held a ferret in their hands."

"You brought Chomp and Snuff?" asked Starah excitedly. "Oh, good, I missed them."

"Ye're no' bringin' those weasels in here," complained Nairnie.

"It's all right, Nairnie," said the sheriff, sounding as if he did not want to disappoint the children, even though Vivienne knew he didn't want the animals in his house either. "And I believe they're ferrets, not weasels."

"Hrumph," scoffed Nairnie, turning back to stir something in a pot hanging over the fire.

"Nairnie, I'm sorry. We should have asked first," said Vivienne.

"It's no' that. It's just that I invited a few people of my own to join us as well, that's all."

"Really?" asked Vivienne. "Who?" Vivienne found this interesting, because she didn't know Nairnie had friends to invite. "Is it Constable Dorson and his family?" Those were the only people she could possibly think of that Nairnie might ask to join them.

"Nay, it's not them," said Zachariah. "Emery told me they had plans with his sister and her family tonight."

"We're here now. I'm sorry we're late, but Gilbert had a lot to do." Vivienne's aunt and uncle walked into the sheriff's home, surprising Vivienne to see them there. They usually never came to town, or even left the castle.

"Welcome," said Zachariah. "Come in, Lord and Lady Mablethorpe." He walked over to Vivienne and said in a soft voice, "well, it looks like Nairnie picked up on the skill of bringing people back together again, too."

"Yes, it seems so," she said, not sure how happy she was that her uncle was there.

"Vivienne," said her uncle, with a quick nod.

"Uncle," she said, nodding back. Then there was an odd silence between them.

"I think mayhap I'll go back to the castle. I'll come pick you up later, Ellen," said Lord Mablethorpe, turning for the door.

"Nay, Uncle. Stay. Please," said Vivienne, seeing that this bothered him as much as it did her. Mayhap Zachariah was right about what he said. Just the fact that her uncle was even here said more to her than any words or apologies ever could. He did really care about her, after all.

"Are you sure you want me to stay?" he asked. "I realize I did some things that made you angry. I'm sorry. It just all happened so fast that I reacted without thinking."

"It's fine," she told him with a smile. "Here, you and Aunt Ellen can sit next to me." She motioned to the bench.

When they were all seated, Zachariah noticed that Nairnie wasn't serving them. Instead, she kept looking back at the door.

"Is something wrong, Nairnie?" asked Zachariah.

"Nay." She turned back around to get the food. "I was just expecting one more guest, but I suppose he's no' comin'."

"You were?" asked Zachariah, wondering how his little house would hold even one more person since they were already smashed together sitting so close at the table. "Whom did you invite?"

Right as he asked, the door swung open and in stepped his brother.

"Isaac," said Zachariah, looking over at Nairnie, who busied herself with putting platters of food on the table. The food was not ornate like that prepared for the King, but there were a few extra herbs on it and it did smell quite tasty.

"How nice to see you, Isaac. Please join us," said Vivienne, looking over and smiling at Zachariah.

"I don't know. There doesn't seem to be enough room for me," said Isaac, looking at the crowd.

"It's all right, Brother, come on in." Zachariah got up and shook Isaac's hand. "I owe you a big thank you for helping identify the assassin. Please, join us for a meal. You can use my chair."

Even though Zachariah had shunned his brother for many years because of his profession, it didn't seem to matter anymore. Isaac proved his worth by being a part of capturing the man who killed Vivienne's parents, as well as helping to stop the assassin from killing the King. Even as a mercenary, he showed his loyalty, and Zachariah had to acknowledge that.

"Why, thank you, Brother," said Isaac, walking in and leaving the door open. "So you forgive me for leaving our family to become a mercenary, then?"

"I'm not sure I'll ever be able to accept that one, but I realize I can't stay angry with you forever," answered Zachariah. "After all, you are family. And as Lady Vivienne says, family is the most important thing of all."

"I'm glad to hear you say that," said Isaac. "Because I've decided to stop being a mercenary and to come back to Mablethorpe for good."

"Really." Zachariah nodded in acceptance. "That's great. But what will you do for a job?"

"Well ... I was hoping that a position to work with you was still open."

"What?" Zachariah couldn't say he was happy with hearing this.

"Oh, that sounds like a grand idea," Vivienne spoke up, probably trying to soften the blow. "If Isaac is working with you, it'll give Constable Dorson more time to spend with his family. Don't you think so, Sheriff?"

"Lady Vivienne, please don't try to help," Zachariah said under his breath.

"I could take all the night shifts, and the emergency calls," offered Isaac. "I mean, it's not like I have children or a wife I need to spend time with, right? It'll free up your time to spend with your daughter."

"Oh, Father, would that mean you have more time to be with me?" asked Starah, snuggling her nose against Midnight's fur. Her big brown eyes stared up in wait for his answer.

Zachariah couldn't tell Isaac *no* without Starah thinking it meant he didn't want to spend more time with her. But by giving his brother a job, it would also mean he'd have to train him and get Isaac to listen to him. That was something that never happened much before, and he didn't know if Isaac was ready to change. Zachariah felt damned if he did and damned if he didn't. Finally, he decided the lesser of two evils was staring him in the face. There was no way he wanted to disappoint his daughter.

"Fine, I'll give you a job, but you can't live here," said Zachariah.

"Thanks, Brother." Isaac plopped down atop Zachariah's chair. "I suppose I can just stay with the whores at the tavern until I can afford a place of my own."

"Sheriff, really?" Vivienne looked over with a scolding scowl. Then he looked over to Nairnie, and she was doing that thing where she squinted one eye and put her hands on her hips. How in heaven's name could he ignore this?

"Dammit, all right, you can stay, Isaac. We don't need any more dealings with whores in this family," he said, meaning their sister, Cassandra, who was a Winchester Goose. Saying *whore* aloud at the table only earned him a glare from every adult there. "I mean, Isaac, you can live here, but only until you can get a place of your own."

"Perfect," said Isaac with a huge grin. He reached out for food from one of the platters, only to be stopped by Nairnie's ladle crashing down over his hand.

"Ow!" Isaac pulled back his hand, protecting it with the other. "What did you do that for?"

"We dinna start eatin' until I say so. That is the first thing ye'll need to learn if ye're goin' to be livin' here, laddie."

"That's right. Watch out for Nairnie's deadly ladle if ye know what's good for you," came a deep voice from the open door.

Nairnie looked up quickly, and smiled. "Bear! Ye're back." She took off her apron and threw it to the ground as she waddled over to the really big man standing in Zachariah's doorway. This man was built like a castle's retaining wall. His arms were like tree trunks. An older man ... his dark hair and bushy beard both had streaks of gray. He reached down and scooped up Nairnie, giving her a big, wet kiss on the mouth, holding her round body close to his. Zachariah wasn't sure anyone was strong enough to pick up Nairnie in that manner, but this man seemed to do so with grace and ease.

"Nairnie, did you want to introduce us?" asked Zachariah, thinking by the time all these people were fed, there'd be nothing left for him.

"This is my husband, Bear," she told them, as the man put her back down on her feet. "Bear, this is Sheriff Fitch, Lady Vivienne, Lord and Lady Mablethorpe, and everyone else."

"I already know Bear," said Isaac, which probably shouldn't

have surprised Zachariah in the least. Considering both of the men's professions. "Actually, I saw him down at the dock looking for you, Nairnie, and told him he could find you here."

"Nice to meet everyone," said Bear, his loud booming voice filling the room, almost seeming to make the walls rattle.

"Is he the pirate you told us about?" Martin looked up with big blue eyes, drinking in the man with a look of amazement.

"Aye, he's one of them," said Nairnie. "Bear was once a pirate captain, but now he is captain of a ship and crew and works for the King instead."

"That's right," said Bear, walking over to inspect the food on the table.

"What exactly do you do for the King?" asked Lord Mablethorpe, seeming a little leery of the man, and Zachariah couldn't blame him. He wasn't quite sure what to think of Nairnie's husband either.

"We hunt down whoever is threatening the King," stated Bear. "He also gives us odd jobs to do, and we see them through without asking questions."

"Oh, kind of like a mercenary," said Isaac.

"Where are the rest of the pirates?" asked Starah, looking a little scared as she clung to her cat.

"Starah, there are no pirates. Those were all just stories, and not real," Zachariah told his daughter, trying to calm her down.

"Well, actually, that's not true." Bear reached out for a bun, managing to grab it and pull his hand back before Nairnie's ladle came crashing down against the plate, making the rest of the buns jump. Unfortunately, her ladle also hit the gravy dish and some of the liquid splashed up on Lord Mablethorpe's tunic. "Sorry about that, my lord," said Bear, shoving the whole bun in his mouth at once.

"It's all right." Vivienne hurriedly wiped the gravy from her uncle's tunic with a hand cloth.

"How did you do that without getting hit?" asked Isaac in awe, still rubbing his hand from where Nairnie's ladle had struck him.

"Ye need to learn to be fast," said Bear. "Like this." He snitched another bun off the platter, quickly tossing it to Isaac and still managing to avoid the dreaded ladle.

"Thanks," said Isaac catching it with one hand. He shoved the whole thing in his mouth at once, probably hoping Nairnie wasn't going to take it back.

"Bear, ye stop that right now," warned Nairnie, making her way over to her husband. "Ye're goin' to teach the young ones bad habits and I dinna like that." She yanked hard on his beard, and he made a face and groaned.

"I knew I should have shaved this off before I returned," said Bear, rubbing his chin. "Nairnie, do you have a little extra food by any chance?"

"Extra food? For who?" she asked, cocking her head and squinting one eye. "Bear, I ken ye good enough to understand that ye're no' just askin' for yerself, are ye?"

"He's not?" Zachariah started getting really nervous now. His house couldn't hold more people.

"We just got into port and my crew hasn't had time to get something to eat yet," Bear explained.

"God's eyes, Bear, if ye want yer crew to join us for supper then send them in, and stop slowing us down from eatin' because the food is gettin' cold." Nairnie turned and stormed back to the other end of the table.

"His crew? As in ... an entire crew? From a ship?" asked Zachariah, not liking the sound of this at all!

"Thanks, old woman," said Bear, throwing Nairnie a kiss. He walked back to the door and stuck his head out, put his fingers in his mouth and whistled. "Come on in, boys, it's all right."

Before Zachariah could object, at least a dozen scraggly, dirty, rugged sailors trudged into his house. One of them had a wooden leg, and some of them were even barefoot. They all stank. Not to mention, that all of them looked to Zachariah like ... pirates. They made so much commotion that it alarmed the dog. Grunt barked, and when he did, Midnight shot out of Starah's arms, running across the table, knocking into the platters of food. Grunt jumped up, his paws hitting the dishes as he tried to get the cat. Then to make matters worse, the ferrets got loose and ran between the sailors' legs and disappeared out the door. Of course, the cat and dog followed and so did Maleine, Wymond, Martin, and Starah, trying to chase them down.

"Well, there are plenty of empty seats now," said Bear, cramming his body atop the bench that the children had just vacated. His crew started to do the same, but Nairnie began hitting each of them with her ladle, sending them running back across the room.

"We dinna eat until ye clean yer hands first," she told them, sending the crew hurrying for the wash basin. "And ye'll eat on the floor. The bench is for the children."

"By God, she really does scare the crap out of pirates," said Zachariah, now having no doubt that the pirate stories were all true after seeing this motley crew.

"Sit down, Sheriff. Ye look like ye need some time to relax," said Bear, leaning his elbows on the table.

"You're telling me," he mumbled.

"We all need some time to rest and relax and just have fun," said Vivienne.

"Then ye're all in luck." Bear smiled, showing his blackened and broken teeth.

"What do you mean?" asked Lady Mablethorpe.

"I mean, my crew and I are goin' to Whitstable next to pick up a shipment of oysters before we have to get back to work for the King. They have the best oysters from those waters that ye can't get anywhere else, and I know how much Nairnie loves them."

"What Bear really means is that he wants me to cook up some oyster dishes for him and the crew," explained Nairnie, shaking her head.

"Thanks, old woman, that would be nice." Bear reached out and slapped Nairnie on the ass, this time getting her fist in his gut.

"Ooomph," said Bear, looking up at Nairnie and smiling. "She's so cute when she's angry."

"Bear, what does this have to do with us?" asked Vivienne.

"I am tryin' to ask all of ye to join us," explained Bear. "I think the young ones might find it exciting to go for a ride on my ship."

"Your ship?" asked Lord Mablethorpe. "Don't you mean the King's ship?"

"Nay," said Nairnie. "The Falcon was my grandsons' ship, but since they're no longer pirates, now it belongs to Bear."

"Vivienne, don't even consider it," warned her uncle. "It's not safe for you or the children."

"It's safe as long as me and my crew are with ye," said Bear, swiping a chicken leg when Nairnie turned her back. "And the beaches are so sunny and the water is so blue. It's a real treasure spot if ye know what I mean." Bear took a big bite of the chicken.

"I think I know what you mean," growled Lord Mablethorpe. "You're a bunch of pirates, and probably have treasure hidden there that you want to collect."

"Gilbert, don't say things like that," scolded Lady Mablethorpe.

"Why not?" asked Vivienne's uncle. "After all, we all know it's true."

"Ye wound me," said Bear, already having devoured the chicken and throwing the bone down on the empty plate in front of him. "We work for the King, like I said, Lord Mablethorpe. We are no longer pirates. If King Edward trusts us, why can't ye?"

"I still don't understand what exactly you do for the King," said Lord Mablethorpe, not seeming to want to trust Bear or his men at all.

"We do whatever the King wants. But mainly we hunting down crooked nobles and people who steal from him," said Bear with a chuckle.

"I think I'd rather not know any more, after all," mumbled Vivienne's uncle.

"So, will you all join us on the adventure?" asked Bear, with a look of amusement mixed with hope in his eyes.

"Sure. Why not?" Vivienne answered with a shrug. "It sounds like fun. And we could all use time to relax on the beach and in the sun."

"Nay, you won't be going, Vivienne," warned her uncle. "None of us will."

"Gilbert, you just made amends with Vivienne," whispered his wife. "Don't ruin it. Besides, I think it's a lovely idea and that we should go as well."

"We're not," growled Vivienne's uncle.

"It's a big ship. There's room for all of you," said Bear, looking over the food, deciding what to snitch next.

"I'm the sheriff in this town and I can't get away," said Zachariah, not sure he wanted to go anywhere with ex-pirates.

"Isaac can help Constable Dorson until you return," said Vivienne. "Oh, please come too, Sheriff. I plan on taking Martin and I'm sure he'd want Starah there for company. The children would love being on a ship. Plus, it would give us time to spend with them, just like we talked about earlier."

"Aye, I'll watch over your house and the town for you while you're gone," offered Isaac, making Zachariah feel no less worried to hear this.

"Well, I don't know," Zachariah mumbled, trying to think of something to get out of going.

"I'm goin', Sheriff, and will be happy to watch over the children as well as cook for everyone, including the crew," said Nairnie. "Ye're no' scared to go on the ship with my husband are ye?"

"What? Of course not," said Zachariah with a chuckle. "Unless he has a ladle too," he added under his breath.

"We can go there and come back in one day, Sheriff," said Bear. "And everyone here is welcome. Feel free to bring your pets too."

"Nay. No pets." Zachariah shook his head, not even able to imagine the animals aboard a ship.

"Grunt has to come with me," said Vivienne. "Unless you'd like to watch him for me, Uncle, since you're not going."

"Me?" Her uncle looked up in surprise. "Nay. I don't think so."

"Are you sure you won't join us, Uncle Gilbert?" asked Vivienne.

"Nay. I don't want to go, and besides, I am lord of a castle. I can't leave it unattended," complained Lord Mablethorpe. "I'm sorry, Vivienne, but Ellen and I will not be joining you."

"Sorry, Vivienne," said her aunt, looking very disappointed. "But I suppose your uncle is right. It wouldn't be good to leave the castle unattended."

"I understand," said Vivienne. "But unless you object, Uncle, I'll be taking Martin, Maleine, and Wymond with me as well."

"Go ahead, I don't care," he said, with a wave of his hand in the air. "Can we eat now? I'm hungry."

"No' until the children return," said Nairnie.

"Here they come," said Isaac. Zachariah turned to see the children and all the animals come through the door.

Martin held on to Grunt's collar and Starah held on to Midnight. Wymond and Maleine each held a ferret. To his surprise, everyone, even the animals, were calm.

"What did we miss?" asked Martin. "Did the pirates do something? Tell me all about it."

"We're going to eat now, Martin, so sit down," instructed Vivienne. "There will be plenty of time to talk to Bear and his crew later."

"Really?" asked Martin, taking his seat. Grunt hurried under the table and rested his chin on Bear's lap. Bear snitched a small piece of meat and gave it to the dog.

"Yes, really," said Vivienne. "We're going on a little trip aboard Bear's ship."

"We are? Hurrah!" said Martin, overly enthused.

"There will be sun and sand and lots of fun," said Vivienne. "And you'll get to experience riding on the sea in a ship."

"That sounds like you'll have a wonderful time, my lady." Maleine sounded a little sad.

"You and Wymond will be joining us," Vivienne told her.

"We will?" Maleine's mood changed, and now she was happy.

"Me? On a ship? I've never been on a ship before," said Wymond, smiling from ear to ear.

"Can we go too, Father? Pleeeeease," said Starah, sitting down with the cat still in her grasp.

"A ship is a dangerous place to be, and I'm not even sure you know how to swim," he told his daughter.

"What does that mean?" Starah pouted and almost looked as if she were about to cry.

Zachariah looked around the room. There were at least a

dozen scary-looking ex-pirates staring back at him, but they weren't half as frightening as the looks that Vivienne and Nairnie were giving him right now.

"It means, I hope you won't get seasick, Starah," he told his daughter. "Because we're about to go on an adventure that I am sure none of us will ever forget."

From the Author:

I hope you enjoyed **Murder at the Joust** and will take a minute to leave a review for me.

Medieval jousts were entertaining, and that is where knights could show off their skills. But like anything else in medieval times, it was also often dangerous. There have been records showing that people sometimes did die at a joust. This includes King Henry II of France when a lance splinter pierced his eye and brain, and he died ten days later. And of course, there were always those who wanted to cheat or ignore the rules of the joust, and would do anything to win.

If you haven't read the rest of the books in my **Harlowe & Fitch Historical Mystery Series**, please do. And be sure to start from the beginning, with **Murder at Mablethorpe Castle** so as not to ruin surprises along the way. Each book holds a new murder mystery that is solved by the end of the story. As the main story continues, answers and clues to the ongoing mystery of the murders of Lady Vivienne's parents as well as the disappearance of her son and brother are slowly revealed.

The next book in the series is **Murder on the High Seas.** You will finally find out more about Nairnie's past life with the pirates. If you'd like to know more about Vivienne's half-brothers, Rowen, Rook, and Reed, be sure to read my romance series called the **Legendary Bastards of the Crown**. It starts out with the birth of the King's bastard triplets in **Destiny's Kiss**. Then it is followed by **Restless Sea Lord**, **Ruthless Knight**, **Reckless Highlander**, and finishes with a spin-off of one of the pirates in **Pirate in the Mist** that also leads into to my **Pirate Lords Series.**

Pirate brothers with their grandmother Nairnie on board? Even the pirates fear this old woman, who thinks nothing of hitting them with her heavy ladle if they get out of hand. Lots of humor as well as mystery, intrigue, and of course, romance as you sail the high seas looking for treasure with **Tristan**, **Mardon**, and **Aaron** in **Pirate Lords.**

And to find out more about Nairnie, please read my romance series called **Seasons of Fortitude**. Nairnie is first introduced as a handmaid and healer in **Highland Spring, Summer's Reign, Autumn's Touch** (Nairnie's background is revealed in this book) and **Winter's Flame**. The four sisters named after the seasons, are cousins who were raised as siblings to the Legendary Bastard triplets.

If you like paperbacks or audiobooks better than e-books, the good news is that my entire Harlowe & Fitch Historical Mystery Series will appear in all three formats.

To see more of my books (over 100 and counting) please stop by and visit my **Website** at **http://elizabethrosenovels.com.** You can also follow me on **Amazon, Bookbub**,

I'd like to now leave you with an excerpt from *Restless Sea Lord,* Lord Rowen's story.

Restless Sea Lord (*Legendary Bastards of the Crown*):

Scotland, Winter 1356

From vengeance and strife, a legend is born.

Twelve-year-old Rowen Douglas looked up from his meal of eel and pottage as the door to the cottage burst open and his father limped in, being held up by their Uncle Malcolm. Rowen's brothers, Reed and Rook, looked up from their game of chess, a game they'd been taught by their father that Rowen could never win.

"Ross!" Their mother, Annalyse, gasped when she saw her injured husband. She'd been tending to Autumn, the baby of the family, while Rowen's two other sisters, Winter and Summer, sat playing on the floor by her feet. "What happened?" Annalyse put the baby down and ran to help her husband. Ross Douglas was a big man with red hair, and had a tremendous skill with the blade. But today, Rowen could see that his father had failed. Many times, Rowen's father returned from battle tired and dirty, but never had he looked so broken, bloodied, and defeated as now.

"'Tis bad, lassie. Verra bad," said Ross, shaking his head, his voice sounding low and gravelly. "Ye'd all better say a prayer." His mangled leg bled profusely, and his green Douglas plaid was now black with soot. Malcolm looked no better.

Rowen's mother rushed around the room to collect water, herbs, and rags to use in aiding her husband.

"It's the English King Edward, isn't it?" she asked softly, looking over her shoulder at her triplet sons as if there was something she didn't want Rowen and his brothers to hear.

"Aye," Malcolm answered for them. "The English king has invaded with his troops and seized the castle at Berwick-upon-Tweed."

"Nay," said his mother, as she wrung out the water from a cloth and tended to her husband's wounds. "Tell me it isn't so."

"The Scots surrendered to him," said his father, with despair in his voice.

"Not only that," added Malcolm, "but Edward Balliol surrendered to the English wretch, and resigned his claim to the Scottish crown."

"Oh!" shrieked Rowen's mother, with her hand covering her mouth.

"The coast is on fire and Edward's troops continue to sack our lands, while his fleet of ships waits at the shore." Rowen's father gritted his teeth, holding his knee, and then half-squinted his eyes as he looked up to the ceiling. "The Scots are burnin' anythin' that could be used by the English, includin' livestock as they flee for their lives! We have no choice. We need to head for the Highlands. We're doomed, Annalyse, doomed I tell ye, and it's all because of the faither of our triplet sons." He shot the boys an angered look, fire in his eyes. Rowen felt confused as to what he meant.

"Ross, quiet!" warned Annalyse, putting down the cloth and hurrying to pick up one of the crying siblings. "We promised to keep my sister's secret, now hush."

Also by Elizabeth Rose

Greek Myth Fantasy Series

Tangled Tales Series

Portals of Destiny

Contemporary Series:

Tarnished Saints Series

Working Man Series

Western Series:

Cowboys of the Old West Series

And More!

Please visit http://elizabethrosenovels.com

About Elizabeth

Elizabeth Rose is an award-winning, bestselling author of over 100 books and counting. She writes medieval, historical, contemporary, paranormal, and western romance. Her books are available as EBooks, paperbacks, and some audiobooks as well.

Her favorite characters in her works include dark, dangerous and tortured heroes, and feisty, independent heroines who know how to wield a sword. She loves writing 14th century medieval novels, and is well-known for her many series.

Elizabeth loves the outdoors. In the summertime, you can find her in her secret garden with her laptop, swinging in her hammock working on her next book. Elizabeth is a born storyteller and passionate about sharing her works with her readers.

Please be sure to visit her website at **Elizabethrosenovels.com** to read excerpts from any of her novels and get sneak peeks at covers of upcoming books. You can follow her on **Twitter, Facebook**, **Goodreads** or **BookBub.** Join Elizabeth's **newsletter** so you don't miss out on new releases or upcoming events.

www.ingramcontent.com/pod-product-compliance
Ingram Content Group UK Ltd.
Pitfield, Milton Keynes, MK11 3LW, UK
UKHW041118071025
8269UKWH00011B/93